kiss me

SUSAN MALLERY

kiss me

HQN™

Doubleday Large Print Home Library Edition

This Large Print Edition, prepared especially for Doubleday Large Print Home Library, contains the complete, unabridged text of the original Publisher's Edition.

ISBN-13: 978-1-62953-561-6

HQN™

This edition published by arrangement with Harlequin Books S.A.

® and TM are trademarks of Harlequin Enterprises Limited or its corporate affiliates. Trademarks indicated with ® are registered in the United States Patent and Trademark Office, the Canadian Intellectual Property Office and in other countries.

Printed in U.S.A.

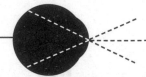

This Large Print Book carries the Seal of Approval of N.A.V.H

This book is dedicated by one of my favorite readers:

To my girlfriends—you add the flavor to my life and laughter to my days. Here's to friends sharing fun, flowers and fabulous food. They say warm friendships are a ticket to a longer life…maybe we'll all push 100!!!

Love,

Nancy

kiss me

CHAPTER ONE

Zane Nicholson believed in listening to his gut. At nine fifty-five that morning, it was telling him that today wasn't going to be a good day.

He glanced out the window at the rolling hills that made up the Nicholson Ranch and wondered if being a farmer would have been easier. Crops didn't break through fences in the night and wander away. Crops didn't try to be born breech. He could be growing corn. Or wheat. Wheat was patriotic. All those amber waves.

He turned his attention back to his paperwork and shook his head. Who was he kidding? He was a fifth generation rancher. The closest he would come to farming was the vegetable garden the ranch cook grew out behind the bunkhouse.

"Hey, boss."

Zane watched his foreman step into his office. Frank Adelman took off his worn cowboy hat, slapped it against his left thigh, then eased into the hard, plastic chair in front of the desk.

A visit from Frank before noon wasn't going to bring good news.

"What?" Zane asked, more resigned than annoyed.

Nicholson Ranch had been annexed earlier this year by the city of Fool's Gold, California, meaning that it was now inside the city's jurisdiction, a decision which the mayor had sworn would be good for him. She said everyone out this way would benefit from more city services, but so far, it had only meant an increase in paperwork. He didn't see the win, though his brother was happy about the faster internet speeds that came from the city laying cable out this way.

"There's a busted pipe in the bunkhouse," Frank said. "Under the kitchen sink. All the boys are out with the herd. I turned the water off, but we're going to have to see to it today. You want me to pull someone in or call for a plumber?"

Zane dropped his pen on the desk and rubbed his temples. What he wanted was a little cooperation from fate. A couple of weeks without a crisis. Apparently that was too much to ask.

He weighed his options. Frank couldn't take care of the busted pipe because they were expecting buyers in an hour or so, and Frank was going to take them around to see the kids. Zane had a meeting with some research scientists from Cal U, Fool's Gold, that afternoon, which meant **he** couldn't take the buyers around. A plumber from Fool's Gold would be easiest, but he might not be able to get someone out today.

"Call in a couple of the boys," he said at last, then shook his head. "It's Monday, right? It always hits the fan on Monday."

Frank grunted his agreement, then rose. The phone rang before he'd even walked to the door.

So much for getting his paperwork finished on time, Zane thought as he reached for the receiver.

"Nicholson Ranch," he said. "This is Zane."

"Hi," a woman said, her voice low and friendly. "I'm calling to talk to someone about facilities. Can you help me with that?"

Zane blinked at the question. "Facilities?

You mean horse boarding? We don't do that here, ma'am. You could check with old Reilly Konopka. Last I heard he was taking in boarders. Or Castle Ranch in town. Ask for Rafe."

The woman laughed. "No. Not facilities for my horse. I meant for my husband and myself. We're coming up for the cattle drive this weekend, and I was wondering if there were any spa facilities. We've been under a lot of stress lately. I was thinking that a couple's massage might be a nice start to our vacation. Maybe deep tissue. Or those heated rocks. Aren't they all the rage right now?"

Massage? Vacation? Cattle drive?

"Ma'am, I have no idea what you're talking about," Zane said, his temper rising steadily as a knot formed in his gut. His gut feeling turned downright ugly.

"Oh." She sounded disappointed. "The website didn't say anything about a spa, but I was hoping. Can you recommend a hotel with a spa in Fool's Gold? We'll come a day early. I do want to be rested before we arrive for our cattle drive on Saturday."

"Ma'am, could you please tell me about

this cattle drive you're expecting?"

"Excuse me? Aren't you an employee of the ranch?"

He was supposed to own it. What was going on? "I'm, ah, filling in," he lied.

"Oh. All right. My husband and I are going on a cattle drive."

She chatted away, giving details, including the website where she'd first found her vacation. While she continued to talk, Zane turned to his computer and typed in the web address. When the site popped up, his jaw dropped. He barely remembered to say goodbye before hanging up the phone.

In less than two minutes he'd explored the site, which detailed all the delights of a Northern California cattle-drive vacation. On Zane's ranch. There was only one person who would dare a trick like that—his brother.

Rage bubbled and boiled into something Zane couldn't begin to name. It filled him until he knew he was going to explode.

Chase had screwed up before, countless times, but compared to this new stunt, all that had been kids' stuff. What had he been thinking?

Zane stood and headed for the door, then stopped himself. He wanted to hit something, throw something, break something. If he went to Chase right now, he would say and do a lot of things they would both regret. He knew the kid saw him as a cross between the devil incarnate and the worst guardian since Scrooge. He also knew Chase was nearly an adult, and if the teen didn't get his shit together, he was going to spend his life screwing up and living with regrets.

Regrets. The single word was enough to calm Zane's temper. He'd lived with them himself, since he was Chase's age. They had a way of eating at a man's insides. Of making him want to outrun the wind, if only he could leave the past behind. But the world wasn't that tidy. Once done, a thing couldn't be undone. He didn't want that for his brother.

Ever since Chase had been a toddler, following him around the ranch, mimicking his every move, Zane had loved him so much, it was painful at times. He had vowed back then to watch out for the kid, to protect him—even from himself.

So instead of going gunning for Chase, he returned to his desk to consider the best course of action. Once and for all he was determined to teach his brother about responsibility so he could become the kind of man who respected himself. The kind of man who didn't have to live with the ghost of blame.

"I've decided not to put you in prison, Ms. Kitzke," Judge Haverston said, looking stern as she peered over her half-glasses. "I believe you had the best of intentions." She paused. "You know what they say about the road to hell."

"Yes, Your Honor."

"There will be no punitive damages. The earnest money will be refunded." She glanced at the paperwork on her wide desk, then gave her gavel a light tap. "I believe we are adjourned."

Phoebe Kitzke remained standing as everyone else in the small Los Angeles courtroom was told to rise. Judge Haverston swept through the doorway leading to her chambers, or whatever it was that judges had. The legal secret place, she thought, looking for humor but unable to feel anything except lingering terror. Hopefully relief would soon follow.

Not going to prison was a good thing, she reminded herself. She'd seen plenty of teenage prison movies when she'd stayed up late watching cable while babysitting back in high school. She knew what sorts of things could happen. Far better to stay on the right side of the law.

Phoebe shook hands with the company attorney and thanked him for his help, then turned to find her boss, April Keller, waiting for her. April was taller than Phoebe—who wasn't?—and the kind of sun-streaked blonde Southern California was famous for. Phoebe had always felt a bit out of place in LA, with her short, curvy physique, and dark hair and eyes.

"Are you okay?" April asked.

Phoebe shrugged. "I'm happy about avoiding prison. I don't have the background to be successful there. As for the rest of it, I'm still pretty numb."

April sighed. "I'm sorry," she said, sounding both miserable and relieved. "For everything. You really saved me."

Phoebe didn't want to go there. If she thought too much about what had happened, she would get angry and say things that would damage an important relationship.

"What about my job?" she asked instead. "Did I save that, too?"

April pressed her lips together and avoided her gaze.

"Great," Phoebe said and pushed past her, heading for the exit. "Let me guess. I've been fired."

"Suspended."

April followed her into the hallway. People milled around them, all going about their legal business. Phoebe hoped the innocent ones would have better luck than she did. She stopped by a battered bulletin board and looked at her boss.

"For how long?" she asked.

"A month." April touched her arm. "Look, I'm going to make this up to you, I swear. I'll pay your salary out of my own pocket."

Phoebe sucked in a breath. "I was suspended without pay?"

April nodded.

Perfect. Just perfect. Phoebe stepped back and squared her shoulders. "I guess I'll see you in a month," she said before heading for the door.

April hurried after her. "Phoebe, wait. I know you're furious with me. You have every right to be angry."

Phoebe stopped. "Actually, the person I'm angry with is myself."

Tears filled April's eyes. "If you hadn't helped me, I don't know what would have happened."

"I know. I'm glad you're okay." She made a show of glancing at her watch. "Look, I have to go."

"Okay, but call me in a couple of days, okay? You can yell at me for as long as you want. I deserve it."

Phoebe nodded, then walked toward the elevator for the underground parking. She tried to tell herself that in the larger picture, she'd done a good deed. Cosmically, she'd just improved her chances of fame and glory in her next life by helping out someone in need. If there was a next life. If there wasn't, she'd just been suspended —without pay—from a job she loved, for something that shouldn't have been her fault, but was.

So far it wasn't the best Monday she'd ever had.

"Phoebe?"

The voice came from behind her, but she recognized it. Recognized it and knew her Monday was about to get worse. She sucked in a breath and turned to find Jeff Edwards standing in the grubby hallway. The same Jeff she'd once loved, promised to marry and had almost moved in with...right up until she'd caught him in bed with an eighteen-year-old intern she was training as part of a jobs program for kids aging out of foster care.

Tall, good-looking, successful Jeff Edwards who had dared to demand all his DVDs back after she'd ended the relationship. Jeff Edwards of the California Bureau of Real Estate.

"You really screwed up," he said, holding out an official-looking envelope. "The board is considering revoking your license."

She blinked at him, unable to believe this was really happening. It was like being involved in a car accident, when everything moved in slow motion. While there was no time to stop the course of events that would change her life forever, there was also no way to avoid the crash.

In a perfect world, she would be able to think of some witty, biting comment to put him in his place. But as her world was spinning in much the same direction as her day, she plucked the envelope from his hands without saying a word. In her first stroke of luck that morning, the elevator doors chose that moment to open, and she stepped inside with as much silent dignity as she could muster. Her only minor victory was the look of shock on Jeff's face as the door gently closed, leaving him standing alone and talking to himself.

Chase typed rapidly on his keyboard, his fingers moving in time with the pounding beat of the song playing in his earbuds. On his screen, a small frame in the corner displayed a montage of images flickering on and off, also in perfect synchroni-zation with the music. He ignored them for the most part—except for the **Sports Illustrated** swimsuit pictures he'd downloaded the previous week. Those very fine ladies got his full attention. When his program started flashing pictures of rock bands, cars and twisted space aliens, he moved his gaze back to the chat box in the center of his screen, and the message waiting there.

Robotic cat failed to attack mice, although it did fall on one.

Chase read the sentence twice, swore, then pulled out a worn notebook and began flipping through the pages.

Did it show any interest at all? he typed. **Can you confirm sensors are working?**

Because in the last test, the sensors had been working fine. At least they'd been registering. But did the robot understand what it was seeing? That was where he and Peter stumbled. Maybe a robot cat was too ambitious, he thought for the thousandth time. Maybe they should have started with the mouse instead. Maybe—

The pounding in his earbuds suddenly went silent. Chase glanced up and saw Zane standing next to his desk, the jack connecting the earbuds to the computer dangling from his hands.

Instantly he hit three keys in rapid succession, activating the macro that sent a message to Peter telling him, due to adult interference, communication would have to cease for now. All his friends had similar emergency escape messages. Some of them were pretty funny. But looking at Zane's angry face and the fury blazing in his eyes didn't make Chase feel much like laughing.

He tried to remember if he'd messed up recently. He'd accidentally broken a couple of plates while cleaning the kitchen last night, but Zane had already yelled at him for that. Plus the level of anger radiating from him wasn't about two broken plates. Which meant Chase had messed up somewhere else. Somewhere big. But it wasn't noon. Except for breakfast, he hadn't even left his room.

Unless Zane had found out about…

Zane didn't say anything. Instead he moved closer to the desk, then leaned over and typed in an internet address. By the time he punched in the fourth letter,

Chase knew he was totally and completely screwed.

He watched the site load in a matter of seconds. A panoramic picture of the town of Fool's Gold nestled into the Sierra Nevada filled the screen. Text scrolled at the bottom. **Come to the Northern California wilderness and experience a vacation like no other.**

The picture faded, replaced by one of people riding on horseback. It was a great photo, he thought, remembering how he'd copied it from another site.

"Start talking," Zane growled as he straightened and fixed Chase with his sternest expression.

When Chase had been little, he'd called it the death-ray look. It used to terrify him. But he'd been a kid then and still unclear on how things worked. Back then Zane had been his big brother and the best part of his world. He'd been too young to know that while he would always think of Zane "as his brother, his family, Zane would only think of him as a constant screwup who always got in the way.

"Well?"

Chase unwound himself from his chair and crossed to the bed. While the death-ray look no longer sent him running, he liked a little distance between himself and Zane.

"It's no big deal," Chase bluffed. "Peter Moreno and I designed a website for our computer science class. Mr. Hendrix gave us an A. He said someday we're gonna be better at computers than he is."

Zane pulled out the chair Chase had vacated and sank into it. After rubbing his eyes, he slowly shook his head.

"Yeah. You got an A in computer science and physics and math and every other subject that interests you. We'll ignore the C in English and the D in history."

Chase threw himself back on the bed. Jeez, were they going to go through all that again? No one at MIT was going to care if he didn't do well in history. It wasn't that kind of college. Of course if Zane had his way, Chase would never get to MIT. Instead he'd spend his life shoveling cow shit and feeding goats.

"I got a phone call about a half hour ago," Zane said.

His carefully controlled voice made Chase

sit up slowly. Even scarier than the death-ray look was the quiet voice. It meant that Zane was doing the best he could to hold on to his temper before it exploded and took out everyone from here to Sacramento.

"A woman wanted to know if she could get a massage before going on her cattle drive."

"Oh. That."

"Yes, that. Why don't you tell me about it?"

Chase swallowed as he remembered what he and Peter had done. It had been a joke that had gotten out of hand. He glanced at Zane and saw a muscle twitch in his jaw. Not exactly a good sign.

"Don't panic," he said quickly. "I've got everything under control."

"Tell me the plan, Chase."

Zane looked like a man holding on to his temper with both hands. Chase wasn't sure how long his brother's grip would last. He started talking as fast as he could.

"Like I said, it was our school project. We had to design a website, then put it on the internet."

"Through the **school**," Zane said, his teeth

clenched. "But you put yours on a host so anyone could access it."

"Um, that was an accident. Reese Hendrix did it as a joke."

Zane's hands curled into fists. "A joke? You advertised a cattle drive. You took reservations. You accepted money."

"Just for a little while," Chase protested. "Look, I know what I'm doing."

His brother stood and crossed to the window. "So people are arriving on Saturday expecting a six-day cattle drive? Was that the plan?"

"No. Don't worry, I've got that taken care of. It was a mistake. When the money started arriving, Peter and I didn't know what to do." Okay, later he'd figured out that sending it back with a letter explaining the mix-up would have been really smart, but it hadn't occurred to him at the time.

"Peter and I are working on our robot, and we needed parts. Peter put in his share, but you wouldn't loan me any money or pay for anything."

"You used strangers' money for your project?" Zane bellowed, turning back to face him. "That's stealing. The whole website is fraud, and I'm sure we can throw in theft for good measure."

Chase sprang to his feet. "I didn't steal. I'd never steal or do those other things."

"Then where's the money?"

"Right here." Chase moved to his computer and started typing quickly. "Peter and I did some day-trading. We figured we'd just borrow their money for a while. After we made a bundle off the deposits, we'd return them and keep the profits. Which was a great idea until the fourth day when we lost nearly everything."

Zane made a sound low in this throat. Chase kept typing, logging on to his brokerage account.

"I know what you're thinking. That we were screwed, right? But then we overheard this tourist at the Fourth of July Festival in Fool's Gold talking about a tech company that was going to announce a new kind of motherboard, and their stock would go through the roof. So we bought as much as we could with what we had left. The announcement is going to be at five today. We'll sell the stock and send back the deposits. I figured we'd tell everyone the ranch burned down or something so they won't show up."

He risked a glance at his brother. "So I've got it covered. I've even written up the letter telling everyone not to come and that we'll be sending their deposits back overnight mail. Pretty good, huh?"

Zane's expression remained unreadable. "You stole their money, lost it day-trading, plan to get it back through insider trading and you're canceling their vacation with less than a week's notice. You think that's **pretty good**?"

His voice rose with each word. Chase had the feeling he was trying to control himself, only he wasn't doing a really great job.

"These people are expecting a vacation. They've taken time off work, bought tickets. You want me to give you an idea of how much they could sue you for?"

"Not really," he muttered.

At that moment his brokerage account popped up. He scrolled down to the value and nearly passed out when he saw it was less than two dollars.

"No!" he yelled. He frantically clicked on the stock trading code of the company to check on recent news articles. A big headline flashed onto his computer screen.

Company President Arrested for Stealing Proprietary Information from Rivals.

He felt more than heard his brother approach. Zane touched the screen. "There seems to be a problem with your plan."

Chase didn't know what to say. This was bad. Really bad. Probably the worst thing he'd ever done. He felt nauseous. He couldn't think. People were going to be arriving for a cattle drive. He didn't have the money to pay them back, and if Zane didn't bail him out, he was probably going to be arrested. Or worse.

"I really blew it," he said more to himself than his brother.

"Looks that way."

Heat flared on Chase's cheeks. He stared at the floor, studying the scarred wood beneath his feet and the scuffs on his worn cowboy boots.

"Sorry."

"Sorry?" Zane swore loudly. "You've pulled some pretty boneheaded stunts in the past, but you've never gone this far before. I expected better." He clenched his hands, as if trying to keep from punching something…or someone. "I always expect better of you. After all this time, you'd think I'd learn."

No punishment, not even a good beating, could ever hurt worse than those words. They made Chase feel small and afraid. His throat tightened, as did his chest. For the first time in years, he thought he might actually cry.

"Now what?" Chase asked.

Zane walked to the door. "Good question. You have a backup plan?"

Chase shook his head. "I g-guess—" His voice cracked, and he had to clear his throat before continuing. "I guess I need to borrow the money so I can pay those people back."

Zane didn't say anything for a long time. When he finally spoke, Chase knew it was going to be bad.

"A loan would be too simple," Zane said. "I'm going to call Raoul and Pia to tell them what you and Peter did. Then I'm going to try to figure out what to do with you. This isn't going to be an easy punishment. I'm going to teach you a lesson you'll never forget."

He walked out of the room without say-ing another word. Chase watched him go. For the first time in his life, he wondered if Zane was going to send him away. Chase tried to tell himself it wouldn't be so bad. He hated the ranch. He wanted to go away, to study computers and lasers and all kinds of cool stuff. Not cattle breeding.

But leaving on his own terms and being kicked out by his only living blood relative were two very different things. He sank back on the bed, feeling alone and scared and a whole lot younger than seventeen.

CHAPTER TWO

Two hours after her court hearing, Phoebe had cleared out her desk, left her pending files on April's desk, purchased a large quantity of chocolate and candy from the See's store and driven to the tall Century City high-rise where her best friend, Maya Farlow, was a producer for a TV entertainment news program.

She smiled at the assistant Maya shared with two other producers, sitting at a desk in the wide hallway. Phoebe tapped lightly on the paneled door, then stepped into a tiny office with a floor-to-ceiling window.

Maya was on the phone, but she motioned for Phoebe to take a seat in front of her desk. Instead Phoebe crossed to the window first and stared out at the north-facing view. To the west lay the Pacific Ocean, to the east, the barely visible high-rises of downtown Los Angeles. And somewhere north was the San Fernando Valley—a suburban mecca everyone loved to mock but that Phoebe actually enjoyed visiting from time to time. The June gloom had burned off, leaving behind brilliant blue skies only possible in Southern California. New York might be the frenetic city that never slept, but LA was cutting-edge cool with a dash of sass.

"Zane," Maya said, her voice tight, "he's young. He did something stupid, but—"

Zane. Which meant Maya was talking to her stepbrother. From what Phoebe could tell, the two had never had an easy relationship.

"When does it start?" Maya scribbled something on a sticky pad on the corner of her desk. "Fine. I'll be there. No, I'm coming. I can't get out of here today, but I'll be there. Just go easy—"

She stopped talking as Zane apparently had hung up on her. She made a face at her phone.

"A room with a view," Phoebe said, taking the seat across from her friend's. "I haven't seen your new digs since you moved. Congrats."

Maya leaned back in her chair and grinned. "Thanks, but I'm hoping I won't be here for long. There's a job coming up at a network. On camera and talking about real news, not these Hollywood fluff pieces. If I have to do one more story about an actress's new hairstyle..." Her smile faded as she studied Phoebe. "Tell me what happened in court. I didn't get a frantic phone call, so I assume you're okay. I still have access to cash if you're going to need bail money."

Phoebe knew her friend wasn't kidding about the cash. Maya would be there for her, no matter what.

"No jail time, no punitive damages." She sighed softly. "The earnest money is to be returned. I'm suspended for a month, without pay, although April says she's going to pay me herself."

"She should." Maya swore. "Let me guess. April just watched the whole thing and didn't utter a word to the judge."

Phoebe nodded. "I'm such an idiot. I actually thought she would say something."

"You mean like the truth?"

"That would have been nice."

"How upset are you?"

Phoebe smiled ruefully. "There's a half-pound box of butterscotch squares from

See's in my car. I'm also planning to stop by the grocery store on my way home and buy a bottle of wine."

"Liquor and sugar. That's pretty bad."

"It's as close as I'll come to a life of crime." Phoebe rested her elbows on her knees and covered her face with her hands. "I know better. That's what kills me about this. What is it with my personality that says I have to earn my place in the world? How many times do I have to be burned before I'll learn to stop helping people? Every time I do, it gets me in trouble." She thought about her unexpected meeting with Jeff outside the courtroom.

"Oh, and the Bureau of Real Estate is considering revoking my license. Jeff stopped by to give me the information himself."

"Did you kick him in the balls?"

"I didn't think about it in time. Bummer." She looked at Maya. "Why am I such a sucker?"

"You're a good person who likes to help people. So what are you going to do now?"

"I don't know. I have a month off. If the board suspends my license..."

She didn't know what would happen then, nor did she want to think about it. After college she hadn't had a clue as to what she wanted to do with her life. Then she'd stumbled into real estate, and for the first time ever, she felt that she'd finally found a place where she belonged. She loved showing houses and getting people good financing and watching their faces light up the day they moved in to their new home. It was her whole life.

"April's a bitch," Maya said.

Phoebe sighed. "She's a single mother with three kids, one of whom is chronically sick."

"You're making excuses."

"I'm telling the truth. She's right. If she'd taken any more time off to stay home with Beth, she could have been fired. So she asked me to fill out the paperwork for the Bauers. My mistake was in listening to her. I knew the paperwork was wrong."

Phoebe had fought with her boss, and a frustrated April had finally yelled at her to just do what she was told and file the stupid things. Which Phoebe had done, even though she'd known better. But through a series of unfortunate events, what should have just been a mistake had ended up starting a lawsuit and a subsequent criminal investigation—the consequences of which had landed her in court. Rather than tell the truth, April had let her take the fall, explaining that Phoebe could afford to be a screwup. If April got fired, there were three kids on the line. Phoebe hadn't come up with an argument to refute that one.

"I didn't think the real estate board got involved in paperwork mix-ups," Maya said.

Phoebe thought about the letter in her purse. The one she'd read while consuming four pieces of almond truffle and a double latte from Starbucks.

"They don't. However the Bauers were April's clients, and I did the paperwork. They're accusing me of taking the credit and money for her sale."

Maya's green eyes widened with sympathy. "Which you didn't do."

"But who's going to believe me?"

"April knows the truth."

"April won't risk telling it."

"So what happens now? You could haul her into court. I could do an exposé."

"Thanks, but I'm looking for a different sort of option." Although what it was, Phoebe couldn't say. "I guess I have a month to find myself a new job." Depending on what happened with her license, maybe a new career. "I love selling real estate. I don't want to stop doing that."

Maya shook her head. "No, what you love is rescuing people. You're the only Beverly Hills agent I know who specializes in starter homes for the financially challenged. You could be making truckloads of money with movie stars and Hollywood execs, but instead you work with newlyweds and single moms on a budget that wouldn't support a rodent family."

Phoebe thought about protesting, but she knew her friend was right.

"I know what it's like to be desperate for a place to belong," she said. She'd lived with the feeling most of her life. One day, she promised herself. One day she would find it, and then she would never let it go.

"Oh, wait." Phoebe brightened. "I do have one movie-star client, but Jonny Blaze doesn't want to buy a house here in LA. He's looking for a vacation paradise home complete with room for a helicopter pad."

"Could you at least sleep with him and take your mind off things?"

For the first time that day, Phoebe laughed. "I wish, but the man actually ruffled my hair and told me I looked like his kid sister."

"That's a drag."

"Tell me about it." Phoebe rose. "I have chocolate calling my name, and you have the rich and famous to stalk. I'm going to get out of your way."

"No way." Maya rose, came around her desk and gave Phoebe a hug. "I'm not leaving you alone. Let's go out for Mexican."

"Are you sure you have time?"

"For you? Always."

Maya had said she needed to wrap up a few things at work, so Phoebe deliberately took the slowest route to their favorite Mexican restaurant. She hated waiting alone in a bar. Instead she took a seat in the foyer and watched the couples and families stream into the popular eatery. Every now and then a single man arrived on his own. She was careful to look away when that happened. The last guy she'd met in a restaurant bar had not only tried to borrow five thousand dollars from her on their second date, but had lied about being married. She was still stinging from the threat of serving jail time and worried about her real estate license—the last thing she needed was a lousy relationship.

Although a good one wouldn't be so bad, she thought wistfully. She wasn't looking for perfect—just a nice guy who would love her, who wanted kids and a regular life filled with things like family car-trip vacations and PTA meetings. A family of her own. Unfortunately she didn't seem to be skilled at meeting normal, stable men. She seemed to attract losers like Jeff the Unfaithful, or married men who wanted money. Maybe instead of looking for a man who obviously didn't exist in her universe, she should think about getting a dog.

Before she could consider breeds or sizes, the front door opened, and Maya breezed in. She was both stylish and elegant in a black suit that skimmed her curves and highlighted her blond hair. Phoebe had been so caught up in her own problems earlier that she hadn't noticed the outfit.

"New?" she asked as she stood and smiled. "It's fabulous."

Maya grinned, then twirled quickly so her suit could be viewed from the back. "It wasn't even on sale, but I couldn't help myself. I love it. This is the suit I bought for my interview with the network, and I've got a green number that matches my eyes for the on-camera audition."

"You'll totally rock the interview," Phoebe said loyally. "And look amazing doing it."

"You're so sweet. Thank you."

Phoebe didn't envy her friend her gorgeous wardrobe. Phoebe shopped at the outlet mall or the Macy's sale rack. With the exception of action-movie stars like Jonny Blaze, her clients didn't want to think their hard-earned money was going to support a designer wardrobe, and she was okay with that.

"I'm starving," Maya said. "And you need a margarita."

They followed the hostess through a maze of wooden tables laden with drinks, chips and oversize plates of fajitas, enchiladas and tacos. The smell of sizzling beef and chicken made Phoebe's mouth water.

The waiter appeared, and they ordered their margaritas and, without looking at the menu, the number three dinner. The busboy was on his heels, leaving chips and salsa.

Phoebe eyed the chips, mentally calculating calories. Not that it was going to matter. By her second margarita, she would throw her eating plan out the window and chow down on everything in sight. In the morning she would try to StairMaster off the calories—with minimal success—and skip lunch. She had been battling the same ten pounds for the past three years. So far, the pounds were winning.

"I have an announcement." Phoebe sipped her drink. "I've realized that I get into trouble every time I help someone. I don't know why, but it happens. So as of now, I'm never helping anyone again. Ever. No matter what."

Maya's green eyes widened. "Wow. That's impressive. I don't believe it for a second, but it's impressive."

Phoebe laughed. "I'm not sure I believe it, either. But I'm going to try."

"Would you mind putting that on hold?

Because I have a pretty big favor to ask. But I think it's going to be good for you, too, so win-win and all that. You have a month off, and face it, if anyone needs a vacation, it's you."

Phoebe frowned. "It's really not in the budget."

"That's why this is so perfect. Actually I'm talking about more of a massive distraction."

"What kind of a distraction?"

Maya's expression turned impish. "The kind that involves a rugged, hunky cowboy."

Phoebe crunched on her chip. As she chewed, she eyed her friend. "You don't set people up," she said when she'd swallowed. "I've listened to more than one rant on the subject."

Maya laughed. "Fair enough. But this isn't a setup. I'm offering handsome man scenery, not a chance at a relationship." Her humor faded as she wrinkled her nose. "Frankly, I don't think Zane is capable of a relationship. His passions seem to be limited to running his ranch and being perfect."

"Zane your ex-stepbrother? That Zane?"

The one Maya had been talking to earlier?

"That's the one." She picked up a chip but didn't eat it. "I got a frantic call from Chase just before you got to my office."

"Your other ex-stepbrother."

"Right. He's Zane's half brother. Chase is seventeen, a complete cutie, a computer whiz and a constant disappointment to Zane. Of course anyone falling short of the ever-perfect ideal is a disappointment. Zane practically had a heart attack when I showed up after his father married my ex-showgirl mother."

Phoebe nodded. While she didn't know the details of Maya's few years on the Nicholson Ranch—they had occurred before she and Maya had met—she'd heard bits and pieces.

"Anyway, Chase screwed up...again. He seems to be making a career of it. But this time, although I really hate to say it, I agree with Zane. He called me right after Chase." Maya took a drink of her margarita. "Chase and a friend set up a website for a school assignment. They offered a cattle-drive vacation. Somehow the school project got on the internet. Don't ask me how. Zane does move steers every spring —it's sort of a back-to-his roots thing with him. He does it the old-fashioned way instead of by truck. He only brings a couple of cowboys with him—mostly the ones who don't talk in more than two-word sentences. He would never take Chase or—God forbid—a tourist. He'd rather be staked out naked on an anthill."

Phoebe saw the potential problem. "Did people actually sign up for the cattle drive?"

"You got it. Even worse—Chase and his little friend collected money. Five hundred bucks a head. Chase took the money and day-traded with it."

"Day-trading? Is he crazy?"

"He's seventeen and immortal. You remember what that was like. He lost everything through some company going under. I don't understand it. Anyway, big brother is refusing to bail him out. Zane says Chase has to learn once and for all that there are consequences for his actions."

"Let me make sure I understand. You're saying Chase sold vacations for a fake cattle drive, and people sent money?"

The two women looked at each other in

silence for a long moment. Phoebe felt her lips twitch. When she saw Maya's eyes crinkle at the corners, she lost it. In unison, they burst into a fit of giggles that drew the attention of the people at the other tables, which only made them laugh harder.

"Who **does** that?" Phoebe asked when she could speak again.

"I know! It's terrible and hysterical. He's an evil genius," Maya said, wiping a tear from her eye. "It's bad. Bad! Stop laughing. I know it's wrong, but it's also just so funny. That's the part Zane doesn't get. Someday, when Chase is a famous inventor, this is going to make a great story."

The waiter showed up with their food, and Maya waited until he left before continuing.

"Zane and I went round and round for half an hour. People are expecting a vacation, and Chase played with their lives. We discussed everything from military school to jail time for the kid. Actually it was kind of interesting to have Zane want my opinion."

"So what did you decide?"

Maya smiled. "What I never would have

guessed. On Saturday morning, a group of city slickers will be showing up on the sacred ground that is the Nicholson Ranch. Zane is going to take them on a cattle drive, along with Chase. He's going to give the kid all the crap jobs, hoping to teach him a lesson."

Phoebe considered the information. On the one hand, she could appreciate Zane's frustration. On the other, she could relate to Chase. She'd been a screwup her whole life, too.

"Did Chase want you to rescue him?"

"Yes, and I was forced to tell him no. But as a way of compromising, I agreed to come along on the cattle drive. When I told Zane, he was actually pleased."

"Why?"

"I've nearly always taken Chase's side. I think he wants me to see him for who he is, or some such nonsense." Maya shrugged, her green eyes darkening. "The thing Zane can't seem to figure out is that I already know Chase. I'm very aware of his flaws. But knowing about them doesn't make me care about him any less. That would be an unknown concept to Zane. Anyway, the point of this story is to invite you along. You love animals and you've earned a vacation."

"A cattle drive?"

"Why not? You claim to like the outdoors, and as long as Zane doesn't open his mouth and actually speak, he's pretty easy on the eyes." Maya grabbed a chip. "You work hard all the time. Do something for yourself. You can use my frequent-flier miles."

The offer was tempting, Phoebe thought. She had a couple of weeks until her interviews, and she **had** just sworn off taking care of the world.

"I'm tempted, but my idea of the rugged outdoors is watering the plants on my patio. I've never been close to a horse. Aren't they big and smelly?"

"They don't smell half so bad as the steers, but we can stay upwind." Maya smiled. "I think we'll have fun. Besides, after what you've been through, you could use a break. You'll be able to think more clearly from the back of a horse."

Phoebe would never in a million years have thought of going on a cattle drive.

But she'd promised herself that she was going to make changes and try new things. She was going to reinvent herself. Maybe the new Phoebe Kitzke would enjoy a cattle drive.

"Okay," she said. "I'll go."

"You won't regret it," Maya promised. "I already have a flight booked for Friday afternoon. I can't get away before then because I have a bunch of video segments to edit. But I was hoping you wouldn't mind going tomorrow. Just to distract Zane. He's so furious with Chase, I'm afraid they're going to get into a fistfight or something."

Phoebe stared at her friend. "You're crazy."

"I know it's a lot to ask, but if you were there, Zane would have to behave."

"I'm not going to show up two days early. I've never even met the man. I can't arrive on his doorstep with no warning."

"Oh, I'd warn him," Maya promised.

Phoebe shook her head. "No. I'll go with you on Friday. Not before." Besides, her no-more-favors vow was only an hour old. She couldn't violate it yet.

Maya shrugged. "Okay. That's fine. I

shouldn't have asked. It's just I worry about Chase. He was so young when his mom died. Zane practically left him to raise himself. Plus, he's really vulnerable right now, what with trying to figure out girls and think about college. And he's the only family I have."

Phoebe grabbed another chip and tried not to feel as if she'd just kicked a kitten. Maya's tactics were completely transparent. She was trying to guilt Phoebe into doing what she wanted. There was absolutely no way it was going to work.

CHAPTER THREE

Phoebe's flight touched down in Sacramento a little after three o'clock on Wednesday. She'd spent most of the flight from Los Angeles calling both herself and Maya names. She absolutely could not believe she'd given in so easily. One or two protests and she was as unyielding as bread pudding.

Now she was going to have to explain her presence to a man she'd never met.

She headed for the baggage-claim area to collect her two suitcases. Not knowing what June weather was like in the mountains, she'd brought plenty of clothes to layer, along with several pairs of jeans, and some boots she'd dug out from the back of her closet. The boots were a reminder of a brief but intense fondness for all things Western.

While waiting for the luggage to arrive, she tucked her headset into her carry-on. When she hadn't been berating Maya and herself, she'd been listening to self-improvement audio books and working on her mind-centering meditation. Unfortunately the former tended to make her doze off and the latter had a three-part breathing technique that started her coughing. Not something to endear her to her seatmates.

She glanced around, noting several men, but no one fitting Zane's description. Maya had claimed he looked like Adam Levine. One of **People** magazine's sexiest men alive.

Phoebe was skeptical and more than a little nervous. What was she going to say to an Adam Levine look-alike cowboy on the drive to the ranch? She'd tried to rent her own car, but Maya had insisted she would never find her way.

Five minutes later Phoebe had wrestled her two bags off the carousel and hooked them together so she could wheel them outside. She remained escort-less. Okay, so she would give Zane thirty minutes, then she would find a shuttle to Fool's Gold and figure out her next move. If she had to she could always—

The sliding doors opened, and a man entered the baggage area. A tall, dark-haired man with incredibly broad shoulders, a cowboy hat and a gaze so penetrating Phoebe knew he could probably tell what color her panties were.

He moved with the kind of stride and purpose of someone who was never indecisive, confused or anything other than in charge. He was gorgeous. Adam Levine gorgeous. Of course.

Any small shred of confidence she might have cultivated from her self-help books went belly-up like a zapped bug. She tried to brush off the last of the peanut dust from the front of her yellow T-shirt and wished for the millionth time in her life that she was tall, blonde, blue-eyed and stunning. Actually, right now she would take any one of the four.

"Phoebe Kitzke?"

The man had stopped in front of her. He had a deep, beautiful voice that made her thigh muscles quiver. This close she could see the multiple shades of deep blue that made up his eyes. He didn't smile. On the whole she would say he looked about as far from happy as it was possible to be while still breathing.

"I'm Phoebe," she said, afraid she sounded as tentative as she felt. Why hadn't Maya warned her? Saying Zane was good-looking was like saying summer in the desert was warm.

"Zane."

He held out his hand. She wasn't sure if he wanted to shake or take her luggage. She erred on the side of good manners and found her fingers engulfed in his.

The instant heat didn't surprise her, nor did the melting sensation. Everything else was going wrong in her life—it made sense for her body to betray her, too.

She mentally jerked her attention away from her traitorous thighs and noticed that he had a really big hand. Phoebe tried not to think about those old wives' tales. She tried not to think about anything except the fact that she was going to kill Maya the next time she saw her.

"Nice to meet you," she said when he'd released her. "Maya says the ranch is some distance from the airport, and I really appreciate you coming all this way to collect me."

His only response was to pick up her

luggage. He didn't bother with the wheels, instead carrying the bags out as if they weighed as much as a milk carton. Uh-huh. She'd nearly thrown out her entire back just wrestling them into the car. While in the past she'd never been all that interested in men with muscles, she could suddenly see the appeal of well-developed biceps.

Zane headed for the parking lot, and Phoebe trailed after him. He didn't seem to be much of a talker. That could make the drive to the ranch incredibly long.

He drove a truck, which didn't surprise her, but the fact that he held the passenger door open for her did. When her foot slipped on the metal step, he grabbed her elbow and gave her a little push into the cab. After stowing her luggage in the area behind his seat, he climbed in himself and settled next to her.

He towered over her as much while seated as he had while standing. Phoebe fastened her seat belt, then gave him a quick glance. Her heart did a one and a half somersault with a half twist at the sight of his profile. He looked good enough to be on a coin.

As Zane drove toward the exit, Phoebe searched frantically for a topic of conversation. Nothing brilliant came to mind. She nibbled on her lower lip as she considered risking the truth. When nothing better occurred to her, she decided to dive right into the cowboy-infested water.

"So this is really strange, huh?"

Zane glanced at her but didn't speak.

She cleared her throat. "Me being here. I mean you don't know me from a rock, and I'm going to be staying at the ranch for a couple of days. Maybe we should get to know each other, so the situation isn't so awkward."

"If you don't feel like you belong, why did you come?"

She spent a good three seconds mentally swooning over the sound of his voice before processing his words. He wasn't exactly welcoming.

"Well, um, several reasons," she said, stalling, then couldn't think of any but one. She sighed. "Maya guilted me into it."

"What did she tell you? That I keep Chase locked in a tower and feed him bread and water?"

Phoebe winced. "Not exactly."

"But close."

"Um, maybe."

Zane's grip on the steering wheel tightened. "She's always had a soft spot for Chase."

"He must be really smart. That must make you proud. I certainly couldn't design a website and entice people to sign up for a cattle-drive vacation."

Zane's ever-so-perfect mouth tightened. "He lied, stole and committed fraud. Pride doesn't much enter into it for me."

Phoebe hunched down in her seat. "If you're going to put it like that," she mumbled and turned her attention to the scenery.

Signs of civilization quickly gave way to rugged isolation. A mile marker along the side of the road announced that Fool's Gold was forty-two miles away.

She'd read up on the little town last night. Their slogan was The Destination for Romance. She cast a sidelong glance at Zane. Somehow, she didn't think the slogan would hold true for her. The man could not be less interested in her.

Mountain peaks rose in the distance. She caught glimpses of white-capped currents in a river that flashed between the thick trees along the side of the road. No doubt the area was teeming with wildlife. Phoebe liked little forest creatures as much as the next person, just so long as she didn't have to worry about them scurrying across the road or showing up on a serving platter.

What would it be like on the ranch? She'd never been on one before, hadn't even seen one except on TV or in the movies.

"So are there lots of cows?" she asked before she could stop herself. "On the ranch, I mean."

Zane didn't spare her a glance. "Some."

"Like twenty?"

He glanced at her then, before turning his attention back to the road. "We run several thousand head of steers. Those are the ones that end up on your barbecue. I have another few hundred head of cows for breeding purposes."

"No bulls?" she asked, unable to keep from grinning.

He sighed the sigh of the long suffering. "A dozen or so."

"A dozen bulls for a few hundred cows?"

Mr. Hunk-in-a-hat, who had put his hat on the seat between them when he'd climbed into the cab, chuckled. "Yup."

"Yet another example of our patriarchal society ignoring the rights of cows."

"You worried about cows' rights?" He sounded both incredulous and amused. "You a lawyer?"

"No. And I'm not concerned about cows' rights. Of course I want them treated humanely, as any civilized person would, but I'm not crazy."

"What are you, then?"

"What?"

He glanced at her. "If you're not a lawyer, what are you?"

"Oh." For a second she thought he'd been referring to her mental state. "I work in real estate."

Fortunately Zane didn't ask any questions about her career. She didn't think that telling him she'd been suspended for litigation would improve his opinion of her. At least he was talking. She tried to think of more cattle-related questions.

"How long have you been in the ranching

business?"

"All my life."

Silence. Zane Nicholson wasn't exactly chatty. Was it her or was it his personality?

"Do you ever sell the cattle for something other than food?"

Zane shifted in his seat. Had he been anyone else, she would have assumed the question made him uncomfortable. But he was too in-charge—too self-assured. Besides, what about it was embarrassing?

"Sometimes I'll sell off a few cows if we have too many."

"That makes sense. What about the bulls? Ever have too many of those?"

"Most of them become steers."

She didn't want to think about that. "So steers are boy cows?"

"That's right."

"What makes you decide who gets to have a really good life and who gets to be a burger?"

"Various factors. I've been working on genetically improving the herd."

"So a new bull with favorable character- istics would get to stay a bull."

He nodded.

"Sounds interesting," she said, because it really was. Who knew that ranchers worried about genetics?

"You're probably not going for things like eye color," she said without thinking.

Zane didn't even roll **his** eyes. "Not really."

"I didn't think so."

"I work with several universities. We have breeding experiments. I also sell to other ranchers."

"Your bulls?"

There was that seat squirm again. "No."

Not bulls? "Cows?"

"Sperm."

Phoebe blinked. "From the bulls?"

He nodded.

"You sell bull sperm?"

He nodded again.

Wow. There really were infinite ways to make a living. So how exactly did one get the sperm from the bull? She shook her head. Not something she wanted to know, she decided. Although she was intrigued by the question of what sort of marketing campaign would be most effective. Still, some subjects were better left unexplored, and this was definitely one of them.

She tried to think of something else to say. Anything, really. But how did one top bull sperm as a conversational gambit?

Maybe it was better if one didn't try.

They turned off the main highway, and Phoebe sat up straighter in her seat, eager for a glimpse of Fool's Gold. Zane had rolled down his window a few miles back, and fresh-scented mountain air filled the truck. A few years ago, a reality show had been filmed in the town. She and Maya had had a standing date to watch it together. Phoebe couldn't believe the place was as quaint as it had seemed on TV, but Maya had insisted it was more so.

Welcome to Fool's Gold, proclaimed a sign surrounded by lush red-and-yellow flowers in the shape of a heart.

Zane turned right onto Lakeview Drive.

Phoebe caught her breath. "It's so pretty!"

To their left, Lake Ciara sparkled in the mid-morning sun. To their right, children played in a large park under the watchful gazes of their mothers and of the mountains beyond. A huge, old oak tree provided shade for a couple stretched out on a pink blanket with their baby.

Just past the park, downtown Fool's Gold rose up, though it didn't rise up very high. She didn't see a building that was more than three or four stories tall, and only a few of those. The shops were neat and tidy. An American flag flew at every corner, and baskets of flowers hung from the other lampposts along the block. A banner spanned the width of the street, advertising the Summer Festival in two weeks.

Zane pulled into a parking spot in front of a two-story blue brick building with a yellow awning. "Mitchell Tours" was painted in bold, white letters on the shop's window.

"I've got some business in here for a few minutes, to arrange for pickup of the other guests later this week," he said. "Do you want to wait in the truck or walk around?"

"I'd love to see the town."

By the time she got her seat belt undone, he was holding open her door. She felt a small flush of warmth as he helped her from the tall truck. Being short had its advantages, she thought. Although he might not be happy she was here, gentlemanly manners were ingrained in him. She had to admit she liked it.

"We'll meet back here in fifteen minutes," he said before turning toward the shop.

"Aren't you going to lock the truck?"

"Not necessary."

The door swung shut behind him, and Phoebe was left standing on the sidewalk, wondering whether she'd heard him right. No need to lock the truck, even with her suitcases in the backseat and his window rolled down? She'd heard about places like that but had always assumed the people who lived there were fictional—or idiots. Zane didn't strike her as stupid, and her body's lingering reaction to his touch confirmed that he was very much a real man.

She turned left on Frank Lane and was pleased to find a bookstore halfway up the block. It made sense to have a print book for when they were out on the cattle drive, rather than relying on technology that would need to be recharged.

"Welcome to Morgan's Books." A trim man with neatly clipped gray hair greeted her with a smile. He wore a brown button-down shirt a few shades darker than his skin and tan slacks with a crisp crease down each leg. "I'm Morgan. Please let me know if you need any assistance. Otherwise, feel free to wander."

"Wandering in bookstores is one of my favorite things in the world," she replied with a smile.

"I like you already."

She quickly found the latest Liz Sutton mystery and was thrilled to see a "Signed by local author" sticker on the cover.

One of her favorite authors lived in this small town? She carried her treasure under her arm as she browsed the fiction section. When she glanced at her watch, she was shocked to discover that twelve minutes had passed.

Somehow, she had the feeling that cowboy Zane would not appreciate being kept waiting. She paid for her book, promised to visit again before she left town, and raced back to the truck.

Zane wasn't there yet. But two old ladies were. They were well into their seventies, both about the same height with white hair and papery pink skin. The thin, curly-haired one with no makeup was dressed in a plush green tracksuit with bright white sneakers, while the plumper one wore a full face of makeup, including false eyelashes, and a prim flowered dress with thick, nude pumps. Oddly, they were sitting on the front bumper of Zane's truck, and the one in the track-suit was pointing a handheld video camera toward the front window of Mitchell Tours.

After a moment of hesitation, Phoebe opened the passenger door of the truck. The old ladies hurried toward her.

"This is Zane Nicholson's truck," the one in the flowered dress said.

"I know."

"Are you with Zane?"

Phoebe glanced at the one in the track-suit, whose video camera was now pointed at her. Since it was about eighteen inches away, she could imagine how huge her face must look on the screen.

"Don't mind me," the old lady said. "Just keep talking like I'm not even here. And... rolling."

"Are you with Zane?" the other one repeated.

"I'm...yes, I guess. Sort of."

"Scoop!" The one in the tracksuit pumped

a fist in the air.

"You're his girlfriend?"

Phoebe looked around, expecting to see the ladies' caretakers coming toward them with white coats and apologies, but although the town was bustling, no one seemed to be paying them any attention. Should she call the police? The hospital? Or was this kind of nosiness normal in a small town? Maybe this was why Zane hadn't locked the truck, because he knew these two busybodies would guard it for him?

Not sure what to do, she said, "I'm here for the cattle drive."

The women exchanged a meaningful look and grinned. Somehow, it made Phoebe even more uneasy.

Just then, the door to Mitchell Tours opened, and Zane stepped out. When he saw the old women, he seemed to falter for a moment, but it happened so fast that Phoebe wasn't sure.

The one in the green tracksuit hurried to the front of the truck, with her video camera pointed toward Zane. "What can you tell us about the cattle drive?"

He shot a look at Phoebe. She shrugged helplessly.

"Sorry, ladies, no time to talk. We have to get back to the ranch."

Relieved, Phoebe pulled herself up into the truck. Zane didn't come to her side to help her this time, but even after this short association with the determined women, she understood that time was of the essence in making a clean getaway. As she settled in the passenger seat, she could swear the video camera was focused on Zane's butt when he climbed behind the wheel.

"Who are they?" she asked under her breath.

"Eddie and Gladys," he muttered, then shot her a dark look. "You told them about the cattle drive?"

"They ambushed me, and, no. They seemed to know about it already." At least that was what she thought the knowing look meant. She could be wrong.

"Who are they?" she asked.

"Just a couple of old ladies who live in town."

"And the camera?"

He sighed heavily. "I have no idea. When it comes to those two, the less you get involved, the better."

"Are you scared of them?"

"Let's just say I know when to take on the bear and when to walk around. When it comes to those two, I walk around."

His mouth turned up at one corner. His face was transformed when he smiled, even when it was a half-smile given half-heartedly. Wow. A sexy cowboy with a sense of humor could be dangerous. And while she'd always avoided danger in the past, for some reason, she found herself wanting to move just a little closer.

Play with fire, she reminded herself. Only getting burned seemed like a small price to pay.

CHAPTER FOUR

"Get ready, Tommy," Lucy Sax told her brother. She kept her voice down, like Mrs. Fortier was always telling her, only this time it wasn't to keep from getting on Mr. Fortier's nerves. She spoke quietly so that no one could hear them.

Her brother shook his head. "I don't wanna."

Lucy planted her hands on her hips and glared at him. "You have to. I can't do it—I'm not any good. You're the best, Tommy. And you know we need the money."

Tommy, ten and older than Lucy by two years, shook his head again. "It's wrong."

Lucy already knew that boys were more important, more special, than girls, but she didn't get that at all. From her viewpoint, boys weren't very bright. Wanting or not wanting didn't have anything to do with it. Need mattered more.

They stood close together by the vending machines in the brightly lit bowling alley. Sound exploded all around them, from the smash of a ball crashing into the pins to the buzzing and beeping of the video games to the frantic laughter of desperate children.

Lucy glanced past her brother to all the nervous couples bowling with children they didn't know and would never adopt. She hated coming to the social events. What was the point? No one was ever going to adopt her or Tommy.

For a long time she'd hoped they would get new parents. She'd agreed to wear her best dress, to smile and be polite. Until one day she'd overheard some adults talking about her and Tommy.

"Mongrels," the man had said. "Not white, not black, not Hispanic." He'd turned to his pretty pale-skinned wife and reminded her that they wanted to adopt a white or Hispanic child.

Lucy had saved her tears until she was in bed and no one would see. Then she'd given in to the sorrow. At the next social event, she'd concentrated on charming the African-American couples, but they didn't seem any more interested in mongrel children. It was then that she realized she and Tommy were never going to find a home. They had each other, and that was all that mattered.

Now she glared at her brother. "I'm going to start doing cartwheels right now," she told him. "While everyone is watching me, you're going to take the money."

He nodded, looking miserable. For a second Lucy felt bad about making him do it, but then she thought about all the times Mrs. Fortier sent them to bed without supper. It was one of her favorite punishments. Lucy had heard her talking to a friend once; Mrs. Fortier had said that at the end of the day, she liked her peace and quiet.

So Lucy and Tommy needed the money for food, and sometimes for clothes. She kept track of every penny, and they never spent it on candy or toys. She was saving, too, so that when they were bigger they could run away together.

But that was for later. Right now she had a plan.

After smoothing her hair, she marched to the front of the bowling lanes. She waited until Tommy was in position, then she smiled so wide her cheeks hurt and started doing cartwheels. Everyone turned to watch. On her third one, she deliberately fell. She'd misjudged the distance and really slammed her knee into the hardwood floor. It wasn't hard to force out a few tears.

Instantly all the adults crowded around her. Lucy did her best to look small and hurt. From the corner of her eye, she saw Tommy moving toward the purses.

"Hel-lo, gorgeous."

Phoebe looked around as she stepped out of Zane's truck. Standing next to the passenger door was a tall teenager with bright, inquisitive eyes and a welcoming smile. He looked enough like Adam Levine to make it easy for her to guess his identity.

"You must be Chase," she said.

"In the flesh. And you're Phoebe." He looked her over from head to toe, then sighed. "Maya said a lot of great things about you, but she never mentioned you were a goddess."

The outrageous compliment made Phoebe laugh. "Hardly," she protested, knowing that with her brown hair, brown eyes and unspectacular features she was little more than average.

"My heart is pounding a mile a minute," Chase said, moving closer. "Want to feel?"

The driver's-side door slammed shut. "Don't you have chores?" Zane growled.

Chase took a step back, and his smile cranked down about 50 percent.

"All done. Even the extra ones you gave me. I got started early so I could be finished to welcome Phoebe." Keeping a wary eye on his brother, he swept his arms open wide. "Here it is. Several thousand acres of Nicholson family ranch. Nicholsons have owned this land for five generations."

She looked around at the rolling hills that stretched out to the horizon. They were a mere fifteen minutes outside of Fool's Gold, but the only signs of civilization were two wind-power generators on a hill miles away. A two-story ranch house sprawled out on her left. To the right were several barns and corrals. Trees crested the nearest hill. In the distance she could see cattle. Lots of cattle.

"Amazing," she said honestly.

"If you're so fired up about playing host," Zane said, his expression both fierce and closed, "I'll let you take care of her luggage and show her to her room."

He put his hat on his head, nodded once at Phoebe and stalked away.

She stared after him for a second. He looked as good from the back as he had from the front. Her hormones yelled out catcalls of appreciation which—fortun- ately—only she could hear. But however impressed she might be with him, Zane obviously didn't return her feelings. He practically burned rubber in his haste to get away.

Chase brightened the second Zane was gone. "How was the drive?" he asked as he walked around to the other side of the truck and pulled her suitcases out from behind the driver's seat where Zane had placed them.

"Good."

"Did Zane talk?"

Phoebe glanced at him, not sure of the question.

Chase hoisted her luggage with the same ease Zane had shown and started for the house.

"He's not much of a talker," he explained as he walked. "I can't figure out if the act of forming words is physically painful, or if he just doesn't have anything to say."

She thought about the drive from the airport. "Things started out well," she admitted. "Then we sort of stalled about twenty minutes into the drive."

Yup—nothing like asking about bull sperm to shut down a conversational exchange.

"Twenty minutes, huh?" Chase glanced back at her over his shoulder and grinned. "I'm impressed. Most people get a grunt. He must really like you."

Phoebe laughed again. "Yeah. He was so overpoweringly impressed he couldn't wait to get away."

She followed Chase up the front steps onto a wide porch that seemed to wrap around the whole house. While the teenager had a long way to go before he was as hunky as his older brother, he was still pretty impressive. Good-looking, funny, easy to talk to.

"I've been had," she muttered more to herself than to him.

"What do you mean?"

"Maya got me out here early by implying you were neglected and pitiful all on your own. I thought I was going to be rescuing a lost waif."

Chase winked. "I am. Can't you tell? Zane practically keeps me chained up in my room."

"Uh-huh. I'm all in tears over your broken spirit."

Chase chuckled, then led the way into the house. They entered a large foyer that opened up into a living room big enough to hold an international peace conference. The furniture—chintz-covered chairs and a matching dark red sofa—wasn't new, but it looked cared for and comfortable. Several other rooms led off the foyer, but Chase headed for the stairs, and Phoebe was forced to follow. She told herself there would be plenty of time to explore later, and the house would be worth the wait.

Even the little bit she could see was amazing. She'd never seen anything like the intricately carved stair rail, and she'd been in plenty of million-dollar-plus mansions.

Old photographs lined the stairway wall, and she caught glimpses of black-and-white pictures of multiple generations of men who looked nearly as handsome as Zane.

At the top of the stairs, the landing led both left and right. Chase went right and stopped in front of a door at the end of the hall.

"You're in Maya's old room," he said. "There are two beds. Normally you wouldn't have to share, but with everyone else arriving, we're a little tight on space."

For the second time since she'd met him, Phoebe saw the humor fade from Chase's eyes. His mouth twisted slightly.

"I don't mind if Maya doesn't," she said. "Plus, I'm here first, so I get to pick the good bed, right?"

Chase's smile returned. "Right."

He pushed open the door and carried her suitcases inside. Phoebe followed. The room was large and bright, done in various shades of lavender. A pansy-print wallpaper decorated the walls from the white chair rail up, with lavender paint on the bottom half. Two beds sat on either side of a big window covered with crisp white curtains. There was a dresser topped with a TV against one wall, two doors on another and a second window on a third.

"There's a bathroom in there," Chase said, setting her luggage on one of the beds. "The other door is the closet."

"It's great."

"Want to see my room?"

Chase might be seventeen, but at that moment, he looked about ten. She nodded.

"I'd love to."

"Sweet."

He led her back down the hall to a room just off the stairs. Phoebe stepped into a messy room with a full-size bed, a massive computer and more electronic equipment than she'd ever seen outside of a Best Buy. Dials glowed, lights flashed, boxes beeped. Circuit boards lay scattered like so many discarded toys.

Chase sank into the only chair in the room and began typing on the keyboard.

"A couple of my friends and I are working on some really great special effects on the computer. You know, for websites. We're also working on a robot, but it's not going that great. I think the main problem is in the programming, but it's hard to tell because everything else is screwed up, too."

He finished typing and pushed back from the desk. Phoebe stepped forward and saw a three-dimensional swirling object on the screen. Chase handed her a pair of 3-D glasses. When she slipped them on and stared at the screen, the spiraling blob seemed to leap out at her.

"I like it," she said, handing the glasses back.

He grinned and rose. "I have a baseball I caught when Zane took me to San Francisco a couple of years ago. It was a fly ball, bottom of the third. Dodgers against the Giants."

He picked up the ball from a shelf above his bed and held it out for her inspection.

"Wow."

"There's also the—"

"I doubt Phoebe wants to see your entire collection of treasures right now."

At the sound of Zane's voice, they both jumped and turned toward the door. Phoebe had a bad feeling that she looked guilty...mostly because she felt that way. Which was crazy. She hadn't done anything wrong.

Zane stood leaning against the doorway, his arms folded over his chest. He looked strong and unmovable. Maya's claims about Chase's broken spirit didn't hold water when compared with the teenager's outgoing personality, but Phoebe couldn't help wondering what Zane was thinking as he studied his brother.

"Is your room all right?" Zane asked her.

She nodded. "Everything is great."

"Maya wants me to take you to dinner in town." He glanced at his watch.

Feel the love, she thought, not sure if she should call him on his lack of graciousness. "You don't have to."

"It's fine."

"Can we go to Margaritaville?" Chase asked. "I could go for nachos."

"What you could go for even more is staying home and finishing cleaning all the guest rooms. There's a pizza in the freezer. Elaine Mitchell's going to pick up the greenhorns and Maya on Friday and bring them out to the ranch in her tourist van. You've got a lot of work to do before they get here."

"But—"

Zane cut him off with a look, then turned back to Phoebe. "Meet me downstairs in an hour."

Phoebe knew a dismissal when she heard one. Due to the fact that she was an uninvited stranger who had shown up with little warning, she didn't feel that she was in a position to complain.

She gave Chase a quick smile, then moved toward the door. Zane stepped out of the way to let her pass. As she walked by him, the hairs on the back of her neck stood up and swayed in salutation.

When Phoebe left her room an hour later, she could hear Chase singing in a bedroom down the hall. She smiled. He was such a cheerful kid, a pure-hearted spirit. Forced to stay home and do chores, he'd decided he might as well make them fun.

She was a little nervous about spending the evening alone with his big brother, though. What would they talk about?

Zane was waiting for her at the base of

the stairs. She stopped on the last step so that when he turned toward her, they were eye to eye.

"I'm sorry I didn't bring anything dressier," she said. She'd changed into white jeans and a pale, dusty purple top with an embellished scoop neckline.

His gaze traveled to her feet and back to her face. She thought maybe she read masculine appreciation in his raised brows.

"You're fine," he said.

So much for any appreciation. On his part, at least. "Give me a moment while I bask in the glory," she murmured and stepped past him to the front porch and then down toward his truck.

Zane got there ahead of her. A neat trick explained by his much longer stride. He towered over her. He'd changed clothes, too, into dark blue jeans and a fitted white T-shirt that showcased his hard-earned muscles. His dark hair was still damp. An image flashed through her mind of him in the shower, water running over his broad shoulders.

He opened the door for her, then helped her into the truck. The masculine scent of his soap and shampoo wafted toward her as he climbed in beside her, making her limbs melt into the leather seat.

This felt like a date. It wasn't, but still. Phoebe sighed. Maya had promised her a distraction, and Zane was certainly that. Too bad he didn't seem to like her one bit.

Phoebe was a little relieved when Zane didn't park outside Margaritaville. After Chase had mentioned wanting nachos, it would seem mean to eat there. Instead she and Zane walked into a place called The Fox and Hound.

The restaurant had lots of dark wood and booths. There were English hunting prints on the wall. Campy, Phoebe thought happily, following the hostess to a booth and sliding in.

She told herself the quivering sensation she felt inside was because she was hungry and had nothing to do with the man sitting across from her. Then she felt bad for lying, if only to herself.

She took the offered menu but didn't open it. When they were alone, she glanced at Zane.

"Do you not like me or is this just your style?"

Zane's gaze was steady. Almost laser-like. She wanted to squirm but didn't. Nor did she look away.

"I like you fine," he said at last.

The low gravelly quality of his voice was so nice, she thought, before the actual words sank in. "Really?"

He sighed. "Why are you surprised?"

"You aren't exactly welcoming. I know you're doing all this to teach Chase a lesson, so it's not like you asked me to visit, but you didn't have to take me out to dinner just because Maya asked you to."

"You didn't have to say yes."

"I was hungry."

"So was I."

Zane knew that he and Phoebe were no longer talking about the same thing. At least not when it came to hunger. She would be thinking fish and chips, and he was thinking more along the lines of naked.

He wanted to tell himself it was simply because he was a man and she was a woman, but he knew it was more than that.

As he'd admitted, he liked her. She was cute and funny. When she looked at him with her big brown eyes, he wanted to grab Tango and ride his horse into the sunset to save something for her. Talk about idiotic. He barely knew her.

Yet there was something about Phoebe Kitzke. An innocence, maybe. No, that wasn't right. It was how she seemed trusting. More fool her. Or maybe him.

Not that it mattered. Wanting wasn't having. She was here as Maya's friend. Possibly to keep watch over him so he didn't hurt Chase. Because Maya wouldn't trust him.

"You're looking fierce," Phoebe said.

Her hair was long and loose. Sexy. He deliberately steered his brain away from that line of thinking.

"My sister brings out the fierce in me."

"Because of how she's always thinking you're too hard on Chase?"

"Maya talks too much."

"She says less than you think," Phoebe told him. "It's more what she doesn't say. She worries about Chase."

"Everybody does."

Phoebe wrinkled her nose. "She worries about you, too."

He raised a brow. "I doubt that."

Phoebe raised her shoulders, then let them drop back into place. "Okay, maybe she doesn't say that exactly, but I know she does. We're friends."

"Being friends gives you insight?"

"Of course. It's not like being family, but it's close."

"Family can be a pain in the ass."

"Maybe," she said, "but it has to be better than being alone."

Maybe if he didn't feel so responsible for Chase, he would be able to enjoy his brother more. As it was, he walked that precarious line between brother and father figure. He spent half the time annoyed with some of the boy's boneheaded decisions and the other half worried the kid was going to screw up his own life.

"An optimist."

"You say that like it's a bad thing."

"It's important to be realistic."

She leaned toward him. "It's important to have dreams. To see the possibilities."

He'd believed that once, he reminded

himself. Before he'd destroyed what mattered most to his father. Before he'd understood that some things were unfor-givable. No matter how much a kid tried to make them right.

Their server came by to take their drink order. Phoebe asked for a glass of red wine while Zane got a beer. When they were alone again, Phoebe leaned toward him.

"Tell me about Fool's Gold."

"What do you want to know?"

He was expecting a question about the tourists, or the history. Instead she surprised him by asking, "What do you like best about living here?"

"It's what I know."

She nodded slowly. "Because you've lived here all your life. I get that. You have a connection with the town and the rhythm of the seasons. You probably have friends from when you were really small."

He stared at her. "You don't need me around for this conversation, do you?"

She laughed. "Sorry. I can get carried away."

"That's okay."

"So do you have friends from when you

were little?"

"Sure."

She glanced out the window. "I like the window boxes with flowers."

"You should see this place at Christmas."

Her eyes brightened. "All decorated?"

"Every inch."

"That's so nice." She jumped a little in her seat. "Oh, wow. Do you get snow? Are we high enough for snow?"

"There's nearly always a white Christmas."

He had no idea why he was trying to sell her on the town. While he liked it well enough, he wasn't looking to join the tourist commission or whatever it was called. What did he care if Phoebe was impressed by Fool's Gold or not? Yet he found himself wanting her to think it was special.

Which made him a fool, and for the life of him, he couldn't say why he was bothering.

C. J. Swanson refused to look at her husband, Thad. Instead she stared out the window and tried to ignore his words. He didn't understand...he would never understand. Yes, the problem was with both of them, but somehow she always felt guilty. As if there was something wrong with her.

"They're just kids," Thad was saying. "Why would you want to deprive them of this vacation?"

"Why is it my responsibility?" she asked before she could stop herself. "Why do I have to be the bad guy? It's not my fault that the couple going with them had a death in the family. It's not anyone's fault."

"C.J...." Thad reached out and touched the back of her hand.

She turned away again. "I can't. You're asking too much. What would be the point? We aren't interested in them. They were horrible. That boy's a thief, Thad. Have you forgotten? His sister is just as bad. She might not have taken the money, but I would bet you anything she put him up to it."

"They're just kids," her husband said in his calm, reasonable voice. Normally she appreciated his willingness to see things clearly, without being blinded by emotion, but today he was really getting on her nerves.

"Con artists, you mean."

C.J. tried not to sound bitter, but she didn't think she was successful. After so many years of trying, after so many disappointments, she felt as if she had finally reached the end of the road.

She and Thad would never have children. Not their own and not any they adopted. She and her husband loved each other. They had a strong, healthy marriage. That would be enough—she would make it enough.

Beside her, Thad turned her hand over and laced his fingers with hers.

"I like them," he said softly.

Her chest tightened. Of course he did. Because he was a good man. Because he always rooted for the underdog, whether it was in his personal life or in the courtroom. After fifteen years of practicing law, he'd been appointed to the bench where he could put all his idealistic notions into practice. Her husband, the man whom she had loved since the first moment she'd seen him seventeen years ago, **would** like a ten-year-old pickpocket and his con artist younger sister.

She turned her head to study his familiar

features. The steady gaze of his blue eyes, the thinning blond hair worn in a conservative cut…not because he was conservative, but because he was cursed with unruly curls that made him look like an aging rock star. She visually traced the lines at the corners of his eyes and the firm set of his full mouth. He was a good man. A kind man. A man who loved her and never blamed her. He knew her better than anyone, knew what he was asking. How was she supposed to tell him no?

"All right," she said softly. "We'll take Lucy and Tommy on the cattle drive. One week, Thad. That's all I'm willing to give them. Please, don't expect to make it more."

He smiled, then leaned forward and kissed her. "You won't regret it."

She didn't answer. Instead she prayed that he was right. Between the two of them, they already had enough regrets for this lifetime.

CHAPTER FIVE

"Goats?" Phoebe asked as she stared at the array of large, open pens. Several horned goats nibbled on their breakfast of hay and some kind of grain. "Didn't you say that the Castle Ranch has goats, too?"

"Those are dairy goats. Heidi makes cheese."

Phoebe shrugged. "And that's different how?"

"These are cashmere goats," Chase grinned. "Just imagine the horror of discovering a cattleman raising goats. They're Zane's most embarrassing secret."

She supposed the romance of the Old West didn't lend itself to goats the same way it did to cattle, but as far as she was concerned, four-legged grazing animals were all pretty much the same.

She'd sure seen plenty on her tour. The Nicholson Ranch was nothing if not huge. As they'd been on foot, she and Chase had only explored a tiny bit of it. She didn't know the going price of cattle on the hoof, or the per acre value of land in this part of the country, but from what she could tell, no Nicholson was ever going to die poor.

Better than that, the land had been in their possession for generations. Phoebe wondered what it would be like to have roots and a history—a place to belong. Family.

"If he doesn't like goats, why does he have them?" she asked.

Before Chase could answer, a man on horseback rode over a crest in the property. One minute there had been green grass and blue sky, while the next a tall silhouette appeared. Zane. Phoebe watched, mesmerized. Her lone experience with riding a horse consisted of slow, sedate turns on a carousel. Not exactly the same as cow roping on the open range.

As she watched, he approached. He moved easily on the horse, riding or swaying or doing something so that he and the animal appeared to be one and the same. It was darned impressive.

As Zane got closer, his handsome features became clearer, which made her breathing increase. Chase might be the charming brother, but there was something mighty fine about Zane Nicholson.

Beside her, Chase groaned. "He's going to make me help Frank put together the kits for the cattle drive."

"What kits?"

Chase grimaced. "Supplies. Tents, eating utensils, first aid, that sort of thing. We have to take it with us and he's basically made me Frank's slave."

Phoebe wanted to ask who Frank was. She also considered pointing out that if Chase hadn't taken money from unsuspecting customers in the first place, none of this would have happened. But before she could say anything, Zane reined in his horse and dismounted. From the second his feet touched the ground, she knew it was going to be impossible for her to form coherent sentences.

However, Zane ignored her, instead turning his disapproving expression on his brother. "Frank's looking for you."

"I'll get there." Chase turned his back on his brother. "I was showing Phoebe the goats."

"Frank's waiting now. Folks'll be arriving

tomorrow. We need to be prepared. If we're short on supplies, you'll have to head into town and pick them up."

Chase muttered something under his breath, but didn't overtly argue with Zane.

"Take Tango with you," Zane said, handing the reins to his brother.

Chase grabbed them, then turned his attention to Phoebe. Rebellion darkened his eyes and tightened his expression. "Sorry to cut this short. Maybe my brother will tell you all about the goats." Some of his annoyance faded as a smile pulled at his mouth. "They hold a special place in his heart."

With that, he left. Zane watched him go, then walked to the edge of the fenced pen and rested his arms on the top rail.

Dinner with Zane hadn't gone as well as she'd hoped. They'd started out okay, but early on, he'd gotten quiet. She wanted to tell herself it was because he had a lot on his mind, but in her heart, she had a feeling he simply didn't find her interesting. Which was too bad, because he was the most compelling man she'd ever met.

"You think I'm too hard on the boy."

His words were so at odds with what she'd been thinking that it took her a second to catch up. "Not unless you're beating him in secret."

She couldn't be sure, but she thought maybe one corner of his mouth turned up. "I've thought about it from time to time."

Phoebe made a quick mental list of Chase's recent infractions, then admitted the possibility that he'd been a handful all of his life.

"Thinking and acting are two different things."

Zane's response was a quiet grunt. She tried to figure out if that was better or worse than a loud grunt. When she couldn't come up with a decision, she turned her attention to the pen in front of them.

"Tell me about the goats," she said.

"What do you want to know?"

Like she had a basic "Ten facts about goats" list she needed filled. "Are they friendly?"

Zane shot her a look that wasn't especially pleasant...or flattering. Okay, so if he didn't like the question he could have volunteered information on his own.

"They can be tamed. It takes time and effort."

Somehow she doubted he was willing to put either into the goats.

"Chase implied it's a problem for a cattle rancher to have goats. Is that true?"

Zane shifted his weight, then stepped back from the pen. "Come on," he said and started walking.

Phoebe figured she had the choice to follow him or not. Even as she told herself he wasn't very social and obviously didn't like having her around, her hormones kicked in, sending instructions to her legs. Before she could decide if she wanted to follow Zane or not, she found herself dutifully trailing after him.

They circled around a barn, passing more pens with more goats. There were dozens and dozens of the horned, furry critters. An entire goat colony. Sort of a Nicholson Ranch Goat-ville.

Zane stopped in front of a pen filled with small goats. Instantly her kitten-and-puppy-loving heart contracted at the sight of baby goats. They were small and sweet-looking with big eyes and dark noses they had yet to grow into.

She crouched down by the fence and sighed. Her heretofore silent biological clock offered a soft but meaningful **tick**.

"Just weaned," he said.

"They're darling."

"They're for sale."

Phoebe gasped. "You're allowing some stranger to rip apart goat families?" The second the words were out, she realized how stupid they sounded.

"I didn't mean that," she said hastily as she scrambled to her feet. "It's not as if goats have an actual social infrastructure that will be disturbed by separation or anything. And if they're old enough to be weaned, then I guess they'll be okay on their own."

Zane's expression remained unreadable throughout her monologue, for which she was really grateful. When she was done, he let the silence linger. A neat trick that made her words echo in her brain, sounding more ridiculous with each replay.

Finally he asked, "What did you say you did in LA?"

"I sell real estate."

"Whereabouts?"

"Beverly Hills."

"Ever been on a horse?" he asked.

"Just a wooden one."

Zane turned away. She thought he might have muttered something under his breath. As it hadn't sounded like "golly darn" she didn't ask him to repeat it.

"Why did Maya drag you out here?" he asked.

Phoebe didn't think telling him that Maya was hoping she would be a distraction, and a possible sex partner, would be something he was longing to hear.

"I needed a vacation," she said. Unfortunately the statement came out sounding a whole lot more like a question.

Zane grunted.

Even annoyed and monosyllabic, he was still intensely appealing. Phoebe liked the way he squinted in the bright sun. Lines formed by his eyes, which gave him the appearance of being wise beyond his years. It probably wasn't true, but hey, this was her bout of physical attraction and she could take it in any direction she liked... as long as she wasn't foolish enough to act on it.

"Chase implied you hate the goats," she said to change the subject and get the attention off her. "Why do you keep them?"

She expected him to say something like they made a lot of money—and based on how much she'd paid for her only cashmere twinset, she knew that had to be true. Or maybe that he was doing an experimental genetic ranch-type breeding program thing with them.

Instead he said, "My dad bought them. He saw them as a way to diversify. He wanted to end up with the biggest herd in the continental US."

Oh, man. Phoebe wanted to stomp her foot on the soft grass and offer up her version of a four letter word. This was not right. Maya had always painted a picture of Zane that was coldhearted, taciturn and humorless. In her mind he'd been more of a robot than a real person. Which had made her instant—and somewhat embarrassing —physical attraction interesting, but not significant. Because there wasn't a real person inside. But if Zane was human and nice, she could be in real trouble. After all, a man who kept goats just because his dad had liked them couldn't be all bad. Right?

"Were you and your father close?" she asked.

"No."

Phoebe almost laughed. For one split second she'd been so darned sure she had a window into the real Zane Nicholson. Her heart had melted at the thought of getting to know the inner man. So much for that theory.

She started to ask why, if he and his father hadn't been tight, Zane bothered to keep the goats, but before she could, one of the kids walked up to the fence and rubbed its head on the corner post.

Phoebe instantly dropped to her knees. "Hi, baby. How are you?" She stuck her fingers through the metal fencing to pet the little guy. The soft fur, or fleece, or hair or whatever it was delighted her. Right before amazingly strong teeth clamped around her fingers.

She screamed. The loud noise frightened the kid into releasing her, and she jerked her fingers back through the fence. Before she could study the damage, Zane grabbed her by her arm and pulled her to her feet. He took her hand in his and examined the injury.

Several things occurred to her at once. First—that they'd never stood this close together before. He was so big, tall and broad that he made her feel positively delicate by comparison. Second—for a man who had spent his morning on a horse, he smelled really good. All clean and woodsy. Third—the instant his fingers touched her, the pain miraculously vanished. Talk about amazing.

"Skin's not broken," he said as he turned over her hand. "Tell me if this hurts."

He bent her fingers back and forth. His warmth sent sizzling jolts of awareness slip-sliding all through her body. Despite the heat filling her, something was wrong with her lungs because it was impossible to breathe. He touched her gently, as if he didn't want to hurt her.

The logical part of her brain turned cynical, announcing that he was simply concerned about a lawsuit by a goat-bitten city girl. The romantic side of her suddenly understood all those country songs about cowboys. What was it that country star Lacey Mills had sung? "Go ahead, cowboy. Rope me in." It was a brief battle, with romance emerging victorious.

Whatever emotional distance she might have been able to maintain was lost the second Zane lightly squeezed her hand and smiled. She'd never seen him smile before. If she'd been able to breathe, he would have taken her breath away.

"I think you'll live," he said. "Just stay away from the goats."

"Okay."

The single word was the best she could do under the circumstances. Zane continued to look at her. Even better, he kept her hand in his, his thumb rubbing up and down the length of her fingers. Over and over. Up and down. It was very rhythmic. And sexual.

Her thighs took on a life of their own, getting all hot and shaking slightly. Her mouth went dry, her breasts were jealous of the attention her hand was getting and her hormones were singing the "Hallelujah Chorus." Obviously she needed intensive therapy...or maybe just sex.

Zane's eyes darkened. The muscles in

his face tightened, and he stared at her with a hawkish expression. Had he been anyone else, she would have sworn that he'd just had a physical awakening of his own. Awareness crackled around them, like self-generated lightning. The tightness in her chest eased just enough for her to suck in a breath, which was really good, because the next second it all came rushing out again when he kissed her.

Just like that. With no warning, Zane Nicholson bent his head and claimed her mouth.

It wasn't a movie-perfect kiss. They didn't magically melt into each other. Instead their noses bumped, and somehow the hand still holding hers got trapped between them. But all that was fairly insignificant when compared with the intense, sensual heat generated by the pressure of his lips on hers.

That part was exactly right. Not too hard, not too soft. When he moved against her, need shot through her body. Had she been breathing again, she would have whimpered. Had he tried to pull away, she would have fallen at his feet and begged him not to stop.

Somehow he released her hand and pulled his free. He wrapped his arms around her and hauled her against him so her entire body pressed against his. The man was a rock. Big, unyielding and warmed by the sun. She wanted to snuggle even closer. She wanted to rip off her clothes and give the goats something to talk about. She wanted—

He licked her lower lip.

The unexpected moist heat made her gasp as fire raced through her. Every singed nerve ending vibrated with need for more. The masculine, slightly piney scent of him surrounded her. Operating only on instinct, she parted her lips to allow him entry. She had a single heartbeat to brace herself for the power of his tongue touching hers. Then he swept inside and blew her away.

It was like being inside the space shuttle on takeoff. Phoebe might not have any personal experience with space flight, but she could imagine. The powerful force between them left her weak and clinging to his broad shoulders. She trembled and needed and ached with equal intensity.

His tongue brushed against hers again. He tasted of coffee and mint and something wonderfully sensual and sweet. His mouth seemed designed for kissing. Maybe it was all that non-conversation. Maybe talking too much undermined a man's ability to kiss. She didn't know and didn't care. All that mattered was the way he stroked her, touched her, teased her. He cupped her head with one hand and ran his other up and down her back. If only this moment would never end.

But it did. A sharp bark from somewhere in the distance brought Phoebe back to earth with a rude thunk. She suddenly became aware of being pressed up against a really good-looking stranger, kissing in front of a goat pen. Apparently Zane got a similar wake-up call, because he stepped back at the same second she did. At least the man was breathing hard. She would hate to think she was the only one who had been affected.

"Okay, then," she said when she realized that all feelings to the contrary, she still could breathe.

Zane continued to stare at her.

She swallowed. "Did you want to say something?"

Anything would be fine. Just any old reaction. As long as he wasn't going to say it was all a mistake. That would really annoy her. Or maybe she was making a big deal out of nothing. Maybe he kissed lots of women out here by the goat pens.

"I have to get back to work. Can you find your way to the house?"

She blinked at him. That was it? Okay. Fine. As long as she didn't try to walk on legs that were still trembling, she could pretend nothing had happened.

"Sure," she muttered. "No problem."

He nodded, then bent down and picked up his hat. She frowned. When exactly had that fallen off? He straightened, opened his mouth, then closed it. She wasn't even surprised when he turned and left without saying a word. It was just so typical.

When she was alone, Phoebe tried to work up a case of righteous indignation. When that didn't work, she went for humor. If nothing else, she had to give Maya credit for the promised distraction. Oh. She also had to remember that as soon as she found out what constituted a treat on the baby-goat food hit list, she would be sure to send a thank-you gift.

Zane figured the morning had been a cheap lesson. If one city slicker could get bit just walking around the ranch, what kind of trouble were ten greenhorns going to get into on a cattle drive? As he headed for the main barn, he considered the potential for broken legs, stampeding cattle and raging cases of poison oak. If he was lucky, that would be the worst of it. He didn't want to consider what would happen if he wasn't lucky.

Most of the time he didn't allow himself second guesses. They were a pointless waste of time. But for once he wondered if he'd made the right decision when he'd chosen to host a cattle drive instead of simply paying back the deposits and taking the money out of Chase's hide with a summer full of rough physical work.

That boy was going to be the death of him.

He jerked open the barn door and stalked toward his office. But instead of entering it, he passed through to the file room—an open area with dozens of file cabinets filled with breeding information, records for the ranch and medical histories for every Black Angus steer, cow or bull to step foot on the Nicholson Ranch. He crossed to the back wall where he studied a map of the area, including his ranch, the Castle Ranch to the east and the Konopka place to the west, and of course, the nearby town of Fool's Gold.

His normal route for the cattle drive took him about a hundred and fifty miles from one end of Nicholson land to the other. It was an easy two weeks of lazy rides, wide-open spaces and plenty of time to just be without the hassles of everyday life. It was also about as far from the main ranch buildings as he could get, outside of coverage from the cell tower he'd had built several years ago. He took a few trusted men, some supplies and Tango, his best horse. Primitive didn't begin to describe the conditions. They were his favorite two weeks of the year.

But not this year. Not with ten vacationers who, like Phoebe, had probably never been on a horse. He would—

Phoebe.

The reality he'd been doing his damnedest to ignore crashed in on him with all the subtlety of a bull after a cow. Desire flared, making him hot, horny and uncomfortable. He swore, stopped, remembered how good she'd kissed, then swore again.

What had he been thinking? Which was a stupid question because he hadn't been thinking. He'd been reacting. One minute he'd been worried that she'd lost half a finger to an inquisitive kid, the next she'd been close and soft and he'd looked at her mouth, then **bam**. He'd kissed her. Like an idiot. Like a man who hadn't kissed a woman in far too long.

The latter was true, but he ignored it, along with the burning need and his throbbing hard-on. She was Maya's friend— someone he barely knew and didn't plan to like. He didn't go around kissing women on impulse. He didn't do anything on impulse. When he figured it was time to scratch an itch, he found someone appropriate. Someone who understood his world and respected his responsibilities. Not brown-haired city girls with big eyes and shy smiles. Not women from LA. Not Maya's friends.

He knew his ex-stepsister had sent Phoebe up to the ranch to keep an eye on him until she could arrive to do it herself. For as long as she'd known him, Maya had made it clear she considered him a potential child abuser who had it in for his brother. Her idealistic view of Chase frustrated him, as did her need to always take his side. The kid was a screwup, plain and simple. If someone didn't take him in hand and fast, he was going to spend his whole life never getting one thing right.

Zane knew the danger of that. Maya thought he didn't care, but she was wrong. He cared enough to be a bastard. Let Chase hate him all he wanted, just so long as the kid had a chance at a life without regrets.

Zane stared at the map without seeing it. Honesty insisted he admit Chase got one thing right. He was a born ladies' man. From the second he'd learned to talk, he'd been charming females into giving him extra cookies and letting him stay up late.

Now that he was a teenager, Chase prob- ably spent his dates charming his way into girls' pants. Zane had given him the safe-sex lecture more times than either of them could count and kept the kid supplied with condoms. The last thing either of them needed was an unplanned pregnancy.

Zane had yet to meet a female who didn't fall for his brother's easy words and open smile. Unlike Zane, Chase always knew the right combination of sincerity, charm and flattery. He wouldn't kiss an attractive woman, then walk away without saying a word. Not that Zane had been talking all that much before he'd kissed Phoebe.

He could talk to the cowboys on his staff, explain the lineage of any of his prize bulls to a potential buyer and go toe-to-toe with the toughest, orneriest negotiator this side of the Mississippi, but with women... especially women like Phoebe...he clammed up tighter than a virgin in church.

The sound of footsteps distracted him. He turned his attention back to the map in front of him as Frank entered the room.

"Sent Chase into town for supplies," the older man said. "I got bad news."

Zane braced himself.

"We needed a couple more tents, and we're a saddle short."

Zane winced. A tent wouldn't be expensive, but a good saddle was. "See if maybe Clay Stryker has one we can borrow. If not, keep track of how much we put out for this. I'll take it out of Chase's summer earnings."

"Sure thing, boss."

Zane moved closer to the map. "We can't take them on a real cattle drive. We'll follow the river toward the edge of our property that borders the Strykers', then turn west here." He indicated the spot on the map.

Frank slid off his hat and rubbed the top of his head with his free hand. "You're going in a circle?"

"A big one. We'll never be more than four hours' ride from either here, the Strykers', or Reilly Konopka's place."

Frank's expression tightened with surprise. "I didn't know you'd started talkin' to him."

"I haven't." If he had his way, he never would. "We have to stay sharp. If there's an emergency, I can't risk us being too far from help."

He knew he could count on the Stryker men, and while Reilly Konopka might be a crusty old pissant of a man who would happily leave Zane out in the cold to freeze to death, he wouldn't turn away a stranger in need.

"Arrange for supplies to be delivered every day. You'll have to write up a schedule for the men. Have Cookie plan a menu this afternoon."

Frank's eyes widened. He looked as if someone had just run over his favorite dog. "Boss, you're not taking Cookie with you."

It was more of a plea than a question. "No one else can cook for shit. What am I supposed to feed them?"

"But without Cookie, one of the boys will have to cook for those of us left behind."

"There's enough stuff frozen to get every-one through a week."

"Ah, jeez." Frank's shoulders slumped. "Why'd you have to take Cookie with you?"

Zane ignored the question. Frank knew he was stuck on the ranch. With Zane gone, Frank would be in charge.

"I'll have the two-way radios with me. With the new tower in place, you'll be able to reach me any time."

Frank was still grumbling about losing the ranch cook for a week.

"Want to trade?" Zane asked flatly.

His foreman pressed his lips together. They both knew taking ten novice riders out on a fake cattle drive through wilderness was nothing short of five kinds of hell. June weather was usually good, but there was always the possibility of a freak snowstorm, a sizable flash flood, spooked cattle, bears, runaway horses, snakebite and saddle sores.

Frank slapped him on the back. "You have a fine time out there, boss. The boys and I will keep things running back here."

"Somehow I knew you were going to say that."

CHAPTER SIX

Phoebe stretched out on her bed, aimlessly flipping channels on the television. Despite the fact there was a sci-fi marathon on one channel, **Sleepless in Seattle** on another and some really great fake diamond earrings on QVC, nothing held her interest. She told herself it was because she was in unfamiliar surroundings. Or maybe it was the fact that except for the cowboy who had delivered her dinner on a tray at six-thirty, she hadn't seen another living being. Well, not a biped. From her window she could see countless cattle, a few horses and even a couple of dogs.

But she knew none of that really mattered. The reason she was restless, edgy and more than a little unsettled had nothing to do with her lack of company and everything to do with a soul-stirring kiss she'd experienced that morning. Strange men were not supposed to be able to elicit that kind of a response from her. She'd always been a kiss on the second date, sex in the third or fourth month kind of gal. More than one potential boyfriend had become frustrated and ended things because she wasn't ready to bare all by week four.

The first time it had happened, she'd been heartbroken. The second time, she'd been resigned. In her world, making love needed to be a significant event. She was interested in emotional connection, not volume. Which put her out of step with a lot of guys she met in LA, but that was okay. She wasn't going to find the sense of belonging she desperately wanted by jumping into bed every fifteen minutes. Which was all really interesting, but not the least bit helpful in explaining her reaction to Zane.

If he'd tossed her to the ground and started ripping off her clothes, instead of being outraged, she would have helped. She would have done it right there, in front of God and the goats. The big question was why?

A knock on the door interrupted her thoughts. She flipped off the TV, then sat up. She'd returned her dinner tray to the kitchen, so it was unlikely anyone was here to bus her dishes. Which left one of two possibilities for her visitor. Chase or Zane.

In her mind, it wasn't even a close vote. She crossed her fingers and walked to the door. When she pulled it open, she fully expected to see Chase standing in the hallway, because that was how her luck was running these days. Yet the man in front of her was tall, good-looking and had a mouth, she knew from personal experience, that could reduce grown women who should know better to puddles of liquid desire.

She blinked and wondered when the finger-crossing technique had actually started working.

"Evening," Zane said.

It was a pretty wordy opening for him.

Phoebe debated inviting him in, then decided it would be too much like an offer to sleep with him. Instead of stepping back and pointing to the bed, which was really what she wanted to do, she moved into the hallway, shutting the door behind her, and did her best to look unimpressed.

"Hi, Zane. How are the preparations coming?"

He gave her one of his grunts, then shrugged. She took that to mean, "Great. And thanks so much for asking."

They weren't standing all that close, but she was intensely aware of him. Despite the fact that he'd probably been up at dawn and that it was now close to ten, he still smelled good. He wasn't wearing his cowboy hat, so she could see his dark hair. Stubble defined his jaw. She wanted to rub her hands over the roughness, then maybe hook her leg around his hip and slide against him like the sex-starved fool she was turning out to be.

"Maya'll be here tomorrow," he said. "Elaine Mitchell is bringing her out to the ranch with all of the greenhorns in her tourist bus."

She had to clear her throat before speaking. "Maya called me about an hour ago to let me know she'd be getting here about three."

He folded his arms across his broad chest, then leaned sideways against the doorjamb beside her. So very close. Her attention fixed on the strong column of his neck, and a certain spot just behind his jaw that she had a sudden urge to kiss. Would it be warm? Would she feel his pulse against her lips?

"She doesn't need to know what happened," Zane said.

Phoebe couldn't quite make sense of his words, and he must have read the confusion in her eyes. They were alone, it was night and the man seemed to be looming above her in the hallway. She'd never thought she would enjoy being loomed over, but it was actually very nice. She had the feeling that if she suddenly saw a mouse or something, she could shriek and jump, and he would catch her. Of course he would think she was an idiot, but that was beside the point.

"Between us," he explained. "Outside. She doesn't need to know about the kiss."

A flood of warmth rushed to her face as she understood that he regretted kissing her. She instinctively stepped backward, only to bump her head against the closed bedroom door. Before she had time to be embarrassed about her lack of grace or sophistication, he groaned, reached for her hips and drew her toward him.

"She doesn't need to know about this one, either."

His lips took hers with a gentle but commanding confidence. Her hands settled on either side of the strong neck she'd been eyeing only seconds ago. His skin was as warm as she'd imagined it would be. The cords of his muscles moved against her fingers as he tilted his head to a better angle.

His hands were still, except his thumbs, which brushed her hip bones, slow and steady. His fingers splayed over the narrowest part of her waist and nearly met at the small of her back. She wished she could feel his fingertips against her skin, but her thin cotton top got in the way.

He kept her body at a frustrating distance from his. In fact, when she tried to move closer, he held her away even as he continued the kiss. Lips on lips. Hot and yielding. She waited for him to deepen the kiss, but he didn't. And she couldn't summon the courage to do it herself. Finally, he drew back and rested his forehead against hers for a long moment.

"Do me a favor," he said. "Try to be a little

more resistible. I don't think I can take a week of this."

Then he turned on his heel, walked to a door at the end of the long hallway, and went inside. She stood in place, her fingers pressed against her still-tingling lips. More than a minute passed before she realized she was smiling.

Phoebe hovered slightly behind Zane in front of the Nicholson Ranch house, watching a cheerfully painted bus chugging along the winding entrance road. As it got closer, the tinny music coming from the speaker mounted on top increased in volume. It sounded like an ice-cream truck. Chase stood by the goat pens, well out of his brother's reach. She couldn't blame him for being nervous. Zane's annoyance with the fake cattle-drive situation seemed to be growing as the bus approached.

She tried not to notice how good Zane looked in his cowboy hat and jeans, but she couldn't seem to help cataloging his impressive features.

Okay, day one his appeal had been interesting. Day two it had been amusing, but this was day three. She needed to get over him, already. Sexual attraction had never been a big part of her life. Sure, she enjoyed the physical perks of a romantic relationship as much as anyone, but she'd never sought them out. To her, the emotional connection was so much more important than the act. So why did she practically have a hot flash every time she was around Zane?

She had a feeling that Maya would be able to offer sound advice. The only downside was having to admit the problem in the first place. Not only was Zane Maya's ex-stepbrother, which made things sort of weird, but Maya had been the one preaching Zane as a distraction. If Phoebe admitted to her attraction, Maya would gloat about being right and tease Phoebe unmercifully. Maybe it would be easier to allow her questions to go unanswered.

Before she could decide, the bus pulled to a stop in front of them. A mural of downtown Fool's Gold had been painted in primary colors on the side of the bus, with "Mitchell Adventure Tours" emblazoned just above the windows. The door at the front opened with a whoosh.

A young girl rushed down the steps yelling, "It's them. Real cowboys."

Zane muttered under his breath to Chase, who had joined them. "You've got little kids involved in this mess?"

Behind her, a small boy and their parents disembarked. The parents seemed to be in their early forties, while the kids were both under twelve. Phoebe found herself playing hostess. She wasn't surprised by Zane's reticence, but Chase could usually be counted on to be a charmer. Maybe the reality of what he'd done was sinking in.

"Thad and C. J. Swanson," the tall blond man introduced himself. "This is Lucy and her brother, Tommy."

The kids didn't look anything like their fair-haired parents. Tommy was painfully thin, with long legs and dark, shaggy hair. Lucy shared her brother's coloring, but instead of being long legged, she was petite and delicate-looking, with a full, rosebud mouth. Both kids had skin that was the most beautiful shade of caramel.

"You two must be excited that your parents brought you on a cattle drive,"

Phoebe said.

The girl, Lucy, shook her head. "They're not our parents. We don't have parents. Are we going to eat soon? Tommy and I didn't have breakfast or lunch today."

Phoebe glanced at her watch. It was after two. Involuntarily she turned to the Swansons, who looked as surprised as she felt.

"We picked them up at ten to catch the shuttle plane," C.J. said uneasily. "They never said anything about not having breakfast. We only have them for this week. The people who were supposed to bring them on this cattle drive backed out at the last minute. Death in the family. There were pretzels on the flight..." Her voice trailed off.

Phoebe returned her attention to the children. Lucy's matter-of-fact statement "we don't have parents" brought back too many memories. She'd lost her folks when she'd been about Lucy's age. With no relatives to take her in, she'd been placed in a series of foster homes. While nothing bad had happened in any of them, she'd never forgotten what it was like to be all alone in the world.

"Do you want to get something to eat?" she asked.

Lucy and Tommy looked at each other, then at her. They both nodded.

Zane said, "Chase, take them to the kitchen."

The party of four trailed after Chase, leaving Phoebe momentarily alone with Zane. Sudden nervousness made her want to wipe her palms on her jeans. Instead she cleared her throat and tried for neutral.

"They seem nice."

Zane raised his eyebrows. "Sure. Skinny, starving kids. I can hardly wait for the rest of the folks to turn up. Maybe we'll have a rock star next. Or some business executive who wants to bring his laptop along so he can work while riding."

She wasn't sure what to say to that, so she ignored his comments. "Thanks for letting the kids go get something to eat."

His gaze narrowed. "What has Maya told you about me?"

The only thing she could think of was her friend's claim that Zane looked like Adam Levine. "Ah, what do you mean?"

"You're surprised that I wouldn't want

kids to starve. I figured she'd claimed I was a jerk, but it sounds like she's also telling you that I'm mean to children."

"No, nothing like that." She took a step back. "Maya thinks you're a little, you know, uptight maybe."

His expression hardened, and she wanted to suck back the words.

"But not in a bad way."

"Right."

Zane turned his attention to the bus. Phoebe got a bad feeling when she caught sight of the worn sandals, tie-dyed T-shirts and woven hats on the next couple to disembark.

"Hey," the man said. "I'm Martin Lagarde and this is my wife, Andrea."

The woman, a thirtysomething brunette with freckles and glasses, shook hands with Zane.

"We're so excited to be here. Martin and I just love being in the outdoors. We've hiked all over, and last year we did a week at a meditation retreat in Hawaii, but we've never done anything like this." She continued to pump his hand as her expression turned earnest. "We really want this opportunity to be one with the land. To experience a different kind of life. The Old West." She finally released Zane's hand. "We're vegetarians. I hope that won't be a problem."

Zane considered them for a moment, then said, "Not for me." He jerked his head toward the compartment beneath the bus that the driver had opened. "Collect your gear and head inside. Chase will show you where you'll bunk tonight."

"Sure thing," Martin said.

He held up his hand for a high five. When Zane simply stared at him, Martin grabbed Zane's wrist and pulled it until it was level with his shoulder, then slapped his hand against Zane's.

When he walked away, Zane turned to look at her. "Two starving kids and tree-hugging vegetarians. I'm going to kill Chase."

Phoebe almost didn't blame him. Despite her lack of experience in the cattle-drive department, even she could see the potential for trouble. Then a familiar figure standing beside the driver caught her attention, and she waved. Maya grinned and waved back.

"It's Maya," Phoebe said.

Zane turned and followed her gaze. "Just perfect," he muttered as his ex-stepsister walked toward them.

"You're looking grim, Zane," Maya said cheerfully when she joined them. "Who died?" She smiled. "Oh, I forgot. You're just being your usual charming self." She squeezed his arm. "You've missed me, I know."

Zane's eyes narrowed. "Like foot fungus."

She laughed and turned to Phoebe. "You're still alive. I see Zane didn't bore you to death."

"Not even close." Phoebe hugged her friend.

Maya waved forward the bus driver, a pretty woman in her fifties. "Phoebe, this is Elaine Mitchell."

"You're the one Maya worked for in high school?" Phoebe asked.

"I am."

Maya put her arm around Phoebe's shoulders. "And this is my BFF, Phoebe."

"Welcome to Fool's Gold," Elaine said with a smile.

Instead of her usual suit and high heels, Maya wore jeans, a long-sleeved shirt and boots. Her blond hair was pulled back in a braid.

"You look like a local," Phoebe said.

"Speaking of locals," Maya began, a note of warning in her voice.

"Oh, shit," Zane said before she could continue.

Phoebe looked toward the bus and immediately saw why Zane's face had gone a little ashen. The two crazy old women who had cornered her at his truck in town had just gotten off the bus. Eddie and Gladys, if she remembered right. The skinny one was wearing stiff, dark blue jeans and a plaid Western shirt with pearly snaps along the front. The plump one, who still looked as if she had asked for one of everything at the cosmetic counter, was wearing jeans, too, and leather chaps with fringe along the sides. They both had cowboy hats perched atop their white curls.

Beside her Zane muttered under his breath. She caught a handful of words. Something about being old, broken bones and a reference to hanging Chase from the lightning rod in the middle of a storm.

"Ladies," he said as he stepped forward. "I'm afraid we don't have enough tents or saddles to add you to the group."

"I already tried to stop them," Elaine said, "but they insisted." She turned to Phoebe. "Eddie and Gladys are known for being a little hardheaded."

"Among other things," Maya added wryly. "That one's Eddie, and that one's Gladys," she said, pointing.

"We're not additions," Eddie said, "we're replacements."

Gladys dug through the large black purse strapped over her forearm and pulled out a checkbook. "We met a nice couple at Ronan's last night, and they couldn't say yes fast enough when we offered to buy their spots on the cattle drive."

"They said they're gonna stay in town and get a hot stone massage every day instead."

"But—"

"We already paid," Eddie said. "Five hundred bucks a pop. Figured it would be worth it if we could see some sexy cowboys. We've taken riding lessons from Shane Stryker, but he refuses to take off his shirt for us. I hope you're not going to be so stubborn."

Phoebe thought Zane might call off the whole thing, after all, but all he did was mutter, "Fine. Head inside, I'll bring your things."

She supposed that novices were a bit of a challenge and senior novices would be even more of one, but to her mind, the older women were quirky and delightful.

"We're mighty excited about this trip," Gladys said. "Eddie here has wanted to go on a cattle drive since she first saw **City Slickers.**" She winked. "Not that either of us have a hankering to help with a birthing, mind you. It looked a tad messy."

Phoebe was charmed.

Eddie reached into her purse and pulled out her video camera. "You never did introduce yourself, little lady. A real cowgirl type?"

Gladys smiled at her friend. "A pretty cowgirl."

Phoebe ducked her head at the compliment. "Thanks, but I'm as much a newbie at this as everyone else."

"We'll watch out for you," Eddie said.

The two women headed into the house.

"Where's Chase?" Maya said. "I want to guilt him into getting my bags for me."

Zane gave a sigh of the long-suffering. "How many?"

"Four, but two of them are small."

"You're going on a cattle drive, not touring the capitals of Europe."

Maya leaned toward Phoebe. "He's always crabby when people invade his precious ranch. Hmm. Actually he's crabby most of the time."

Zane's scowl didn't seem to affect Maya, who linked arms with Phoebe, then used her free hand to blow Zane a kiss. Just then, Chase stepped outside. With a whoop, he ran to Maya. She opened her arms wide and pulled him close.

"Hey, sis," Chase said, lifting her off her feet and swinging her around. "You look good."

"You've grown some," Maya said in obvious delight. "You're taller."

Chase set her down and kissed her cheek. "You forgot better-looking."

Maya grinned at Zane. "You must take after your mom."

Their teasing seemed to bother him. Phoebe saw his jaw clench as they continued to banter back and forth. Maya had always said that Zane didn't appreciate her special relationship with Chase, but Phoebe wasn't sure that was true. Watching Zane stand by himself made her wonder if instead of being annoyed by their closeness, he felt left out and lonely. She knew she would if she were him.

She shoved her hands into her back pockets and considered the possibility. Honestly, it was tough to imagine someone like Zane feeling lonely or inadequate or any of those emotions experienced by lesser mortals. Maybe she was assuming a tender heart where one didn't exist.

They said goodbye to Elaine, grabbed the last of the luggage she'd left on the ground, and took it into the house. The guests had congregated in the large living room. Phoebe noticed that Eddie and Gladys made it a point to speak with each of the children. She wondered whether they had grandkids that they saw on a regular basis.

"Do we have enough beds to sleep

everyone tonight?" Maya asked Zane quietly. "Phoebe and I can get a hotel if you want and then join you tomorrow morning."

"We should be fine," he said. "Besides, if anyone's going to be kicked out of his bed tonight, it would be Chase."

"Poor boy." Maya moved next to Chase and hugged him protectively.

Phoebe knew she was kidding. Even so, she didn't agree with Maya's teasing. Zane might be stern and difficult, but this time he was right. Chase had really messed up by offering a fake cattle drive to vacationers. Because of him, Zane was now responsible for all these people. She wanted to say something supportive to him but couldn't think of anything that didn't sound stupid. Or obvious. The last thing she needed right now was Maya figuring out that she was more than a little attracted to Zane.

She satisfied herself with trying to convey empathy with a glance. His dark blue eyes seemed more intense than usual, but maybe that was proximity. She found her gaze drifting down to his lips and her mind zipping back to the kisses that they'd shared. She tried to tell herself that him being a good kisser was meaningless. That sort of a skill didn't say much about a man, except that he'd either kissed a lot of women or had innate talent. Even as she mentally tried to change the subject, she found herself remembering that Jeff had been a lousy kisser—and more than a bit of a toad—and wondering if Zane came by his talent naturally, or if he'd earned it through lots of practice.

Charles Elvis Monroe, otherwise known as Cookie, glared at Zane. "You're bringing kids along?" he asked in disbelief.

Zane didn't bother answering. He wasn't bringing anyone along voluntarily. Instead, he was a reluctant host and caretaker, all in the name of teaching Chase a lesson.

"I figured you'd want to know," he said, then stepped out of the way as Cookie opened the refrigerator and pulled out an armful of lettuce.

"Kids," the old man muttered. "I'd ask what you were thinkin' when you agreed to all this, but I'm guessin' you weren't thinkin' at all." He sighed heavily. "I'll make sure I got some stuff along that they'll like."

He drew his thick, gray eyebrows together. "Anything else?"

Zane thought about Andrea and Martin Lagarde. He cleared his throat and took a step back so he was close to the kitchen's exit.

"There's a couple from San Francisco. They're vegetarians."

Cookie slammed the lettuce onto the counter and spun around to glare at Zane. "What did you say, boy?"

Zane remembered the first time he'd met the older man. He'd been called all the way to Sacramento to make bail for a few of the cowboys. Apparently the usual Saturday night carousing had gotten out of hand. When the party had finally broken up, they'd been making time with several teenage girls on the shy side of eighteen.

After listening to the list of charges and the men's explanations, Zane had fired two of the men on the spot, had given three a second chance and left the last one—already on probation for fighting—in jail to serve his time. Cookie had been in the last cell. When Zane had finished his lecture to the men he'd sprung, the old cook had straightened and asked where Zane's spread was located. Zane had told him. Six weeks later Cookie had shown up. Instead of a resume, he'd baked biscuits, grilled steaks and put together a fudge brownie sundae good enough to make ice sweat. Zane had confirmed there weren't any outstanding warrants on the man, then had hired him on the spot.

That had been ten years ago. Zane had never learned why the old man had been in jail. Cookie didn't talk about his past, but then Zane rarely looked into other people's histories. Cookie was grouchy, opinionated, stubborn about only working with good quality food and disappeared for three weeks every year without saying where he was going.

Zane stood his ground. The fact that Cookie had never started a fight didn't mean he couldn't be pushed too far.

"Vegetarians."

Cookie muttered something under his breath. "I ain't cooking no tofu. I'll quit first."

"Fine by me. You cook what you like. I just wanted you to know."

"Vegetarians." Cookie washed his hands,

then attacked the lettuce.

Frank walked into the kitchen. "Everything's all set, boss. Tents, saddles, supplies. Cookie's wagon is loaded, except for the fresh stuff. We have a schedule set up. You'll get a delivery every afternoon."

Zane nodded. "You get a look at the folks?"

His second in command did his best to keep his expression neutral, but Zane saw the corner of Frank's mouth twitch.

"You mean the fact that you've got to deal with Maya's mouth, some old ladies and a couple of kids?"

Cookie picked up a lethal-looking knife, then reached for several tomatoes. "You left out the good part, Zane. Tell him about the damn nut eaters."

When Frank looked confused, Zane shrugged. "Vegetarians."

This time Frank's entire mouth jerked, but he controlled his humor. "Sounds interesting."

"Tits are interesting, boy," Cookie growled. "Vegetarians are just plain stupid. If people want to eat leaves and grubs, then they should go live in the forest. Root around with those ugly truffle pigs and get away from my table."

"What time is supper?" Zane asked.

Cookie snarled something under his breath, then walked to the back door and stuck his head out. "Billy, you got that there barbecue ready yet, boy?"

"Yes, sir. Coals are hot and gray. You wanted them gray, didn't you, Cookie?"

"What color gray?"

There was a pause. "Sort of medium."

"Huh." Cookie closed the back door and grinned at Zane. "I screw with him because he makes it so easy. Dinner can be ready in half an hour."

Zane glanced at his watch. "Okay. We'll have everyone in the dining room by then."

"What about **those** people?" Cookie practically spit the last two words.

Zane knew who he was talking about. What would Andrea and Martin be eating?

"Let them make do."

He left the kitchen with Frank on his heels.

Zane had given his guests a couple of hours to settle in and had asked them to collect in the living room at five-thirty. He walked into the large room and found them talking with each other.

The old ladies were playing some kind of game with the two kids while the temporary foster parents looked on uneasily. The tree huggers were admiring pictures of the area, while Maya had helped herself to a drink from the bar. And Phoebe... He braced himself for his unexplainable but very real attraction to her. His brain might know that she was all wrong, but his dick kept pointing in her direction.

She sat next to Maya on the sofa. When he walked in with Frank, conversation gradually ceased. He did his best to offer a warm and welcoming smile, then wondered why he bothered. Charming people was Chase's job. Zane was the mean-ass brother who worried about work schedules and getting the payroll out. His busy days didn't leave much time for charm.

Still he wanted to put everyone at ease before he offered them a chance to back out on what might be the disaster of a lifetime.

"I have some announcements," he said when he had their attention. "First," he looked at the kids. "Our neighbors brought over a couple of saddles for the kids. They're worn but serviceable. However, the plan was for a six-day ride. This is a tough pace for some seasoned riders. I'm concerned about the children being able to keep up."

As he spoke, the boy looked a little worried, but his sister got a stubborn expression he recognized from dealing with Maya. The foster parents shifted uncomfortably, but didn't say anything.

That seed planted, he turned to the next issue. Trying to appear apologetic, he smiled at Andrea and Martin.

"We weren't aware we were going to have vegetarians on the cattle drive. At this point, we can't offer you a special menu plan. Meals will be served family style, so you can take as much or as little as you want of any one dish, but there won't be any vegetarian entrees."

Martin seemed okay with the information, but Andrea—who Zane suspected wore the pants in the family—appeared outraged.

She took a step toward him. "Are you aware of the havoc your steers cause the environment? And what about pigs? Ninety percent of the corn grown in this country goes to feed pigs. If Americans cut down on their pork consumption by as little as fifty percent, we could send almost half our corn crop to other countries—"

Andrea stopped suddenly when her husband lightly touched her arm. She glanced around. Everyone was staring at her.

She pressed her lips together. "I'm not a meat eater."

"I understand," Zane told her. "But we're not equipped to provide you with vegetarian meals. I'm more than willing to refund you the price of the vacation, including your airline tickets, and arrange for you to fly home in the morning." He turned to the couple in charge of the children. "I would be happy to do the same for the four of you."

He was hoping that with more than half the group gone, the old ladies would feel strange about staying by themselves. Not that they were known for a sense of appropriate behavior.

Maya stretched her legs out in front of her and swirled her glass. "Zane, how generous. And here I thought you were committed to the cattle drive."

He ignored her. "Just let me know."

Eddie stood up. "Now hold on, Zane," she said with a smile. "There's no reason to get all fired up because Andrea here won't eat meat. I'm sure your cook can make some extra vegetable dishes for her and Martin. As for the kids—" She smiled at them fondly. "Gladys and I are happy to help out. We love kids."

She crouched down in front of Lucy and Tommy. "You two live in the city, don't you?"

Tommy still looked worried, but he nodded.

"Ever been on a horse?"

The boy shook his head.

"Ever want to be a cowboy?"

A slight smile pulled at the boy's mouth.

Eddie rose and faced Zane. "See there? He wants to be a cowboy. This young man and his pretty sister need to spend a little time in the outdoors."

Gladys slapped Zane on the back. "You're a good man to be so concerned about everyone, but I say let's have at it. We're all here for an adventure, and you're just the man to provide it."

Andrea looked mollified. "We have wanted to try something new," she said to her husband. "I guess we could work around the food choices."

"I'd like to try," Martin told her.

Even the temporary foster parents looked less apprehensive than they had.

Zane knew when he'd been bested, and he didn't try to argue. He'd given it his best shot.

"We'll meet again after supper, and Frank will explain what you should bring and what should be left behind at the house. Then you can turn in early. We'll head out just after dawn."

CHAPTER SEVEN

"You don't mind sharing?" Phoebe asked when she and Maya retreated to their room after dinner.

"Of course not." Maya sank down on the bed by the window, then looked around the room. "It's so weird to be back. Maybe that's why I don't come home very often. It's too strange."

Phoebe thought about her own lack of roots and how she would love to have a home to go back to. She settled on her bed. "If it were me, I'd come back every chance I got."

"I believe that." Maya flopped down on the bed and stared up at the ceiling. "Looking back, I was so young. I thought I was mature and together, but I was a kid." She looked at Phoebe. "This was the first house where I felt safe."

Phoebe knew her friend had grown up in Las Vegas. Maya's mother had been a stripper who had constantly been on the lookout for a man to rescue her. Then

Zane's father had come along. After a whirl-wind courtship, they'd married, and Maya and her mother had moved to Fool's Gold and the Nicholson Ranch.

"Safe is nice," Phoebe said.

"It is." Maya sighed. "I liked seeing Elaine. She's the lady who drove us in today. Elaine Mitchell. I knew her when I lived here before. I worked for her the summer before college. We've always kept in touch."

"Mitchell Adventure Tours," Phoebe said, then tilted her head. "Wait a minute. Mitchell, as in Del Mitchell?"

Maya groaned. "Don't say that name. Yes, Del. My one true love." She wrinkled her nose. "At least that's what I thought back then. The first time I saw him, I swear I heard sound-track music. We were convinced it was going to last forever."

It hadn't, Phoebe knew. And these days Maya rarely got involved with a guy for very long. Giving her heart wasn't an option. Phoebe knew most of the reasons. While they made sense, she still felt badly for her friend. At least one of them should be feeling the buzz on falling in love.

"When was the last time you saw Del?"

she asked.

Maya sat up. "It's been close to ten years. He travels all the time. Elaine rarely mentions him in her emails. I make sure I see her when I visit, but I've never run into him."

"Maybe he's not hot anymore."

Maya laughed. "That would be nice, but I suspect he's still just as attractive. Not for me, of course."

"Of course," Phoebe murmured, wondering if any of those sound-track feelings were still lingering for her friend. Not that Maya would ever admit it.

Phoebe glanced at the clock and groaned. "We have to pack."

Maya picked up the small duffels and saddlebags that had been left on the foot of the bed and tossed one of each over.

Phoebe shook her head. "I brought way too much stuff."

Maya pointed to her open suitcase and the pile of makeup bags, jeans and shirts next to it. "You and me both. Looks like I'm going to have to settle on sunscreen and mascara. And eye makeup remover, or I'll look like a raccoon." She glanced at Phoebe. "You, of course, don't have to worry about your eyelashes fading into nothing. They're thick and dark all on their own. If you weren't such a good friend, I'd have to hate you."

As Phoebe collected her own clothes and toiletries, she didn't bother pointing out that she would gladly give up her eyelashes for about two inches in height, along with blond hair. Or big boobs. They would be nice, too.

"Poor Zane," Maya said as she folded a T-shirt. "I almost feel sorry for him. Eddie and Gladys are a handful at the best of times, and what's with those kids?"

Phoebe stacked the clothes she knew she had to take in one pile and the ones she would leave behind in another. The problem was all the things she wasn't sure she would need. They made up the largest pile.

"What about the kids?" she asked. "I thought they were cute."

"Agreed, but out of their element."

"Count me in with them."

Phoebe felt as unsure as little Tommy had looked at the prospect of six days in the great outdoors. She already liked the ranch and had enjoyed looking out at the expansive view, but she had a feeling she was wildly unprepared to ride the range.

"Why are those people with them?" Maya asked. "C.J. and Thad seemed the most unlikely parents."

"I don't get it, either," Phoebe admitted. "They're not their regular foster parents. C.J. said that the people who were supposed to accompany the kids had a family emergency. C.J. and Thad were called in for backup." She thought about the time she'd spent going from foster family to foster family. "I hope Lucy and Tommy have a good time."

"They will. Eddie and Gladys seem ready to adopt them, if only for the week. But enough about munchkins. I'm surprised Zane gave in so graciously about the cattle drive. His last-minute attempt to get the thing canceled was impressive. I guess he decided the pain wasn't worth whatever lesson Chase might learn."

"Can you blame him?" Phoebe asked. "He's taking on a lot."

Her friend raised her eyebrows. "Are you defending him? Ooh, I like that." Maya pushed her clothes aside and flopped onto her stomach. "So big, bad Zane is getting to you, huh? Tell me everything that's happened."

Phoebe busied herself with a choice between a bulky sweater and a flannel shirt she could fit into her bag. "He's not getting to me. I just don't think he's the devil incarnate, which is how you've described him."

"I have not."

Phoebe rolled her eyes. "You said he was heartless and lacking normal emotions. From what I've seen, he really cares about Chase, and even you."

Maya hooted. "Me? He loathes me, when he bothers to think of me at all. I drive him crazy."

Phoebe didn't agree, but there was no point in arguing.

"At least tell me you think he's good-looking," Maya said.

Phoebe grinned. "Pure Adam Levine, just like you promised."

"I guess that's something. I suppose my plan to get the two of you into bed was just wishful thinking on my part."

"Not gonna happen."

Phoebe was pleased that her voice sounded normal. There was no way she was going to let Maya know about the sizzling kisses she and Zane had shared. Not only did she not want them analyzed, she had a feeling it had been a once-in-a-lifetime occurrence. Well, twice in a lifetime. Sort of like the planets aligning, or winning the lotto. There was no point in mentioning that Maya's fantasy had also become her own.

"I just know if he would cut loose, he could be a really fun guy," Maya said as she sat back up and reached for another T-shirt. "Okay, maybe fun is too strong, but he could be less of a stick-in-the-mud. He needs a woman. Of course when he had one, it's not like he knew what to do with her."

Phoebe nearly dropped the jeans she'd been folding. "What are you talking about?"

"Zane was married before. Didn't I tell you?"

Zane? Married? Why did the thought surprise her so much, and why did she suddenly feel stricken?

"No. You forgot to mention that."

"Probably because it didn't mean anything."

"I'm sure it did to Zane." And it certainly did to her, although she couldn't say why.

"Maybe." Maya shook out the contents of her makeup bag and began sorting through the items on her bed. "But it's not as if he loved her. Zane married Sally to provide Chase with a mother. He's such an idiot. He actually told her that about a year into the marriage."

"Chase?" Phoebe asked with a frown.

"No, Zane. I never got all the details, but I think Sally was pushing for kids of her own. Zane refused and finally explained that he'd married her so Chase would grow up with some stability. Hardly the romantic declaration designed to get a wife's heart to fluttering. Especially when she thought they'd married for love. She split. Zane got worried about losing the ranch, but all Sally wanted was compensation for duties performed. I heard that she calculated a salary equivalent for the time she'd been married to Zane and presented him with a bill."

Maya laughed, as if she found the whole situation amusing, but Phoebe couldn't help thinking how sad it all sounded. Zane marrying someone he didn't love to provide his brother with a mother. He'd done the wrong thing with the best of intentions. How many times had she done exactly the same thing…and gotten burned?

"I guess it's not completely his fault," Maya said reluctantly. "I know he had a tough time after his dad died."

"Meaning?"

"My former stepfather loved Zane's mother so much, he never recovered from her death. From what I could tell, he barely noticed Zane. The old man married a few times to try and forget, but it never worked. Instead he made everyone's life hell."

Phoebe's tender heart clenched at the thought of Zane's pain. "He's had to deal with a lot," she murmured.

"I guess. But he still acts like he's got something stuck up his ass. Look at how he is with Chase."

"You always talk about him as if he doesn't care about anything, but didn't marrying Sally prove that he worries about his brother?" she asked. "And what about the cattle drive? He's doing it to teach Chase an important lesson. You love Chase. You should be pleased that Zane's willing to show him how to be a good man."

Maya's green eyes widened. "Oh, my. Someone has it bad."

Phoebe shook her head. "You're wrong."

"Am I?"

"Absolutely."

Maya didn't look convinced, and who could blame her? Phoebe didn't have it bad...but she did have it.

It was close to midnight when Phoebe realized she wasn't going to be able to sleep. Maya had crashed shortly after ten —no doubt the result of working twenty-hour days all week so that she could take time off. Phoebe should have been tired, but instead she felt restless.

She pulled jeans on over her pj bottoms and grabbed her jacket, then walked barefoot along the hall and down the stairs.

The house was still, with that hushed quality that comes when everyone is asleep. Phoebe noticed that a few lamps had been left burning, probably for the safety of any guest who felt compelled to wander in the night.

As it had the first afternoon she'd arrived, the house impressed her with its high ceilings and open floor plan. While the furniture in place worked, she could easily imagine other styles fitting well with the moldings and hardwood floors. In the least expensive neighborhoods of Beverly Hills this place would get at least three million. On the exclusive streets, the price would come close to doubling.

At the front door she paused to check for an alarm system, then remembered where she was and laughed quietly. She doubted Zane went in much for motion sensors or perimeter alarms.

She opened the door and stepped out onto the porch. The night was even more still out here, and cold. She was surprised she couldn't see her breath. It would be warmer down in Fool's Gold, but the ranch was at a higher elevation. Her toes curled against the freezing temperature of the painted wood, but she didn't retreat. Instead she walked to the railing and looked down at the storybook town nestled on the shore of the little lake. Then she stared up at the inky, black night.

There were thousands of stars. Even on the clearest night in Los Angeles, she'd never seen half this many.

"I should have paid attention in astronomy class," she murmured, then smiled. "Okay, I should have taken astronomy in the first place."

She tilted her head in an effort to find something easy like the Big Dipper and the North Star. She found the former, but couldn't remember if the North Star was off its handle or did she need to look for the Little Dipper first. Then, as she took in the endless sea of twinkling lights, she became aware of a...presence.

Milliseconds before she turned, she heard a footfall. Had she been anywhere but Zane's ranch, she would have panicked. Strange footsteps at night in the city were never good news. But this was different. Despite her unfamiliarity with her surroundings, she felt safe. Besides, the odds were good that she knew who was out here with her.

She turned and saw Zane approaching. In the dim light of the porch, he was little more than a shadowy silhouette, but that only added to his appeal. He wore a thick, leather jacket that hung open. Unlike her, he still wore the clothes he'd been in that day. He was imposing and more than a little out of her league. She probably should have run for the hills, or at least her room. Instead she hugged her arms to her chest and wondered if she'd been in bed long enough to make her hair stick up in weird places.

"Couldn't sleep?" he asked as he approached, then stopped by the railing next to her.

She shook her head. "I guess I'm too excited about the cattle drive."

"It's keeping me up, too, but not from excitement."

The simple statement caught her unaware. With a few words, he expressed a vulnerability that made her heart squeeze, even as her hormones hummed a Dixie Chicks song about cowboys and being taken away.

It was the night, she told herself. Or

maybe it was just the man. Regardless, wouldn't this be a good time to suddenly be witty and charming? Or even gorgeous. She would settle for gorgeous and not funny, as long as she didn't have to talk too much.

"I know it's a big responsibility," she said when she neither transformed into a super-model nor thought of anything brilliant to say. "But you seem to have everything figured out. I'm sure it will be fine."

He sighed. "Want to guarantee that in writing?"

"Would it help if I did?"

"No." He stared up at the sky. "I couldn't get them to leave."

"Yes, well, you tried."

He grunted. She guessed that trying and failing didn't count for much in his world. Yet another strike against her. She screwed up all the time.

"At least everyone seems really nice," she said.

He turned so he stared at the house. His face was in the light now, and she could see the humor crinkling the corners of his eyes. "Even Andrea?"

She thought about the other woman's forceful personality. "Well, she's not easily likable, but I'm sure that once we get to know her, she'll be lovely."

He stared at her. "You're a 'glass half full' kind of person, aren't you?"

"I try to be." She leaned against the railing as well, mimicking his pose by putting her elbows on the wood and gazing upward.

"I think it's important to have a positive attitude in life," she said. "To look for the opportunities."

"You're too busy worrying about everyone's feelings to see an opportunity coming a mile away." His gaze narrowed. "How'd you and Maya get to be friends?"

Phoebe blinked at him. He'd barely known her forty-eight hours, and in that time, they'd spent less than an hour or two talking. Yet he'd managed to sum up her character in a single sentence. Even more amazing...he'd been right. How did he do that?

She **was** too busy helping people to advance her career. She often made choices based on her heart rather than her desire to get ahead. From what she'd figured out, opportunities went to the ruthless, and she could never seem to act in a way that put her best interests first. Not if it meant stepping on someone else.

She shook her head, then returned her attention to Zane. "What was the question?"

"How'd you and Maya become friends? You're nothing alike."

"You mean she's a successful TV producer on the fast track and I'm not?"

He shrugged. "I was thinking more in terms of personality."

"That, too." She rubbed her right foot against her left calf and tried to ignore the chill seeping through her. What were a few shivers when compared with a midnight conversation with her own private fantasy?

"We met in college, when we were freshmen. Maya was talking with a bunch of people. You know how she is. Always the center of attention."

She paused, but Zane didn't speak. So she continued.

"She had this big cup of coffee, which she accidentally spilled all over me. She insisted on taking me back to her place so I could get cleaned up. We started talking, and by the end of the morning, we were friends."

Phoebe didn't mention how lonely she'd been at college. While the foster homes hadn't been the most idyllic setting, after the death of her parents, they'd been all she'd known. At eighteen, she'd had to leave, and it was like losing her family all over again.

"I didn't have anyone," Phoebe said. "Maya took me in and made me feel a part of things. She's been a good friend."

"I never thanked you for your help today," he said. "I figured Chase would do all the talking when those folks started arriving. Most of the time I can't pay him enough to shut up. But he didn't say a word."

"Maybe he was overwhelmed by the enormity of what he's done."

One dark eyebrow lifted slightly. "I wouldn't bet on that if I were you."

"You don't think he's remorseful?"

"Not yet, but he's going to be." Zane paused, then shook his head. "He's not the only one who didn't think things through. I'm just as guilty. Making him go on the cattle drive he'd created seemed like a good way to teach him a lesson, but now that everyone is here and we're heading out in the morning…"

"It's not what you thought," she said, finishing his sentence.

Zane looked at her. She had the sudden thought that maybe she wasn't supposed to participate at that level. She was about to apologize when he nodded.

"That's right."

She shivered again, but this time the involuntary reaction had nothing to do with cold and everything to do with the tingles skittering through her. What was it about this man that got to her? Standing here in the night, freezing her butt off, probably looking like cat gack, she couldn't help thinking there was nowhere else she wanted to be and no one else she wanted to be with.

"I need to have my head examined," she murmured before she could stop herself.

"Why?"

She laughed. "Just on general principal. I'm from Los Angeles. We're all into that sort of thing."

The sound of Phoebe's laughter drifted through the night. Funny how it sort of got inside Zane and made parts of him all tight. And not just his crotch, although that was plenty hard right now. There was also a pressure in his chest, and his gut.

"Some lady called and wanted to know if we had hot stone massage," he said.

Phoebe looked at him and grinned. "What did you tell her?"

"That she was coming to the wrong place. As Frank asked just yesterday, who gets a massage with a rock?"

"They're very popular. I think it has something to do with the heat. It relaxes the muscles."

"An LA thing."

"Most of the best things are."

"Oh, you're one of those, are you? A fan of La-La Land."

She wrinkled her nose. "We don't call it that anymore. You can make fun all you want, but until you've lived there, you'll never understand the appeal."

"Living there wouldn't help."

She laughed again, which was what he wanted. He liked how the sound cut through him and made him want her more. He felt like one of his bulls, ready to tear through a fence to get at the female of his choice. He liked that he wanted her, even though the wanting was different from any he'd experienced before. Even though it felt dangerous.

What was there about this woman that tapped into such a deep-rooted need? Was it the way she smiled, with an almost innocence? The shape of her face, the scent of her? Was it the sway of her dark hair against her cheekbones as she moved her head? Was it the delight she took in her world? A delight that made him feel as old as dirt?

Even standing here on the porch, he wanted her. His fingers curled into his palms, when what he really wanted to do was touch her cheek. He wanted to trace her profile, feel the silk of her hair, then lower his head and kiss her.

It wouldn't stop there. One kiss, then another, then his hands would be all over her, tearing at clothes, baring her body, and then he would push her up against the wall of the house and—

He shut down that part of his mind, mentally turning his back on the erotic image. He became aware of the silence, of the night, of the sound of her breathing. Awareness sparked between them. He ignored that, too.

"It's late," he told her. "We've got an early start."

She nodded once, then turned toward the house. Before she went inside, though, she looked at him.

"Are you going to be okay?" she asked.

The question stunned him. No one ever bothered to ask. They assumed. He was Zane Nicholson—a man in charge. **The** man in charge.

"I'll be fine," he assured her.

Phoebe offered one of her soft smiles, then stepped into the house. "See you in the morning."

"'Night."

He watched her go and knew he would be seeing her again the second he closed his eyes.

Lucy turned onto her stomach and shoved the fluffy pillow under her head. It was big—nearly as big as herself. She liked the way it was both squishy and firm. She liked the bed and the sheets and pretty much everything about the room. She and Tommy even had their own bathroom.

"Did you smell the towels?" she asked.

Her brother turned and stared at her. "No." His expression said he didn't know why he would want to.

"I did. They smell good. Like flowers, but not 'xactly. Not like the towels there."

The "there" in question was Mrs. Fortier's house, but Tommy would know that. There, towels and sheets smelled funny. Not bad like the time a sick cat had crawled under the porch and died, but sort of thick and goopy. Like something old had been wrapped in them for a long time. Plus the towels and sheets weren't nearly this soft. Lucy rubbed her face against her pillow again. It almost tickled her skin.

"I like this house," Tommy said. "It's really big, but nice."

"Yeah." She flopped onto her back and stared up at the white ceiling. It was late, and they should be asleep, but everything was too strange.

Tommy turned on his side to face her. Their beds were sort of close together, but not too close. Lucy liked that.

"Zane's real big," her brother said.

"Scary."

Tommy tried to deny it, then nodded quickly, as if he didn't want to get caught agreeing with her.

"I like Chase," Lucy said. "He smiles a lot."

"C.J. said they're brothers."

Lucy didn't want to think about C.J. or what she said about anything. C.J. made her feel all cold and shivery every time she looked at her and Tommy. Thad was different. He seemed to like them, but C.J....she didn't want them there.

Lucy almost told her brother that, but she knew he wouldn't believe her. He never believed anything she said about the adults they met. He always said they were nice and kind and looking for kids just like them. Lucy knew better.

"Zane and Chase kinda look like brothers," she said instead, "but Zane is a lot older. I wonder why."

"They're still family," Tommy said.

Lucy glared at her brother. He had a really stupid look on his face, like he was thinking about them being part of a family.

"Forget it," she said. "We're never going to find anyone who wants to adopt us."

"We might."

"No."

She hated saying it, hated how it made her feel, but she knew one of them had to see the truth. Wanting and wishing were scary enough, but believing…that was the worst. Believing made her insides hurt.

She blinked really fast so Tommy couldn't tell that she suddenly wanted to cry.

"Dinner was good," she said to distract him. "Maybe we'll go the whole week without being sent to bed hungry."

"You think?"

"Maybe."

Tommy pulled up his covers. "What did you think of C.J. and Thad?"

"She hates us."

"No, she doesn't."

"She looks at us the same way Mrs. Fortier does. Like we did something bad when we didn't."

"But Thad—"

"No." She turned away from her brother. "It doesn't matter. So what if he's nice and likes us? Boys might be more special than girls, but in families, you know who decides. She does. Not him. And she doesn't like us at all."

CHAPTER EIGHT

Phoebe set her Stetson on her head, then turned to gaze at herself in the mirror.

Jeans, boots, hat. All she needed was a six-shooter, and she could pass for Jesse James…well, almost.

A week ago if someone had told her she would be heading out on a real, live cattle drive she would have laughed in disbelief. But now that she was actually here, she could barely keep from dancing from foot to foot. So far everything about the ranch was too cool for words—and that was excluding the Zane factor.

She collected the saddlebags and small duffel that she'd packed the night before and walked out of the bedroom. Maya had gone downstairs a few minutes before, grousing about the limited amount of gear she was allowed to bring.

Phoebe would have liked a few more of her possessions along as well, but she could manage without for a few days. She would just have to—

She stepped out into the clear morning and instantly came to a stop. Everyone had collected in front of the house. Eddie and Gladys were over by the corral, taking video of the cowboys at work. The men seemed to be enjoying the attention, even showing off a little. C.J., Thad and the kids were clustered together but not talking. Maya smiled up at a handsome, older cowboy, but none of that mattered to Phoebe.

Without warning, without knowing why, what it meant or how to stop it if she wanted to, she found her gaze settling right on Zane. As if she'd known where he would be at that exact instant. As if he had some magical power to draw her attention only to him. As if he were magnetic north to her female compass.

She paused, willing him to look up and see her, but he remained in an intense conversation with one of the cowboys. Oh, well. Maybe next time.

Eddie and Gladys called out to one of the cowboys who was riding his horse out of the corral. He grinned at whatever they said and encouraged his horse to rear up on its hind legs. The two old women applauded.

Chase stood next to Maya. They looked good together, Phoebe thought. Both tall, both attractive. His dark good looks contrasted with her fair skin and blond hair. Chase said something Phoebe couldn't hear, and Maya laughed. She touched his arm in a gesture that was both affectionate and comfortable. As if they'd always been family.

An uncomfortable twinge caught Phoebe by surprise. It wasn't that she didn't want her friend to have family, it was just that Phoebe couldn't help wanting the same thing for herself. She turned to see if Zane had noticed the exchange and was stunned by the starkness of his unguarded expression. For a single beat of time, she saw into his very soul. The loneliness there, the need to fit in and be a part of something more than himself blindsided her. He understood, she told herself in amazement. He wanted it, too. She thought about what he'd endured with his family and wasn't surprised.

But then he blinked, and the emotions disappeared as if they had never been.

Had she imagined it all? Had she projected

her own wants and desires onto him because she found him sexually intoxicating, and she wanted them to have something significant in common?

"It's way too early to be thinking such deep thoughts," she murmured to herself.

The sound of hoofbeats caught her attention. She turned and saw two mules pulling a large covered wagon. Phoebe wanted to rub her eyes to make sure she hadn't imagined the sight, but there they were. Like something out of the History channel. A real, honest-to-goodness covered wagon and mules.

The old man driving the contraption fit the part perfectly. He wore a faded red shirt and ratty jeans. An old battered cowboy hat had been pulled low over his grizzled features. One of his cheeks stuck out way more than the other. Phoebe's feelings of romance about the Old West quickly turned into a horrified gag when he turned and spit tobacco on the ground.

"Here comes another cowboy," Gladys said.

"I don't want him. He's old," Eddie replied. "You can have that one."

"I don't want him!"

Hiding a smile, Phoebe quickly turned her attention to the mules, who were so darned cute with their perky ears. She noticed two more being pulled behind the wagon. This pair was laden with several duffels and cloth sacks tied together. With their big eyes and sweet faces, they looked charming.

"All they need are straw hats with little bows or a crown of flowers," she said.

Unfortunately Zane walked by just then, and the look he shot her told her that he had not only heard her, but he thought she was an idiot. She wanted to hurry after him and explain that thinking the mules would look cute in hats wasn't the same thing as actually wanting them in hats, but she didn't. In his mind, thinking it was probably as bad as buying the hats.

"This is Cookie," Zane said to the group. "As you may have guessed from his name, he's in charge of feeding us all while we're gone. You had a sample of his cooking last night."

Thad patted his belly. "Then I think we're all going to weigh at lot more at the end of this week than at the beginning. Hope the horses don't mind."

"Oh, we'll ride them pounds off you," Cookie said with a grin. Then his good humor faded. "Well, don't just stand there staring," he yelled. "Hand over your gear. We haven't got all day. Snap to."

Maya bent down and picked up her duffel. Phoebe followed her.

"Hey, Hot Stuff," Cookie said to Eddie as Chase hoisted her bag into the wagon. "You look good enough to eat."

"You better not try," Eddie replied.

Maya grinned. "Have you missed me, Cookie?"

He winked at her. "Like you'd give an old coot like me the time of day."

Maya put her hand on her hip and gave an exaggerated bump and grind. "Cookie, for your biscuits I'd do just about anything."

The old man cackled. Phoebe handed him her duffel. Cookie looked her over, then winked. She gave him a smile and tried not to think about the plug of tobacco stuck in his cheek.

Andrea was next. She handed up her bag but didn't move on. Instead she narrowed her gaze. "You are careful when you cook, aren't you? I would hate to think you'd contaminate our food with your filthy habit."

Cookie's mouth got all pinched and thin. "You doing the cooking, or am I?"

"I suppose you are."

He nodded. "Just so we're both clear on that."

Andrea turned away. She muttered something to Martin, who patted her arm. Chase carried Gladys's duffel to the wagon.

Cookie looked Gladys over. "Nice. Just give a holler if you ever get lonely. I can be real good company."

Andrea sniffed. "How disgusting. Is he going to come on to all the women? Can't he be controlled?"

Chase passed by Phoebe and leaned close. "You'll notice Cookie didn't say a word to the vegetable princess there."

Phoebe had to turn away to hide her grin.

When all the gear was loaded, Zane had them line up. He walked in front of them, staring at each of them in turn, then calling out a name. When he paused in front of Phoebe, she felt the heat of his gaze all the way to the insides of her bones. Although he only stared at her for a second, it was enough to get her heart up into the serious-cardio-workout range. When he moved to Maya, her body returned to normal. She felt like one of those special flowering plants that only blooms in full sunlight. When Zane wasn't around, she withered.

As Zane finished calling out names, several cowboys appeared leading horses. There was a brass nameplate on each bridle, corresponding with what he'd called out. Phoebe looked for a horse named Rocky.

When he appeared, he was a brunette with legs that turned dark on the bottom. His mane and tail were black, as well.

Phoebe offered Rocky a tentative smile. He did not respond.

"Listen up," Zane said. "Who here has been on a horse before?"

Eddie and Gladys raised their hands. Martin's went up, too. Zane asked about their riding experience.

"Shane Stryker gave us lessons last summer, and then we rode as elder warriors in the Maá-zib parade last year," Eddie said.

"We offered to go topless, to be real authentic, but Mayor Marsha wouldn't let us."

"Since then, we go out to the Castle Ranch about once a month to keep our muscles limber," Gladys added.

Martin said he'd had lessons as a kid.

Zane explained the basics of riding a horse. While the guests weren't working cowboys, on the trail they would be expected to help with the care of their horses. That meant making sure the animal had plenty of water, taking off the saddles in the evening and basic equine grooming. Using his horse, a rust-colored gelding, he demonstrated how to mount.

Phoebe looked from Zane's horse to hers. They seemed to be about the same size, at least in height. Rocky was a bit on the lean side with long legs.

Speaking of legs—she glanced from hers to Zane's. There was a difference of several inches in length, which meant there was no way she would be able to put one foot into the stirrup and swing her way up to the saddle the way he had. She needed a chair or bench or stool or something.

Right as she realized the problem, Zane turned toward her. Her heart sprouted wings and did a quick turn around her chest, but before he reached her, Chase appeared at her side.

"Ready?" he asked.

She shifted her attention to Zane, but he'd already moved over to help Gladys. She swallowed her disappointment and smiled at the young man.

"Is there a stepping stool?" she asked.

"Sure." He laced his fingers together and held them a little above knee high.

Phoebe wrinkled her nose. "I don't want to hurt you."

Chase winked. "Not possible, even if you are a goddess."

"Oh, right. What is it with you cowboy types? You and Cookie should get together and write a book of pickup lines."

"We're talkin' about it." He touched the side of her leg with his finger. "Come on, Phoebe. Show everyone how it's done. Put your left foot on my hands. We'll count to three, and you'll spring on up to the saddle."

She wasn't too confident about the whole

"springing" part. Rocky's saddle looked really high up. There was also the worry of springing too far and finding herself sliding off the other side, which wasn't how she wanted to start her morning.

But if she planned to go on the cattle drive, she had to get her butt onto a horse… literally. Sucking in a breath for courage, she grabbed the front of the saddle with both hands, placed her booted foot onto the man-made step Chase offered, then counted to three.

As she pushed off the ground with her right foot, Chase lifted her high into the air. She swung her leg over in an almost graceful move and found herself plopping down on a very hard, very small saddle.

Until that moment, Phoebe had always thought Western-style saddles were huge. But now that she was in one—and about forty feet from the ground—she felt as if she were perched on something the size of a saucer. Rocky shifted, which made her grab for the saddle horn.

"Do I have to be up this high?" she asked.

Chase chuckled. "You'll get used to it."

She had her doubts.

Chase fiddled with some buckles on the saddle and adjusted the stirrup so that she could rest her foot in it. As he worked, he put a hand on her calf.

"The best part," he said with a wink.

Of course Zane was close enough to hear, and he scowled at his brother. "Keep your mind on your work."

Chase responded by rolling his eyes.

Eddie and Gladys got on their horses with an ease Phoebe envied. Kind of embarrassing, being shown up by two septuagenarian cowgirls. Maya was also at home several stories in the air. After Chase adjusted Maya's stirrups, she rode over to Phoebe and reined in her horse.

"How are you doing?" she asked.

Phoebe shrugged. "I'm trying not to look at the ground."

Maya laughed. "You'll get used to it. Remember, the trick is to move with your horse. Try to relax into his stride so you're not bouncing. If you don't, you'll be sore for days."

Phoebe had a feeling she was going to be sore for the rest of her life, but she was determined to tough it out. She hadn't been on a vacation in years, and with her future looking doubtful, she had a feeling she wouldn't be on one again for a long time. So she'd better enjoy this one.

The two children were given scaled-down versions of real horses. They both looked as apprehensive as Phoebe felt. C.J. watched as Chase checked their stirrups.

"Are you two all right?" she asked. "We can still change our minds about this."

The question was reasonable enough, but Phoebe couldn't shake the feeling that C.J. wanted the children to say they didn't want to go, which made her feel badly. Lucy and Tommy looked at each other and grinned.

"We're going," the little girl said.

"Listen up," Zane said. He eased into his saddle as if he'd been born to it.

Well, duh, Phoebe thought with a smile. He had.

"We're heading out," he continued. "We're going to take things slow, letting the cattle set the pace. You'll each be assigned a place alongside the herd. Don't try to direct your horse, because he has a better idea of where we're going than you do. If you get into trouble, give a shout."

"We'll be fine," Gladys said.

Famous last words, Zane thought, wishing he could believe them. All the novices looked as if they could be blown off their mounts by a stiff wind. He didn't usually allow for second-guessing, but he was about to make an exception. Deciding to go forward with the cattle drive had been about the stupidest idea he'd ever had.

"Ready to go, boss?" Frank asked as he rode up.

Zane let his gaze settle on the two kids, then he shook his head. "No, but we're leaving anyway."

Frank grinned. "Me and the boys are taking bets on who falls off their horse first. You're gonna have to let us know who it is and when it happens for the pool."

Zane pulled his hat down low. For the first time in years, he wanted to be somewhere other than the ranch. Greenhorns. The whole lot of them. Frank and the boys were right. Someone would be tumbling from a horse, and if Zane was lucky, that would be the least of his troubles.

"Have fun," Frank said with an expression that announced "better you than me."

Zane nodded. "I know you're not much for praying, but you might want to put in a good word with the Almighty."

"Sure thing, boss. You're going to need all the help you can get."

Zane nodded. "You'll be able to reach me on my cell phone. We'll be staying within range of the towers."

"I'll be here."

Zane wished he would be, as well.

A sharp whistle warned him that his life was about to stampede out of control. Seconds later a dust-colored steer with a half bit-off ear appeared, followed by rows of cattle.

"Line 'em up," Zane yelled.

He and Chase quickly moved the greenhorns into position. Zane trotted to the front and took off his hat.

"Move 'em out," he yelled, and they headed east.

CHAPTER NINE

Chase would rather have his teeth pulled out by rusty pliers than admit the truth, but he was having second thoughts. It was only midmorning on the first day and while nothing had exactly gone wrong, he was getting a bad feeling about the whole cattle-drive experience. Fifty steers didn't sound like many during a conversation at dinner, and most cattlemen could control three times that many without thinking twice. But their motley crew wasn't exactly made up of average cattlemen.

There were kids and old ladies. Maybe, just maybe, he'd really been an asshole when he'd taken everyone's money. Maybe he should have thought about the consequences of day-trading and then trying to get it all back based on a stock tip that had been as realistic as a steer siring twin calves. Maybe—

He coughed and tried to move out of the cloud of dust. It was a futile effort. Zane had positioned him at the rear of the herd, the worst place to be. No doubt he'd considered it fitting punishment for his screwup half brother.

Chase tugged his hat lower and thought about tying a bandanna over his nose and mouth. He had a clean square of cloth in his jeans pocket. But somehow using it felt like giving in or admitting he'd been wrong.

He **had** been wrong. Chase winced as the realization settled on him like too heavy a load. He'd been impulsive and arrogant and a fool. His insides felt all twisty and hard. Guilt, he acknowledged. Pure guilt.

The obvious solution was to admit he was wrong and apologize to Zane. Only that had never worked in the past. His brother didn't care about apologies. Zane talked about not getting it wrong in the first place, which Chase was in favor of...if only he knew how. Zane seemed to always know the right thing to do. He never made a mistake. Good thing, because Chase made enough for both of them. And every time he got it wrong Zane would give him that look. Not the death-ray one—although it was bad enough—but the one that said he was disappointed. Again.

He slumped in the saddle, prepared to spend the rest of the morning feeling sorry for himself. Up ahead the cattle moved at their slow, steady pace. At least the weather was halfway decent, he thought. Plenty of sun. It would warm up during the day and—

A scream cut through the sound of steer hooves thudding on packed ground. Chase straightened, then swore as Andrea's horse cut sharply to the left and headed directly into the thick trees on the side of the trail. The woman still clung to the saddle, but with all the low branches she was likely to encounter, that wouldn't last for long.

Chase swore again as he turned his mount and headed after her. There was no reason for her horse to take off like that, not if she hadn't done something she shouldn't have. Zane had been real careful to choose calm horses for everyone. But regardless of the reason, the fool woman was his responsibility.

He ducked as his horse raced through the trees. Up ahead came the thrashing of something large moving at a fast speed, and without much regard for the potential danger.

"Help me!" Andrea screamed. "Oh, God, don't you dare jump."

The instruction was followed by a long, high-pitched yelp, then an awful silence that made Chase's throat go dry.

He rounded a couple more trees, then saw Andrea barely clinging to her horse. She was more off the saddle than on, with her left leg flopping around and both hands holding on. Chase kicked his horse once and the animal moved closer. He had to duck under a low branch, and then he was able to lean low and grab the runaway's reins.

The horse instantly slowed. Andrea continued to slip. She gave a cry of alarm, but Chase caught her arm before she slipped too far, and he helped her back into the saddle.

"You saved my life," Andrea said as she pressed a hand to her chest. "I thought I was going to die for sure."

"Are you all right?"

She shook her head, then drew in a deep breath. "I'm fine. That jump. It was so high and we were flying, then we came down with a thump, and I couldn't stay in the saddle."

Chase looked her over, but there didn't seem to be anything wrong. She was a little shaken but still functioning.

"Your horse doesn't usually take off like that," he said. "What happened?"

Andrea smoothed her hair away from her face. "I'm not sure. I was just humming to myself and—" She broke off and stared at him. Her eyes widened. "Oh, my. I was humming and sort of bouncing to the music and I must have accidentally kicked him."

She leaned forward and touched her mount's neck. "I'm so sorry. I would never have kicked you on purpose."

Her horse didn't respond, but that didn't seem to bother her. She returned her attention to Chase. "I don't even know what to say. Really. You were great."

Just then Zane rode up. "You all right?"

Andrea beamed. "Your brother saved my life. I think I accidentally kicked my horse, and then we were racing through the trees, and he jumped over a stump, and I was hanging from my saddle. I just knew I was going to fall, and then Chase was there."

Zane didn't spare him a glance. "So

you're not hurt?"

"Just my pride." Andrea slowly turned her horse to face back the way they'd come. "No more humming for me."

Zane took the reins and headed toward the trail. As he passed Chase, he gave him the death-ray look. Chase knew what he was thinking. If Chase hadn't messed up in the first place, none of this would be happening.

It was just unfair, he grumbled to himself as he headed back to the dust cloud at the rear of the herd. He'd made a mistake, and now he was being punished. But was that enough for Zane? No. Nothing was ever enough.

He broke through the trees and found Maya waiting for him.

"Everyone all right?" she asked.

"Andrea's fine," he said. "Not that it matters. This sucks. I can't make what I did right, and that's what he can't forgive me for. Saying I'm sorry doesn't matter for shit. You know? Like it's my fault that I can't change the space-time continuum and rewrite the past. So sue me."

Maya lowered her sunglasses and looked

at him. "Are you about finished with the pity party or should I go get some chips and drinks?"

"I'm just about done. Except that, no matter what, it's not going to be right. At the end of this cattle drive Zane's going to be just as mad at me as he is now. Punishing me won't make him happy."

"I'm not sure Zane is capable of being happy," Maya said. "But that's not the point. Everyone makes mistakes."

"Not ever-perfect Zane."

"Even Zane," she insisted. "The difference is the whole world doesn't know when he gets things wrong."

"I wish they did. It would even the score."

She nodded in sympathy. "I know it feels really unfair right now, Chase, but the truth is this time you—"

He cut her off with a flick of his hand. "I know. This time I went too far, even for me. I deserve to be punished. I am being punished, and when all this is over, do you think for one second, it's going to be okay with Zane? Do you think he'll ever let it go?"

"He won't talk about it."

"Sure. But it will still be there. We'll both

know it."

She nodded. "You're right. Zane doesn't hold a grudge, but he's not exactly forgiving, either. I'm sorry, Chase. You have to live with the fact that your brother is a hard-ass. Under normal circumstances I'd consider his tight butt one of his best features, but this time I mean it in a bad way."

He winced. "Don't talk about Zane that way. It grosses me out."

"What? Zane and any woman or Zane and me?"

"Zane and you. You're my sister."

She grinned. "Don't sweat it. Zane and I have never had even a flicker of interest between us." She tilted her head. "Maybe Zane and a woman isn't such a bad idea, though."

"Ha. That would require him to have an actual conversation that wasn't about business. I'm not sure he can."

"I suspect that under the right circumstances Zane can be charming."

Chase stared at her. Maya held up one hand. "Okay. I take it back. I can't imagine him being anything but himself. Still, he must have needs. Doesn't he get lonely?"

"Zane doesn't have weaknesses, remember?"

"Not that he'll let us see, but that doesn't mean they don't exist. Is he seeing anyone?"

"No. There hasn't been a steady woman since Sally."

Maya looked surprised. "Does he date?"

"I don't know. I guess. Maybe. When he goes to town or maybe on his business trips."

"How often does he do that?"

"A couple times a year."

"Maybe his bad temper comes from not getting laid," she said.

"Another problem I can't fix," he grumbled.

Maya started to respond, then shook her head. "Hold on. Phoebe looks like she's in trouble. I'll be right back."

He watched as she rode on ahead. About fifty feet in front of them, Phoebe was doing a piss-poor job of turning around her horse. Maya demonstrated how to tug on the reins, and Rocky slowly rotated in the direction Phoebe indicated. Chase urged his mount to trot forward so he could join them.

"What's up?" he asked, mindful of Andrea's close encounter with the forest.

Phoebe shifted on her saddle. "I was wondering about rest stops. When do we make them? And where? I haven't seen any facilities. Is there a campsite or something?"

Chase stared at her. Maya's mouth dropped open.

"What?" Phoebe looked from one to the other. "What did I say? Are you trying to tell me that real cowboys don't go to the bathroom?"

Maya reached out and patted Phoebe's arm. "I thought you knew."

Phoebe's eyes narrowed. "Knew what?"

"We use nature's restroom."

Chase knew it was rude to laugh, but he couldn't keep himself from grinning as Phoebe's eyes widened with horror.

"Outdoors? In the bushes? But what about sanitation? What about washing my hands?"

"What about back to nature?" Maya asked.

"I'm not sure I want the two of us to be that close."

Chase shook his head. "You don't get out much, do you?"

"Not like this." Phoebe swallowed. "We're not going to be showering, are we?"

"We have camp showers," Chase said. "Big bags of water you hang in the sun so they get warm."

She winced. "Sounds really great. I can't wait." She looked at Maya. "You didn't say anything about this when you talked about an exciting vacation on a cattle drive."

Maya didn't look the least bit contrite. "I forgot."

"Like I believe that." Phoebe carefully turned her horse around again. "I need to get back to my place in the herd."

When she was gone, Chase nudged Maya. "What about Phoebe?"

His former stepsister shook her head. "I considered it for a while, but I'd worry that Zane wouldn't treat her right."

"Hey. What about me? I deserve a break. Phoebe's nice and I think Zane might like her. He talks to her more than to anyone, and I think I've seen him watching her. If he was distracted by her, he would get off my back. You should want to help me out here."

"I'm not sure you've earned the privilege of having Zane off your back."

"You have to help me."

"Sorry, kid. You're on your own with this one."

When they stopped for lunch, Phoebe walked around in an attempt to get feeling back into her butt. She wasn't too keen on "nature's restroom," and the tingling in her fanny was kind of strange; but aside from that, she found she was starting to like her time in the outdoors.

Although Rocky still scared her a little, she didn't think he would try to bite her or throw her, which was a step in the right direction. She tried to be considerate and not flop around too much in the saddle. When she'd dismounted, she'd been careful to pat Rocky's neck and thank him for the ride, although she wasn't 100 percent sure he'd understood what she was saying. Still, it had been a start to what she hoped would be a pleasant working relationship.

She walked along the edge of the grove of trees where they'd stopped. The air was just warm enough for comfort, the blue sky seemed to stretch on forever, and there were mountains not that far away.

Phoebe had never much thought about being away from the city. She'd lived in Los Angeles her whole life, and her idea of back to nature was new plants for her patio. Her various foster parents hadn't been big on camping trips or hiking in the foothills, and as an adult, she'd never considered the option of getting away. But now that she was here, in the wilderness, she found that she liked it.

If she'd thought about it ahead of time, she would have expected silence, but it wasn't quiet at all. There were all kinds of birds flitting around, along with small creatures making rustly noises in the bushes. The cattle had a symphony of their own— the rhythm of their hooves, the grunts and occasional moos. She wished she knew more about this part of the country. She would like to be able to name the trees and the small yellow flowers. Maya knew as little as she did, and when she'd asked Chase, he'd rolled his eyes and reminded her that he was seventeen. His interests lay more in the direction of computers and girls than flora and fauna. Since she hadn't brought her cell phone along on this stroll, that left only Zane, but she couldn't actually bring herself to ask him to give her a botany lesson.

So she contented herself with admiring the leaves and walking around small bushes until some feeling returned to her butt. Then she walked toward the stream they'd passed a few minutes before stopping.

Cookie had provided everyone with a hand towel and some kind of soap that was supposed to be ecologically safe to use in the wilderness. The nature-friendly cleanser had made Andrea and Martin happy.

The brush seemed to get sparser the closer she got to the stream. She found a dry spot at the end and crouched in front of the rapidly flowing water.

For a minute or so she simply watched the bubbling and gurgling progress of the stream. The air smelled fresh and damp, with a hint of coolness that teased at her cheeks. She unfastened her watch and set it on a flat rock, then squeezed the soap over her hands and rubbed until there was a thin lather. Then she plunged her hands into the stream.

A fish brushed her, and she jerked her hands out of the water with a little shriek. Unfortunately her hands were still slick and she had to drop them into the stream again to clean them.

Ew.

She reached for her towel. As she picked it up, she heard a slight rustling from behind her.

Standing quickly, she turned, but there wasn't anyone there. No animals, either, at least not any she could see. If some furry resident had been spying on her, she'd probably scared him off with her scream about the fish. Even if she hadn't, nothing around here was big enough to be a problem, right? She rubbed her hands on her towel. It wasn't as if there were bears or anything. Or snakes.

She shivered and took a step back. A sudden loud rustling on her left made her jump again. She whirled around and covered her mouth with her hand as something very big lunged toward her. Something huge and scary and—

"I heard you scream," Zane said as he stepped out from behind a tree. "What happened?"

Her first instinct was to throw herself at him and beg him to protect her. Good sense intervened, and she settled for taking a step toward him and offering a shaky smile.

"Nothing. I'm fine."

"Uh-huh."

She cleared her throat and went for the casual smile. Her attempt at nonchalance wasn't helped by her instant and oh-so-familiar physical response to the man's nearness. It was the usual list of reactions —faster heart rate, weaker thighs and knees, dilated blood vessels and hormones performing bits from the balcony scene in **Romeo and Juliet.**

"I might have called out in surprise," she admitted when it became apparent he wasn't budging without some kind of an explanation. "A fish touched my hand."

"Hey, you almost caught your dinner."

She caught a glimmer in his eyes and laughed. He wasn't as humorless as some people might think.

"How are you holding up?" he asked.

She tossed her towel over her shoulder and smiled. "Great. I really like the riding. Except for my..." She cleared her throat. "I'm not used to sitting on a saddle."

"Butt numb?"

"A little."

She waited for him to say it would get better, but when he didn't, she filled in the silence.

"Rocky seems nice. He's a little tall for me, but I guess that's a good thing in a horse."

Zane's blue eyes continued to stare straight at her. His lips didn't move, but somehow she heard the word "idiot" as clear as if he'd shouted it from those snow-covered mountaintops.

"You don't actually want short horses," she continued, even though she knew it was a mistake to keep talking. "Except maybe for children. You don't have any, do you? Children, I mean. Not short horses."

He was quiet a long time before he answered.

"No."

"I didn't think so. Maya didn't mention any. Plus, I probably would have seen them at the house, huh?"

He tugged on the brim of his hat. "You about ready to head back?"

"Sure. I just need to get my watch."

She relished the excuse to turn away. Man, oh, man, had she really said short horses would be good for children? Could she have sounded more stupid? Had there been a wall nearby, she would have banged her head against it a few times, just to give herself something to think about other than feeling humiliated.

As there was no wall, she crossed to the flat rock where she'd left her watch.

"It's gone."

Completely. There was the rock, and on top of it was exactly nothing.

She checked around it to see if it had fallen off, then checked her pockets, but she hadn't put it there and forgotten about it.

Zane walked over to stand next to her. "What did it look like?"

"My watch? It was silver. Not expensive or anything. Just a regular watch."

"Shiny?"

"I guess."

"Raccoons."

Determined not to say anything stupid for at least the next ten minutes, she considered his single-word statement. Raccoons? Okay. He probably hadn't started a word-association game, so what did he mean?

Going with the safest response, she cautiously repeated, "Raccoons?"

"They like shiny things. Take off with them whenever they can."

"You're saying a raccoon stole my watch?"

"Probably."

She really wanted to point out that they couldn't possibly tell time, but knew instinctively that was a bad idea.

"Can I get it back?"

"Sure. If you can find it."

Could she? She glanced around at the underbrush, the trees, the stream.

"Is it safe for me to go exploring?" she asked.

"You're not likely to be attacked by raccoons, but you'll probably get lost, fall down a ravine, break your leg and starve to death. But if the watch is that important to you, have at it."

She felt herself deflating. "You don't like me much, do you?" she asked sadly.

She half expected Zane to stalk away, but instead he exhaled and shook his head. "Sorry."

She blinked. "What?"

"I said I'm sorry."

Had the earth stopped turning, or had the taciturn, hunky cowboy standing in front of her just apologized?

"I—you—" She paused for breath. "That's okay. I guess it was a stupid question."

"No. It was a reasonable question under the circumstances." He shoved his hands into his pockets. "I get a little sarcastic sometimes."

"Let's call it a dry sense of humor."

He half nodded in acknowledgment. "You'll never find them, and even if you did, your watch would probably be all broken up and rusty from them dunking it in the water. Don't leave out anything they'll take. Shiny jewelry, another watch."

"I don't have another watch. Not with me."

"You need to know the time?"

"Just when the meals are."

"Cookie rings a bell."

"Really? Just like in the movies?"

"Yeah." One corner of his mouth turned up as he spoke. It wasn't exactly a smile, but it was close enough to get her breathing up to Mach 3.

"Come on," he said. "It's nearly time for lunch."

He started back toward the camp. Phoebe followed him happily.

"You think the raccoons could ever learn to tell time?" she asked.

He glanced at her. "You're kidding, right?"

"Maybe I have a dry sense of humor, too."

"City girl."

He was probably insulting her, but the way he said the word made her feel almost tall and, if not blonde, then certainly high-lighted.

"I think Rocky likes me," she confided.

"I'm sure he does."

CHAPTER TEN

"This is a hamburger," Andrea announced with all the enthusiasm of a schoolteacher discovering a student with head lice.

Cookie glared at her. Zane figured his annoyance at having someone question him about his food overrode his natural inclination to flirt with the ladies.

The old man used his spatula to lift up the meat patty and stare underneath it. "Yup. Looks like hamburger to me. Now if you like I could fry you up some bacon to go on it, but I don't have nothing fancy. None of them designer cheeses or guaca-mole."

Andrea pushed her plate at him. "I can't eat this."

Cookie's thick eyebrows drew together. "Listen here, little lady. I've been making burgers since before you were spitting up on your mama's shoulder."

Andrea turned to her husband. "Martin, it's a hamburger."

Martin cleared his throat. "We're vegetarians, Cookie."

Cookie frowned and looked at Zane who could only shrug. The cook shook his head.

"I heard tell you don't eat meat. Don't make sense to me."

Andrea shuddered. "Meat is unhealthy, inhumane, and if you knew all the wasted land spent growing food for livestock you'd understand why a non-animal-based diet is so much—"

"You crazy?" Cookie asked, interrupting her.

Andrea looked unamused by the question. "Absolutely not. I am concerned about my health and the state of the environment. Now, I'm requesting an alternative for my lunch."

Cookie glanced at Zane who shrugged again, then the cook picked up a clean plate. He put a grilled burger bun on first, flipped it open and set lettuce, tomato and cheese on the bottom half. Next he slapped on a mound of potato salad on the plate along with a scoop of cut up fresh fruit, then handed the plate to Andrea.

"Next," he bellowed, glaring at Martin.

Andrea opened her mouth, then closed

it. "Fine," she murmured from between clenched teeth.

Martin stepped up to Cookie and offered a tentative smile. "Is the beef hormone free?" he asked.

Andrea swung on him. "Martin, you wouldn't consider actually eating that, would you?"

From where Zane was standing, Martin looked more than a little interested in the juicy burger his wife had refused.

"If it's hormone free," he said, not meeting her gaze.

Zane stepped forward. "I don't use feed with antibiotics in it," he told Martin. "The steers are healthy, prime beef."

"Fresh, too," Cookie said with a wink. "Just last week this one was on the hoof."

Andrea thrust her plate at her husband and made a beeline for the bushes. Martin paled and said the meat-free burger would be fine. Cookie shrugged as if to say it was his choice, but Zane wasn't fooled. He collected a plate and took the burger neither Andrea nor Martin had wanted.

"I don't guess they'll be asking any more questions," the cook said with a cackle.

"Serves 'em right," Chase said as he joined them.

Zane glared at them both. "They're our guests. Paying guests. Cookie, I want you to figure out something those two can eat. Chase, finish up your lunch, then check on the cattle."

"But, Zane, I've been working all morning."

"So has everyone else. We wouldn't be here if it wasn't for you, so I suggest you do your best to not cause more trouble."

Chase grabbed his food and stalked off. Cookie watched him go.

"You're hard on the boy."

"He's earned it." Zane grabbed a fork and napkin. "You hear me about those two?"

Cookie's mouth twisted. "They're vegetarians, Zane. You gotta let me have a little fun."

"They're my responsibility."

"Aw, hell."

Cookie grumbled as he tended the cook fire, but Zane knew the old man would respect his request. He depended on his crew, and they rarely let him down. If only he could say the same about Chase.

He headed toward the group of canvas

and metal chairs that had been set up for the meal. The kids were sitting a few feet away from C.J. and Thad, close to the wagon. Neither of them were eating.

Just perfect, he thought as he stopped next to them.

"Don't you like your lunch?" he asked.

The girl—Lucy—looked up at him. Her light brown eyes were wide and full of mistrust.

"We heard what that man said. About the burgers."

The boy nodded, then swallowed. "Are we really eating a cow?"

Zane silently ran through five swear-words, using some in combination, damning Cookie, the tree huggers and Chase most of all. He set his plate on an empty chair and crouched in front of the kids.

He knew in his world that the reality of food coming from something in the garden or one of the four-legged critters out in the field was no big deal, but these were city kids. They might know that meat came from animals, but they'd never spent the day riding next to steers, then dining on one just like them.

"You two in school?"

Tommy looked at his sister, then nodded.

Zane smiled. "I was. A long time ago. Right after the dinosaurs died out."

Lucy's mouth twitched a little. "You're not that old."

"Gee, thanks. Okay, so maybe it was a little after the dinosaurs, but not by much. I remember this one kid everybody liked to pick on. It wasn't fair and it wasn't nice, but we did it. Do you two have someone like that at your school?"

Lucy nodded slowly. "It used to be us, but I can beat up a lot of kids, even if they're bigger than me. Tommy can, too, but he doesn't like to do it."

Zane let that go. He had a point, and it wasn't that beating up on other kids was a bad idea.

"So you understand about teasing people, even when it's not very nice," he said. "That's what Cookie was doing. He was teasing Andrea and Martin about the hamburgers. Grown-ups do that, even when they should know better."

Thad shifted his chair closer to Lucy. "Zane's right. I'm sure Cookie's sorry for what he said."

Zane doubted that, but he wasn't going to contradict the guy. Not when Lucy's expression of mistrust began to fade.

Thad picked up his burger and took a bite. "Cookie sure knows how to make good food."

Zane reached for his lunch and sampled the hamburger. He didn't have to fake his pleasure.

Tommy exchanged a look with his sister, then picked up his burger. "I'm hungry," he said.

Lucy went for a small nibble and chewed.

"Better than the ones at school?" Thad asked.

She swallowed and shrugged. "We get a hot lunch, but we don't hafta pay for it like other kids. We get a piece of paper that says it's free."

Zane watched as Thad glanced first at his wife, then back at the girl. "What about McDonald's? Are Cookie's burgers just as good?"

"I can't remember," Lucy said. "Tommy and me haven't been to McDonald's for a real long time. Not since before staying with Mrs. Fortier."

"She says that taking kids to restaurants is too expensive," Tommy added. "And that fast food is a waste of money. But sometimes she and Mr. Fortier have it for dinner."

The boy sounded wistful as he spoke. Zane saw C.J. turn away as if she didn't want to hear any more.

Zane took his plate to an empty chair and sat down. As he ate, he glanced around at Eddie and Gladys talking with Maya and Phoebe on the far side of the camp. Phoebe met his gaze, blushed slightly, then looked away.

He found himself wanting to know what she was thinking. He had a couple dozen other questions for her as well, the most pressing of which was would she join him in the privacy of a grove somewhere for a quickie up against a tree.

Real romantic, Nicholson, he thought grimly. That was sure the way to convince a lady of his intentions. What was wrong with him? He hadn't had it this bad since he'd been sixteen and so hot for Aurelia Ronwell that he'd driven into Fool's Gold three nights a week on the pretext of studying with her.

While she'd talked about their classes in school, he'd fantasized about becoming a man in the secret darkness of her young body. When their relationship had ended, all he'd earned for his trouble was two sightings of her bra strap, half a dozen gut-twisting tongue kisses, a slapped hand for trying to touch her breast and straight A's. The grades hadn't been worth the agony. Right then and there he'd vowed to never let a girl make him act like a fool again.

He'd lost his virginity that summer to a college girl he'd met at the Summer Festival. Sheryl had been working one of the concession stands, and he'd helped her out when she'd had a flat tire. One thing had led to another. She'd given him his first blow job in the front seat of his truck. At the crucial moment, he'd nearly put his foot through the floorboard. That night he'd stayed with her at her place, and she'd shown him the possibilities between a man and a woman.

When he'd dragged his butt back home

about ten the next morning, his father hadn't said a word. He'd driven to town, and when he'd returned, he'd handed Zane a bag containing several boxes of condoms.

"Don't get her pregnant," his old man had said. "Save the babies for the woman you love."

Zane had always followed the first part of that advice, if not the rest of it. He'd been careful to always use protection, regardless of what the woman in question claimed about being on the Pill. He'd learned to find partners who understood that he was only looking for temporary relief and not happily-ever-after. As for having babies with the woman he loved...he'd learned the hard way what loving a woman did to a man. How nothing else mattered and how losing that woman made a man angry and bitter.

He'd watched his father nearly drink himself to death in the first few months after Zane's mother had died. He'd heard the cursing, the angry conversations with God, the crash of glasses hitting the wall in the middle of the night. But the worst of it had been when he'd walked into his father's office and found him holding a gun to his head. In that moment, twelve-year-old Zane realized that nothing he did, nothing he was, would ever matter.

His father had stared at him, his eyes bloodshot, his skin gray.

"I have to be with her," he'd said. "I can't live without her."

Zane had wanted to protest that he couldn't live without his mother, either, but somehow he managed. He wanted to yell that he was still a kid and that it was wrong for his dad to want to die and leave Zane alone. But he didn't say anything. He just stood there—watching.

Eventually his father had put the gun away. They'd never talked about it, but every day when Zane came home from school, he wondered if his dad would still be there. Every night as he lay in bed, he listened for the sound of a gunshot.

Zane shook off the memories. His father was gone. The old man might not have paid much attention to his oldest son, but he'd taught him a good lesson. Love turned a man inside out. It ripped him in two and destroyed his world. Better to keep things simple. Better to want than to need.

He turned his attention back to Phoebe, to the curve of her cheek and the way she tucked her hair behind her ears. To the swell of her breasts and the question of what she would taste like if he licked and kissed his way from her toes to the sweet, salty wetness between her thighs.

Dammit all to hell, he thought as he tossed down his fork. All it took was one image like that in his brain, and he was hard as a rock. He was too old to be that out of control. Yeah, it had been a long time since he'd had a lady friend to visit in town, but so what? He often had long stretches without relief. That didn't mean he had to go around all jacked up like a kid in puberty. It was embarrassing.

Besides, Phoebe wasn't like the women he usually chose. She wasn't divorced, widowed or old enough to know better. She had **happily-ever-after** scrawled across her face as clearly as if it was a tattoo. He knew her type, and he steered clear of them. Sally had been like that, and he still felt badly when he thought of how their marriage had ended.

Nope, he knew what was right, and that meant staying away from the brown-eyed beauty with the full mouth and big heart. When they got back to the ranch, he would make a point of going to Fool's Gold or maybe Sacramento to find himself a nice woman looking for a little uncomplicated action.

C.J. ignored the chill in the water as she washed her hands after lunch. She used the towel Cookie had given them, then hesitated, not sure if she should wait for Thad to finish or make her escape while she could.

She knew he wanted to talk, and she had a feeling she knew what he was going to say. After this many years together, she understood how his mind worked and what he was thinking. The thing was, she didn't want to hear it.

"Lucy and Tommy seem to be having a good time," he said.

Trying not to feel trapped, C.J. nodded. Thad was a good man, she told herself. One of the things she loved about him was his goodness.

"Their foster situation doesn't seem suitable."

She sucked in a breath. "We have no way of knowing that. You know how kids exaggerate. Besides, that's not our responsibility. We're here to make sure they have fun and stay safe. They're doing both."

She braced herself for Thad's response, but he surprised her by not saying anything. In a way, his refusal to remind her that children were everyone's responsibility made her feel empty inside. As if he had finally figured out there was no point in trying to convince her that adopting any child would be better than having no child at all.

He'd never understood, no matter how many times she'd explained. He was softhearted and she... C.J. handed him the towel, then started back toward camp. She wasn't sure what she was. Of course she felt badly that Lucy and Tommy seemed unhappy in their foster home. She wasn't a complete bitch. But their unhappiness had nothing to do with her. It wasn't her fault, and she was in no position to fix the situation. She couldn't fix anything—certainly not herself.

Thad caught up with her and touched her arm. She stopped walking but refused to look at him. Instead she stared at the bright green leaves on the tree next to them, then at the patterns and colors of brown making up the bark.

"C.J.?"

She squeezed her eyes shut, then gave in because she'd loved him from the first moment she'd seen him back in college. She opened her eyes and stared at his face.

He smiled gently, then brushed her cheek with his fingers.

His gentleness, his compassion, made her throat ache.

"I wonder if we could figure out the actual odds of there being something wrong with both of us," she said bitterly. "Is there some statistical table we could consult to find out the mathematical impossibility of our situation? It's so unfair. Why couldn't it just be one of our faults? I want someone to blame, even if it was me."

He slipped his hand to the back of her

neck and drew her close. "There's no fault in any of this."

"There should be."

"Blaming won't help. It's just one of those things."

She pressed her face into his shoulder and inhaled the familiar scent of him. Soap, fabric softener and that indefinable essence that would allow her to pick him out in a crowd, even if she was blindfolded.

"You're so reasonable," she whispered.

"Is that bad?"

"Sometimes. Sometimes I just want to scream and pout and be unreasonable. Sometimes I think I won't stay sane any other way."

"You're fine," he assured her, then kissed her forehead.

Fine. She felt a lot of things, but none of them were fine.

A loud shriek of laughter followed by a splash made her step back. Irritation flared in her like an out-of-control bonfire.

"They're in the water. I told them to stay out of the water, but of course they didn't listen."

Thad smiled. "They're kids. It's their job

to do things like play in streams."

"The water's freezing. They'll get sick."

"They'll dry and be fine."

He headed toward the sounds, his steps eager, as if he wanted to be with those two children. C.J. walked the other way.

She knew it was wrong, she knew it made her heartless and cold, but she couldn't seem to be around those children without wanting to yell at them. There was an anger festering deep inside. It fed on her like a parasite. Sometimes the rage woke her up in the night, and sometimes she was afraid.

While the cause was clear, the exorcism was not. Maybe because sometimes she thought the anger was the only thing keeping her alive. Without it, she would be completely empty. But was a life of anger and resentment any way to live? What had happened to the bright, happy, caring woman who had married Thad? When had her heart turned hard and dark? And when had she stopped caring about their future?

Phoebe tilted her arm toward her to check the time, then remembered that her watch was gone, a casualty of her own citiness and the inquisitive nature of raccoons.

Zane said they were moving out in ten minutes. She figured she would hear everyone mounting up, and until then, she would keep moving.

Feeling had returned to her butt, and with it came the promise of stiffness in the night. Phoebe glanced around to make sure no one was watching, then rubbed her hands against her fanny. Unused muscles had a way of letting her know when they'd been pushed too far. She had a feeling that by the end of the week, she would have a greater appreciation for her sensible office chair back at work.

"Except I'm not returning to work," she reminded herself aloud. "Not for another couple of weeks after I get back."

She didn't want to think about that so she quickened her pace. As she circled around the next cluster of trees, she saw the herd of cattle clumped together.

Maya had said there were only fifty or so, but Phoebe would have sworn there were at least twice that number. So many heads and hooves, so many colors. She would have thought steers were all brown, but these were different shades, ranging from beige to black.

A few of them glanced up when she approached, but most ignored her. Maya had complained about the smell, but Phoebe didn't mind it. The scent was more appealing than being caught in traffic on the San Diego freeway and then rolling down her window.

She was admiring a very dark brown steer when one of the animals broke from the pack and headed toward her. The steer was big, with dark eyes, a half-bitten ear and a bell slung around its neck. She wasn't sure if it was going to charge or anything, so she took a step back. The animal kept on coming. Before she could decide if she should run or not, it reached her.

She froze in place, part terrified, part curious. The steer seemed to look her up and down, then it sniffed the front of her shirt.

"Hey, girl," Phoebe said tentatively. She slowly reached out her hand and lightly brushed the soft hairs above the steer's nose. The steer snorted once, then stretched its head down to pull at the bright green grass at Phoebe's feet.

"Huh. Are we friends now?"

The steer didn't answer.

She decided to take the silence as a yes. "So are you enjoying the cattle drive? Do you like the exercise?"

She patted the animal's neck, then bent down to examine the bell more closely. As she did, she happened to glance at the animal's tummy and realized "it" wasn't a girl. Nor was it all male.

She winced in sympathy. "That had to hurt. But I'm sure you were really young when that happened and don't remember much." At least she hoped he didn't. Something told her the removal of his testicles hadn't taken place in a vet's office.

"This is my first time on a cattle drive," she said. "My first time on a real horse. Rocky is really nice. Do you like horses?"

Phoebe knew it was silly to be talking to a steer, but she had to talk to someone. There was always Maya, but as most of Phoebe's thoughts were about Zane, and her friend was his ex-stepsister, the situation was complicated.

"I guess the real problem is that I'm

attracted to Zane," she told the steer. "Some of it is he's really good-looking and some of it is..." She paused to try to figure it out. "I'm not sure. A chemical reaction maybe? Destiny?"

The last word surprised her. Destiny? She didn't believe in that. People weren't fated to be together. She'd never wanted to believe that life happened according to a plan, because that meant some force had wanted her to grow up without a family of her own—without someone to love her. Could the universe really be that cruel?

"So I really can't explain it," she told the steer. "Still, he's very nice. Zane, I mean. And a good rancher. Maya told me that. I don't think he likes the goats much. They were cute, except they bite. Did you know that?"

She suddenly caught a glimpse of large bovine teeth and took a step back. Baby goat nibbles had startled her. If this big guy wanted to take a go at her, he could probably chomp off her hand. She carefully tucked her fingers into her back pockets and continued the conversation.

"At first I didn't think he was very friendly.

But he's sort of started talking to me, which I like. I think he feels alone, too, so we have that in common." And he'd kissed her which she wasn't going to mention to the steer. "But I think he figures I'm an idiot. Which I'm not. I'm from LA. It's not like I grew up knowing how to do all this ranch stuff."

"Does he answer back?"

Phoebe gasped, then spun around, only to find Zane on his horse, Tango. The two of them were right behind her.

She felt the instant flush of heat on her cheeks as embarrassment flooded her. She wanted to throw herself in front of the herd and be trampled. She wanted to ask how much of her muddled, one-sided conversation he'd heard.

But Zane's dark blue eyes were unreadable, nor did he offer the information.

She cleared her throat and tried to smile. "He, um, isn't much for conversation. Are we heading out?"

Zane nodded. "Rocky's waiting." He turned Tango back the way they'd come, then paused and glanced at her over his shoulder. "I wouldn't mention this to Rocky," he said, jerking his head at the steer. "You don't want your horse getting jealous."

Phoebe's mouth dropped open. Fortunately Zane was moving away and didn't notice. Wow. He'd been humorous. And charming.

"Did you see that?" she asked the steer. "Maybe he doesn't think I'm a complete idiot. Isn't that the best?"

CHAPTER ELEVEN

Canvas was not generally a fabric Phoebe thought of as confining, but when it was sewn into the shape of a tent and wrapped around her body, she started having second thoughts. Somehow she'd thought there would be more room. But her sleeping space was barely wide enough for her sleeping bag. Her saddlebags were pressed up against the wall, and her duffel fit down by her feet. A tent for one was not a place for a party.

There was also the issue of the ground. Perhaps if she'd thought it through, she might have considered that earth was, by nature, hard. Very hard. It was the kind of hardness that defied even an air mattress which, by the way, squeaked when she moved on it.

Then there was the whole outdoors thing. It was all much...bigger than she'd ever thought. Bigger and maybe a little scary, but in a good way. In an exciting, I'm-so-alive way.

She shifted on her sleeping bag, not yet ready to crawl into it and sleep. She was tired but also surprisingly alert. And tingly. There had been wine with dinner.

She was a pretty cheap date, with a single glass making her giggly and a second giving her a buzz. She'd downed her limit of two and still felt the delightful sense of blurriness that softened the crueler edges of the world into something beautiful and appealing. The two glasses of wine were also responsible for her need to go use nature's restroom.

Phoebe sat up and immediately bumped her head on the roof of her tent. After feeling around for her boots, she found them and pulled them on. She was still wearing her light jacket, so all she needed was a flashlight, and she was set.

The second she stepped out of her tent she became aware of the noise. There were hoots and clicks and rustles and swishes. Over to her left she could see the remnants of Cookie's fire, carefully contained within a ring of stones. To her right were the other tents. Low conversation drifted to her, although she couldn't make out the words.

She clicked on her flashlight, then headed away from the camp. After a few minutes of walking, she did what she'd come to do and headed back. She stepped around a tree and ran smack-dab into something big, hard and unyielding and she dropped her flashlight.

Even as panic ripped through her, an essential part of her being recognized Zane.

"Out looking for your watch?"

There wasn't enough light for her to see the details of his face. He was all shadows and outlines, a quick stroke of a man who made her body long to surrender.

"I've let it go," she said.

"That's probably wise."

She told herself she should head back to her tent, or maybe just bend down and pick up her flashlight. But she couldn't seem to move. Breathing was as much as she could manage.

She shivered, but not from the cold. Was it anticipation? What was it about the night, or was it just the man? Did he know?

"Zane?"

She had no idea what she was asking or what he might answer. Yet she liked the sound of his name. She liked saying the word and having it fill her mouth with its strength.

"It's late," he said. "You should probably be in bed."

She didn't know what to say. However she might want to believe that was an invitation, she had her doubts. Still, a girl could dream.

"I'll walk you back."

"Okay."

She waited for him to take a step, or to bend down and pick up her flashlight. Then he did bend, but not toward the ground. Instead he bent just enough to brush her mouth with his.

The soft, gentle contact took her breath away. Warmth flowed through her like a sigh. His hands settled on her waist at the exact second she raised herself on tiptoe and wrapped her arms around his neck. She tilted her head as he angled his. Her mouth parted just as his tongue swept along the seam.

The first taste of him made her want to moan as he explored her, delighting her with every caress. She arched against him, wanting to feel his hardness against her curves, his strength surrounding her. Their kiss was all hot surrender. Need burned through her body, making her breasts swell as her nipples tightened in anticipation.

He kissed her deeply, sucking on her tongue when she darted into his mouth. His big hands slipped from her waist to her rear where he rubbed and squeezed. The movements both aroused her nerve endings and soothed the sore muscles. She groaned.

He raised his head. "You like that?"

The unexpected question blanked out her brain. It took her a second to catch up.

"Well, um, yeah. It feels good because you're touching me and because I was on a horse all day."

Apparently he was done talking because he didn't respond to her comment. At least not with words. When she'd finished speaking, he lowered his head so that he could kiss the side of her neck. Phoebe had never considered that much of an erogenous zone, but then she'd never had Zane pressing his damp lips against her skin. Nor had he ever licked the suddenly sensitive skin or nipped right below her ear.

Goose bumps broke out all over her body. She wanted him to keep doing that kissing, nipping, licking thing pretty much everywhere. If he could make her feel that delicious with just a few kisses on her neck, imagine what he could accomplish on bare breasts and—

She froze. His hands had moved from her backside to the button of her jeans.

Okay. The kisses were good. Better than good. They were extraordinary, but this was a little fast. They were outside. She wasn't sure she knew him that well.

But before she could figure out exactly how to explain that they'd exceeded her comfort level, two things happened. The first was that he drew her earlobe into his mouth and sucked. It didn't sound like much. Had someone described the event to her she would have been mildly impressed, but not overly so. However, having it actually happen was very different.

The combination of his teeth gently grating on her skin and his tongue flicking back and forth was the most erotic experience of her life. A sad statement on her sexual experiences, but still true. At that point, ground or no ground, she was willing to go all the way.

The second thing that happened was that Zane slid his hands inside her panties. Yup, those big, warm, manly man hands were right up against bare skin. But instead of slipping between her thighs, he moved his hands over her behind and dug his fingers into sore muscles.

It was heaven. Pure and simple paradise. Even as he kissed his way along her neck, his palms circled, his fingers kneaded, and she sent up the white flag of surrender.

"Don't stop," she breathed, meaning both the kisses and the massage. It wasn't supposed to be this good. They weren't even doing anything that bad and yet she was melting from the inside out.

He shifted slightly and returned his mouth to hers. She reached for his head and dug her fingers into his hair. She kissed him with a franticness that defied reason. It shouldn't have been sexy, but it was. Intensely so. The sensations were beyond believing.

The sound of laughter cut through the night. Phoebe tensed slightly, suddenly aware of their surroundings. Zane must have heard it as well, because his hands stilled, and he broke their kiss.

Reason returned and she wanted to wince. Had she really begged him not to stop?

"I, um, want to tell you—" She broke off, not sure what she wanted to say to him.

She looked at his face, but the night was too dark for her to be able to see what he was thinking. Besides, how was she supposed to think when the man's hands were still down her pants?

"I have to know," he murmured.

Know? Know what?

Before she could ask, he moved his right hand across her hip to her belly, then slipped it down between her legs. His fingers slipped across slick, swollen flesh. They both sucked in a breath.

He pulled his hand free and carefully zipped and buttoned her jeans.

About fourteen thousand questions flashed through her brain, but she settled for the most important one.

"What did you have to know?"

"That you wanted it, too."

He took her hand in his and brought it

to his crotch. She had a good idea of what she would find there, but even so, the thickness, length and hardness of his erection made her want to whimper.

All righty, then. They both liked the kissing and touching. An interesting fact that should have absolutely no bearing on their lives. Really.

"Go to bed, Phoebe," he said.

She had a feeling he meant by herself.

Zane bent down and collected her flashlight, which he pressed into her hand. Then he turned her in what she guessed was the direction of the camp and gave her a little push. She felt dazed. As if she'd just been given laughing gas, and some kind of potent sex drug. She felt giddy and giggly and light enough to float. Zane Nicholson might not be big on conversation, but the man obviously knew his way around the bedroom...not to mention her body. She couldn't wait for morning, when she got to tell Rocky all about it.

Zane was up before sunrise, mostly because he hadn't slept more than a couple of hours. He told himself the reason was his concern over the greenhorns in his care, which was about 60 percent true. The other 40 percent had a whole lot more to do with a big-eyed brunette with full lips that could drive a man to insanity and back with a single kiss.

He finished storing his gear and stood in the quiet morning. He was tired, on edge and horny. His body ached, his mind raced and he couldn't stop thinking about how Phoebe had felt in his arms mere hours before. Intense longing gripped him. He did his best to remind himself that wanting her had nothing to do with liking her. He didn't know her, although he would admit what he did know, he liked.

He sighed. A man shouldn't have to deal with women or even sex before coffee.

He headed toward the cook fire. Cookie already had a pot bubbling. Zane poured himself a mug, then gulped down two mouthfuls of the steaming liquid. Heat and caffeine jolted his system.

The old man shuffled around from the side of the wagon. "We're having eggs this morning," Cookie announced. "Hell if I know if them tree huggers are gonna eat.

I made pancakes yesterday, but we're on the trail. I'm not Emeril Lagasse. I can only do what I can do."

Zane drank more coffee. "Don't sweat it. Andrea will eat when she gets hungry enough. Martin, too, although he seems like less trouble than his wife."

Cookie grinned. "Less like a pain in the ass, you mean."

"They're our guests," Zane reminded him warningly.

"That don't change what they are." He set down the big fry pan he'd been carrying and held up both hands. "I'll be good."

Zane didn't believe that for a second, but he hoped Cookie would at least keep his opinions to himself.

Fifteen minutes later, everyone was up and moving around the camp. Zane sent Chase to make sure no tent poles or stakes were left behind. Involuntarily, he found himself glancing over at Phoebe's tent, as if he were waiting for her to appear. When the flaps finally opened, he was rewarded for his patience in a big way. She chose to back out.

That perfect, curved fanny he'd been

fondling the previous night wiggled into sight, followed by the rest of her. The hand not holding the coffee mug curled slightly as he remembered the feel of her bare skin against his palm and the sound of her rapid breathing. She'd been hot, ready and wet. When he'd slid his fingers between her legs, it had been like going home. Under other circumstances, namely them being alone, he would have lowered her to the ground and eased both their aches. As it was, he'd been left to wonder if she'd had as much trouble sleeping.

He drained his mug and took a step toward her. But before he could get there, Chase appeared.

His younger brother grinned at Phoebe, then took her saddlebags from her and slung them over his shoulder.

"So you're one of those special women who looks even more beautiful in the outdoors," Chase said with a wink. "I should have guessed."

Phoebe laughed. "Maya already warned me that you shamelessly flatter women and that it doesn't mean anything."

"Sometimes that's true, but in this case,

I'm simply stating the obvious."

Zane turned back to the fire and poured himself another cup of coffee. Chase's ability to charm the opposite sex was an innate talent, like being good at math or having a great singing voice. Most of the time Zane found his brother's machinations amusing. But not this morning. Instead something dark swirled inside of him. He wasn't jealous—that would imply an interest in Phoebe that wasn't there. Besides, Chase's talk was cheap. But he couldn't seem to make the twisting go away, nor could he find a reason to move to the far side of camp.

"How'd you sleep?" Chase asked.

"Okay. Everyone talks about how quiet it is in the wilderness at night, but I thought there was a ton of noise."

Zane wanted to turn around and look at Phoebe's face as she spoke, but he forced himself to stay by the fire.

"Ready to take your tent down?" his brother asked.

Phoebe sighed. "I wanted to check my sleeping bag one more time. I'm missing an earring."

"Is it shiny?"

"Of course. You're going to tell me it's raccoons, aren't you? I've already heard about them. The thing is, if they took my earring, should I go ahead and leave them the other one so they have a matched set?"

One corner of Zane's mouth twitched as he pictured a raccoon with Phoebe's earrings dangling fashionably.

"It's your call," Chase said.

"I want to make sure I keep my cell phone tucked away. With my luck, it would be taken by a raccoon family with relatives in Madagascar."

Chase laughed. "Come on. I'll help you look for your earring."

Zane turned to tell his brother that he would take care of that and that Chase could move on to another tent, but just then Maya strolled up. She reached for his mug and took it from him. After draining it, she handed it back.

"So how's the head cowboy this morning?" she asked. "Are we dealing with friendly Zane or crabby Zane?"

He poured more coffee. "I'm always friendly."

"If only that were true."

There was something about her words and the way she didn't look at him as she spoke that got to him. He sighed. "I never disliked you."

"Wow. Talk about a compliment. Wait. Don't say anything for a second. I want to feel the love." She dramatically clasped her hands together over her heart, then shrugged and dropped them to her sides. "Sorry. I know you didn't hate me or anything. You were very generous in your tolerance. You tolerated me and you tolerated my mother. Not that I blame you for that. She was obviously in it for the money."

Zane didn't know what to say. Maya's mother had been a Las Vegas showgirl when Zane's father had met and married her.

"It wasn't all her fault," he told Maya. "My father never loved her. He shouldn't have married her."

"I don't know. Their marriage might have been hell, but I enjoyed my time on the ranch."

Zane remembered a gawky blonde blossoming into a beautiful young woman.

Maya had been the sort of serious, responsible child flaky parents often produce. She'd ignored the neighboring young men, had concentrated on her studies and spent all her spare afternoons with Chase.

The summer after she'd graduated from high school, things had changed. She'd fallen for a local guy, then had bailed on all of them when she'd headed off to college.

He passed her the mug. She took it and held it between her hands.

"Your father expected you to run things, but he wouldn't let you make any decisions," she said, looking at him over the steam. "I remember a lot of teeth grinding on your part."

Chase and Phoebe laughed about something. Maya turned to watch them. "He's growing up."

Zane was aware of that. "His stunts are getting worse."

"He'll always be a handful, but you've done a good job with him. He's going to be a good man."

Zane wasn't sure about that—not yet. But if it was in his power, he would make sure

Chase didn't have to live with the bitterness of too many regrets.

"'Morning, folks," Gladys said as she crossed the camp. She collected mugs for herself and her best friend, then poured coffee for both of them. There was a slight tremor in her hand, but overall, the two elderly women seemed sprightly despite the early hour and the long day yesterday.

"Fine morning," Eddie said with a smile. "There's nothing like sleeping in the outdoors."

Maya stretched. "I don't know. There's something to be said for a feather bed and heated towels."

The two kids raced into the clearing, with C.J. and Thad trailing after them. Andrea and Martin followed.

"Chow's on," Cookie yelled as he banged on the large triangle bell he'd brought with him. "Get it while it's as hot as these two hot young things." He winked at Eddie and Gladys.

People jostled for position. Zane stepped out of the way. He told himself he was being polite, but he was also watching to see exactly when Chase and Phoebe emerged from the close confines of her tent.

Ten seconds later, Chase popped out, shaking his head. Phoebe followed, looking defeated. Zane took that to mean that they'd been unable to find her earring. His gut churned at the thought of them looking together, heads bent close, arms touching.

He stalked over to the wagon and grabbed a plate, then took his place in line.

Andrea was up in front. Cookie held a ladle full of scrambled eggs over her plate. His dark expression warned there would be trouble if she refused. Martin—apparently smarter than his wife—nudged her elbow so that her plate shot toward the grumpy old cook.

"We love eggs," Martin said. "I have to say that so far the food has been really delicious."

Cookie grunted and scooped more eggs for his plate, then thrust out two platters. One was covered with bacon and sausage, the other had flaky biscuits. Andrea blanched at the sight of so much animal flesh in one place. She took a couple of biscuits and stumbled away. Martin hesitated.

"Bacon's real good," Cookie said with a

sly wink. "It's the real thing. Lean and tasty. Not like that store-bought crap you get in the city."

Martin reached for the serving tongs. He'd nearly picked them up when Andrea's voice cut through the morning. "Martin, what are you doing?"

Martin backed away as if faced by the devil himself. "Nothing. I'll be right there." He took three biscuits, then scurried toward the chairs.

The kids were next. They took some of everything Cookie offered. Thad took a plateful as well, but C.J. only wanted coffee. Eddie and Gladys pretended not to like Cookie's flirting as they collected their breakfasts and walked toward the chairs. Maya moved up behind Zane.

"I want to be like them when I grow up," she whispered.

Zane glanced at her. "A cougar?"

She rolled her eyes. "You know what I mean. They're not letting age stop them from doing anything. They're still having adventures. I wonder if they get lonely sometimes."

Zane saw the longing in Maya's eyes.

From his observation, she had always both yearned for and feared romantic love.

"If you're lonely, find some guy and settle down," he said.

"Oh, right." She stepped in front of him and held out her plate to Cookie. "Because charming, sensitive types always fall for lady shark news producers."

"You don't want some sensitive man," Cookie told her. "You want a real man."

Maya laughed. "Not you, Cookie. You're too much man for me. You'd plain wear me out."

"That I would."

Zane listened to their banter but didn't join in. Unlike Maya, he didn't want romantic love. Not because he mistrusted it, but because he knew what it did to a person. He'd grown up with parents who loved each other to the exclusion of all else, and he'd always felt like the third item on a list of two. Love wasn't the great gift everyone claimed. Love isolated, and sometimes it even destroyed. From what he could see, it cost too much and didn't offer enough in return. He'd spent his whole life avoiding love, and he had no plans to change.

CHAPTER TWELVE

Phoebe delighted in the beauty of the morning. A light breeze teased at her hair, the sounds of the birds provided a tinkling melody for the background beat that was the hooves of the cattle. Despite her relatively sleep-free night—erotic fondling and kissing by Zane did that to her—she felt happy, energized and alive. So when Rocky meandered toward C.J. and her horse, Phoebe didn't pull him back into line, even though C.J. wasn't the friendliest person on the cattle drive.

The two women rode next to each other for several minutes before Phoebe thought of something to say.

"Have you and your husband taken many foster children on vacation?" she asked.

C.J., a blonde woman in her early forties, shook her head. "We've never done anything like this before. We wouldn't have except the people who had agreed to bring Tommy and Lucy on the cattle drive had a death in the family and were unable to go.

Rather than let the kids be disappointed, we agreed to accompany them."

Phoebe nodded. The words sounded fine, but there was something about her tone that wasn't right. Was C.J. here out of obligation rather than preference? The thought made her feel sad.

"I grew up in foster care," Phoebe told the other woman. "My parents died when I was seven. There wasn't any family, so I became a ward of the state."

C.J. looked at her. "You were never adopted?"

Phoebe shrugged. "It wasn't like it is now. Prospective parents had no way to meet kids like me. For the first year, I was in shock over losing my folks. If anyone came around looking, I doubt I made a very good first impression."

C.J. nodded. "We've seen some children like that. Their eyes are so sad. Do you remember your family?"

"Not as much as I would like. I have a few memories, some pictures. After a while, the kids I met in the various homes became my family."

"Did you think about getting adopted?"

C.J. asked.

"Sometimes. We'd talk about it. I knew my parents were dead, but other kids I'd met had just been abandoned. They would make up stories about what it would be like when their parents realized they'd made a mistake and came to get them. Even if we said we didn't care, we all secretly wanted to belong to a family."

Phoebe smiled sadly at the memory. "I wanted a big house with a couple of dogs and a cat that slept on my bed at night." She'd imagined parents, too, but they'd been vague figures, and she'd always felt guilty—as if her emotional needs made her disloyal to her dead mother and father.

"The babies were never around long," she continued. "A few of the toddlers were adopted, too, but the older kids never had a chance. I've heard that these days there are parties to introduce prospective parents to available children."

"Thad and I have been to a few of those." C.J. pushed up her sunglasses. "They're so awkward and difficult. The children are on their best behavior and the adults...well, I'm not sure what they're thinking. I just know Thad and I felt strange. As if we were shopping for a child. We met Lucy and Tommy at a park party a few months ago."

"They seem like nice kids," Phoebe said.

C.J.'s mouth tightened into a straight line. "They have some problems."

No one could grow up in the foster-care system without having some scars, she thought, but didn't say anything to C.J. The other woman was smart enough to have figured that out for herself.

"We can't have children," C.J. explained in a rush. She stared straight ahead as she spoke. "There's something wrong with both of us. I couldn't believe it when I found out. If only one of us had been the problem, we could have used in vitro fertilization or a surrogate mother, or something."

"I'm sorry." Phoebe didn't know what else to say. The pain of not being able to have a child—she knew what it was like to feel separate and alone. Although C.J. did have Thad.

"Once we realized we wouldn't be having a child of our own, we went the adoption route. Two days before we were approved, I was diagnosed with breast cancer. That knocked us right off the list." Her voice turned bitter. "Private adoption won't work, either. No single mother wants her child raised by a woman who had cancer. So we decided to try foreign adoption."

"What country?"

"Kazakhstan. We were supposed to get a little girl. She was about seven months old. But she got sick, and they wouldn't let us go get her. While we waited, another couple went to get another child, who turned out to be our little girl's brother. The agency gave them permission to take them both. Then the agency director was arrested on charges of accepting bribes. It's been a mess."

C.J. shrugged as if to say it didn't matter, but Phoebe knew better. Nothing mattered more.

"Thad and I decided that we've had plenty of signs from the universe. We're just not meant to have a child. We're very happy together, and that's going to be enough."

Phoebe didn't believe that for a second. She wanted to point out that Lucy and Tommy were right here and available to adopt. Or, if not them, then there were hundreds of other children desperate to belong. But she didn't say anything. C.J. already knew. Maybe she was one of those women who felt she could only bond with a baby or a very young child.

"Considering all you've been through, it was really nice of you and your husband to agree to take care of Tommy and Lucy for the week."

C.J. shook her head. "I didn't want to." She laughed harshly. "Don't I sound like a bitch? But it's true. Thad talked me into it. Now that we're here," she said as she glanced at Phoebe, "I tell myself that we're doing something nice, and that's a good thing. But I can't help being angry about how unfair it all has been."

Phoebe wanted to say it was unfair for the kids, too. None of them had asked to be orphaned. None of them had asked to be alone. She still remembered every birthday she'd spent after her parents had died. That had always been the worst day.

Oh, sure, there was a party, a cake and a few presents, but it wasn't the same. There hadn't been anyone to hold her and talk about the future and love her. There hadn't been cards from grandparents and dinners with aunts and uncles. No older cousins had teased her, no younger cousins had gotten in the way. There hadn't been any family at all. After all this time, that was still true for her.

Late that morning Phoebe found herself riding next to Zane. She wasn't exactly sure how that had happened. Okay, maybe after they'd stopped for a bathroom break she might have maneuvered Rocky kind of close to Zane so that when they started out again, his was the horse Rocky followed. But she hadn't been sure the plan would work. And now that she was bouncing along beside him, she wasn't sure what she was supposed to say.

The day was still beautiful with clear skies and a slight nip in the air. She could smell the trees and caught occasional whiffs of cattle. Her butt hurt, but not enough to distract her from the pleasure of being so close to Zane. It was like being sixteen again and assigned to her crush's study group. The afternoon practically crackled with possibilities.

She wondered if he was thinking about their kiss. Had he relived it over and over again, as she had? Not that there was a way to ask. She might find Zane a little more approachable than she had when she'd first met him, but he wasn't exactly an open and friendly guy. Even if he was, she doubted she would be comfortable plopping down next to him and saying, "How about that kiss? Pretty amazing, huh?"

It had been amazing. Erotic, exciting, arousing and bone-melting. Kissing him didn't just make her want to make love with him—although she was certainly becoming more open to the possibility—it made her want to get to know him. She wanted to find out about the man behind the handsome face. Who was Zane Nicholson and what did he dream about? What made him happy and what made him sad? Had he ever been in love or had his heart broken? Had he—

Phoebe mentally backtracked. Maybe she didn't want to know about women Zane had loved. She had a bad feeling that when compared with them, she would come up short. Not that she wanted him to fall in love with her. She barely knew the man. But still, there was something about him. Something that made her wonder about the potential for more.

"You're quiet," Zane said.

As she wasn't even sure he'd known she was riding sort of next to him and a little behind, she jumped slightly. Rocky turned around to glare at her, as if reminding her that it was his back her fanny thumped on.

She patted his neck by way of apology and considered Zane's statement.

"I didn't want to interrupt if you were thinking about something important." Like them. Like what had happened last night. Like the fact that he'd had his hands on her bare ass and his fingers between her legs. A shivery tingle twisted low in her stomach at the memory.

"Are you enjoying yourself?" he asked.

For a second Phoebe was terrified that she'd spoken her thoughts out loud. Heat flared on her cheeks, and she ducked her head.

"You'd said you hadn't been on a horse before. Do you like it?"

Cool, sweet relief trickled through her. Was she enjoying herself on the cattle drive? Of course.

She sucked in a breath, then exhaled slowly. "Rocky's being very patient with me," she said. "Sometimes when I mess up he gives me this look that tells me I'm annoying him, but otherwise we're getting along."

She glanced at Zane and saw he was staring at her with a look of incomprehension.

"Don't you and Tango get along?" she asked.

"We're best friends."

She thought there might be a little sarcasm in his voice, but she ignored it. "Are the cattle doing okay? Is it healthy for them to walk this much every day?"

"Do you think they should be riding instead?"

"I don't know. You're the cattle expert."

"They're fine. As long as we keep the pace slow, they'll even put on weight. They're grazing on good quality land." He smiled. "For them it's a four-star restaurant."

Phoebe's heart hitched a little as Zane's mouth curved up. His eyes crinkled at the corners, and his face relaxed.

"Do they have names?" she asked.

To his credit, his smile only wavered a little. "Just Manny. He's the lead steer."

"The one with the bell?"

"That's him. The steers all have a place in the herd. They go to the same spot every day. If this were about a hundred and twenty years ago and we were taking the cattle from Texas to Kansas, they'd walk that whole distance in formation. If a steer got sick, he'd drop back until he was better, then return to his original position."

"Has Manny always been the leader?"

"Pretty much. I take him with me whenever I move cattle. He's calm and doesn't mind crossing water."

"We met. He seems very nice."

Zane tugged on his hat and muttered something like, "You'd make friends with a tree," but Phoebe wasn't sure she'd heard him correctly, so she didn't comment.

"Manny's pretty tame, but watch yourself with the other steers. Remember what happened with the goats."

She instantly thought of the kiss they'd shared outside the baby-goat pen, then realized he probably wasn't talking about that. Ah—she'd been bitten by a kid.

"The steers have much bigger teeth," she said. "Would Manny bite me?"

"No."

"Then I'll only talk to him."

"That's probably best."

She glanced at him. Zane looked as if he'd just swallowed lemons.

"Don't you want me talking to Manny?" she asked.

"I don't care one way or the other."

"You think I'm crazy."

His dark blue eyes crinkled as he grinned. "Crazy's a bit strong."

"I like animals. I don't have any pets of my own, so I like to spend time with other people's."

"Cattle aren't pets."

"I know. Manny would probably be tough to housebreak and I sure wouldn't want to be the one cleaning up his accidents."

She shifted on her saddle. They'd just broken free of the trees and were out in the open. The sky stretched out for miles, as did the grassland. Small trees provided pockets of shade.

"It's not like this in LA," she breathed.

"Is that where you're from or did you move there after high school?"

"Born and bred. A back-to-nature outing for me is a trip to the beach or hiking in Griffith Park." She glanced at him out of the corner of her eye. "You don't strike me as the city type."

"I don't mind visiting, but after a few days it gets too noisy and crowded."

"I like being around people, but I can understand the appeal of this kind of beauty." She inhaled deeply. "No smog and you have a satellite dish."

"There's also Cookie's biscuits."

Phoebe sighed. "They're pretty amazing. If he opened his own restaurant, I bet he'd make a fortune."

"Cookie's not a real people person."

She thought of his over-the-top flirtations with the female members of the group and his annoyance whenever anyone turned down one of his dishes.

"Okay. Maybe he doesn't have the service industry temperament, but I like his cooking."

She watched as the herd moved into the

open pasture. The steers stayed in their basic formation, but spread out more and began to eat. In the distance, she saw an animal that looked far too large to be a cow.

"Is that an elephant?" she asked.

He gazed in the same direction and nodded. "That's Priscilla. She lives at the Castle Ranch."

"They breed elephants?"

He chuckled. "No, they rescued Priscilla. See that little dot to her right? That's her donkey."

"The elephant has a pet donkey?"

"Fool's Gold is a strange place."

Strange and wonderful, she thought. What would it be like to live in a place where people would rescue an elephant, and where they treated strangers like new friends?

"Maya mentioned you make a cattle drive every year. Are we following that same route?"

Zane pulled his hat low over his forehead. "No. Usually I take a few hundred head north. That trip takes about three weeks. We didn't have that long, so we're going in a different direction."

"What happens after your steers arrive? Is it like summer vacation for them?"

"Not exactly. In early September I round 'em up and ship 'em out."

Phoebe winced. She didn't want to think about where the cattle might be going. She knew it wasn't Club Med. Her stomach flopped over, and she hoped they weren't having burgers for lunch again.

"Is that what your father did?" she asked. "Is it a family tradition?"

"He sent the cattle up north, but didn't take them himself. My grandfather did, when he was alive. And his father. There have been five generations of my family on the land."

She tried to imagine that and couldn't. "The house isn't that old, is it?"

"The one we have now was built in the sixties. The original place was torn down."

"I'm sorry to hear that. Too many old buildings are destroyed to make way for the new. In LA, something from the thirties is considered ancient." She looked at him. "It must be nice to have such deep roots."

"It's all I know."

What would it be like to belong to a place?

To be part of history and know that in another hundred years, the family would still be there?

"What about your family?" he asked.

"I don't have any. My parents died when I was seven, and they were both only children who had lost their parents while still in their teens. If there are distant relatives, I could never find them. So it's just me."

She tried not to sound wistful as she spoke. Her life was her life.

"You said you sell real estate?"

"I do, and I love it. There's something very satisfying about seeing someone find the perfect home."

"What's your house like?"

"I live in an apartment."

"Why?"

A simple question. Phoebe considered her answer. Money was a factor. The Los Angeles housing market wasn't exactly for the financially challenged. While she did all right at her work, she didn't move in the million-dollar circles that guaranteed a six-figure commission-based income.

There was also the sense of not being deserving. Maybe it was growing up in foster care where she'd been expected to earn her way by helping with the younger children. Maybe it was just her personality. Six months of therapy three years ago had left her more confused than ever.

"I rescue people," she said.

Zane raised his eyebrows. "That's why you live in an apartment?"

"Sort of. I find wonderful houses for other people, but not for myself. I don't know why. Am I scared? Am I waiting for something?" Like marriage, although she didn't want to say that to Zane. "I rescue people, sometimes dogs, but after I was bitten the last time, I steer clear of strays."

"What kind of people?"

"Anyone in need. There was a homeless lady who was hit by a car. No one stopped, so I took her to the hospital myself. Sometimes I find runaways or battered women trying to escape their abusive husbands."

"How do you find them?"

"I don't know. Maybe they find me. Maya says I carry around a sign that says I'm an easy target. I prefer to think I'm a good person doing the right thing. It's just that sometimes it doesn't go well."

"You mean they take money from you?"

"Yeah, or there was the time I took on an intern, a girl who had aged out of the foster-care system. She was eighteen and had nowhere to go. She couldn't afford college, so I was going to give her some experience and then help her find a way to pay for real estate school. One day I came home early and found her in bed with my boyfriend. Then there was the thing with my boss."

Zane hesitated, as if he didn't really want to know, then asked, "What thing?"

She told him about the problem with April. How she'd nearly ended up in jail and was now being investigated by the real estate board.

"I'm trying to stop rescuing the world, but it's a tough habit to break. That's why I'm here. I needed to get away."

Away from all the questions and the worry that she might lose her license. She loved her job. Without it… She didn't want to think about that.

"Who rescues you?" Zane asked.

Phoebe reined in her horse and stared at him. Zane stopped, as well.

"I don't need rescuing."

She couldn't. Being needed was safe, but needing? No. She didn't want to go there. Needing something or someone meant being vulnerable. It meant the risk of not getting. The pain of not asking was a lot easier to stand than the pain of being refused or rejected.

"Everybody needs to be taken care of some of the time," he said.

"Do you?"

"I'm the exception."

She wanted to say that she was, too, only she didn't feel all that strong. Sometimes she wanted to hand all the responsibilities and worries to someone else for a while. Not completely, or forever, but just to get a break. She'd often thought that was what a good marriage would mean. Sometimes she would take on all the burdens, and sometimes her husband would. Most of the time they would share them.

If Maya heard her say that, she would call Phoebe a Pollyanna and remind her life wasn't that simple. Phoebe had always thought it should be.

Zane urged his horse forward. Rocky

dutifully fell into step.

"If you're in Los Angeles and in real estate, you must work with rock singers and movie stars."

Phoebe laughed. "Not exactly. I mostly specialize in starter homes. The problem is I work in an office in Beverly Hills, so finding the right place at the right price can be a challenge."

"You're in Beverly Hills and you find cheap houses?"

She winced. "Now you sound like Maya. I like working with people who really need a home. I'm not the rock-star type, although I did work with Jonny Blaze once. You know, the action star?"

"I know who he is."

"Oh. Well, he's really nice and not all that scary, like he is in the movies."

"Who's in the movies?" Chase asked as he rode up.

"Jonny Blaze. Zane and I were talking about movie stars I've worked with, but he's the only one."

Chase's eyes widened. "You know Jonny Blaze? That's awesome. He kicked some serious ass in his last movie. What's he like? Did he have a bunch of groupies hanging all over him? He came to Fool's Gold last year for a golf tournament, but I was working that weekend." He shot a dark look toward Zane. "Is he really short? I read that a lot of action stars are short."

Phoebe laughed. "He's over six feet. I know because he patted my head and told me I reminded him of his kid sister."

"Jonny Blaze. You think you could get me his autograph?"

Before Phoebe could answer, Zane cut in.

"Is there a reason why you're not in back of the herd where you belong?"

His cold voice chilled the pleasure out of Chase's face. The teenager's eyes narrowed. "Cookie sent me to tell you he wants to stop and fix lunch."

Chase wheeled his horse around and rode off without waiting for a reply. Phoebe watched him go, then turned back to Zane. He met her gaze.

"You think I'm too hard on him."

"I think that you have trouble walking the line between being his brother and being his father. I don't think Chase makes it easy for you. But at least you have each other. When I was growing up, I used to wish there was someone to tell me they loved me. However much you yell at Chase, he knows in his heart that you care. That counts."

CHAPTER THIRTEEN

After lunch Zane rode west until he reached a ring of stones on the edge of a grove of trees. He checked his watch, then dismounted and sat on a fallen log to wait. Ten minutes later he heard an engine. The sound grew louder as the vehicle approached. Frank drove the ATV around the trees and came to a stop by the edge of the stones.

"Hey, boss," he said as he cut the engine. "How's it going?"

Zane rose. "You really want to know?"

Frank grinned. "Probably not. You haven't had to call in help for a medical emergency. That's something."

"That it is. How are things back at the ranch?"

"Smooth as shit, boss. Tim broke a finger, one of the goats chewed through part of the fence. We got a couple of buyers coming next week. The usual."

Zane walked to the trailer attached to the ATV and peeled back the cover. Three ice chests were stacked side by side. He flipped open the first one and found fresh meat, eggs and butter. A second one contained milk and canned soda, along with bottled water. The third held bags of ice. Fresh produce filled a couple of cardboard boxes and there was feed for the horses.

"Good job," Zane said. "I'll lead you to camp. I sent Chase and the greenhorns ahead with the steers. You and Cookie can load up the supplies while I join every-one else."

"Sure thing. Cookie said he wouldn't need another delivery for two days."

Zane squinted at the sky. In two days they would be completing their first loop and be fairly close to the ranch.

"That'll work," he said. "I'll phone you the night before and tell you where to meet me."

Except for the afternoon and evening spent by the river, they were always close enough to a cell tower to call the ranch. Zane had planned the circular route such that they would only spend two nights by the river. He figured even his citified guests could manage to stay safe in the wilderness that long.

He mounted his horse and headed back the way he'd come. Frank followed. When they reached the wagon, Cookie jumped down and headed for the trailer.

"You bring any strawberries?" the old man asked. "I got me a hankering for short-cake. I'll put a bit more sugar in my biscuits and split 'em open. I told you I wanted heavy cream. Did you bring any? Seems to me you weren't writing things down."

Frank snorted. "Cookie, I wrote everything twice just to make sure I didn't forget something. It's all here. Why don't you go through the supplies before you start flapping your lips at me? Give a man a chance to screw up, why don't you?"

Cookie grumbled under his breath.

Zane turned his horse north. "I'll leave you two to work this all out. Cookie, you know where we're camping tonight. I'm taking the long way. You should be able to load up and still beat us there."

"I'll have the campfires burning bright," he promised.

"Frank, I'll see you in a couple of days.

Let me know if there are any problems at the ranch."

"Sure thing, boss. We'll be fine. You just keep your cowpokes riding straight." Frank grinned as he spoke.

Zane grunted instead of replying and urged his horse forward. If his second in command thought this was all so damn funny, maybe Zane should put Frank in charge of the cattle drive for a few days. That would worry the humor right out of him. Not that he blamed Frank. If their positions were reversed, Zane would find the situation pretty amusing. Fifty cattle and ten greenhorns. What the hell had he been thinking?

As Frank had said, at least there hadn't been any disasters and no real trouble. Except for Phoebe. She was a nicely curved, sweet-smelling, sexy, trouble-filled bundle of big eyes, gorgeous legs and a butt that fit his hands as if the two had been made for each other.

He had it bad. Wanting her was one thing. But liking her was something else. She was an animal-loving ditz who would bond with a rock if given the chance. She wouldn't know poison ivy from honeysuckle. Her idea of the great outdoors was probably spending an evening on her balcony in the middle of Los Angeles. They had nothing in common. They were barely the same species.

But he liked her.

Not just her body or her scent or the way her eyes widened and darkened when he kissed her. He liked that she spoke her mind, even when it was crazy. That she cared about people. She was soft-hearted, which should have made him think she was an idiot. But he didn't. He thought she was sincere.

"Sincere," he muttered. "A patsy."

But he spoke without conviction. She'd nailed his problem with Chase in one try. That Zane didn't know how to walk the line between being a father and being a brother.

He wanted better for Chase than he'd had for himself. Wasn't that what parents always said? Zane did want that for his brother, but he didn't know how to make it happen. He didn't know how to save him from regrets. Zane tried. He would have done anything to keep Chase from having the same empty feeling Zane had when he thought about his own life.

As Chase's surrogate father, he wanted the kid to make the right choices. As Chase's brother, he wanted him to feel that he was good enough. That he was important. That he mattered.

Zane shook his head. Had he succeeded on even one of those points? The tightness in his gut told him the answer was no.

"You think Cookie would give me some ice to put in a bucket?" C.J. asked her husband when they'd finished rubbing down their horses. "I'd like to sit in ice water for a while."

Thad stretched out his arm to hug her and pull her close. "If you promised to eat meat, I think Cookie would do just about anything."

C.J. chuckled. "Andrea isn't making friends with him, that's for sure. While I appreciate her beliefs, shouldn't she have made sure she could get vegetarian meals before she and Martin signed up? After all, the purpose of the vacation is to herd cattle. Doesn't that imply beef to you?"

He kissed the top of her head. "Maybe she didn't read the fine print. Martin seems nice enough. I saw him sneaking a strip of bacon this morning when Andrea wasn't looking."

"You're kidding. Good for him." C.J. wrinkled her nose. "Why does he let her push him around?"

"Men have always done foolish things for the women they love."

"Oh, really? What foolish things have you done for me lately?"

He raised and lowered his eyebrows. "I'd be willing to do several tonight."

"In a tent?" She made herself sound more shocked than she really was.

"In a tent. Out of a tent. Your call." He leaned close and dropped his voice to a whisper. "How about if I start by massaging your aching fanny?"

"That works for me."

They made their way into the camp. Andrea's shrill voice cut through the quiet of the afternoon. C.J. winced.

"I wonder what she's complaining about now. It's not just that she's a vegetarian, it's that she's so rabid about it. She told me she'd brought 'feminine' supplies with her so that if I got my period, I was to let her know. Apparently she has special tampons she buys that are organic or unbleached or made out of recycled paper or something."

Thad sighed. "Poor Andrea. She must be very unhappy. She could take a lesson from Eddie and Gladys. Those are two women who know how to live."

C.J. wasn't thrilled about the shift in topic. While she agreed that the old ladies seemed to be extraordinarily happy, she couldn't help thinking they had probably been blessed with trouble-free lives.

"Hey, Thad! Look what we found."

C.J. stiffened as she heard Tommy's voice. Lucy and her brother broke through the trees on the edge of the clearing. The boy held something in his hand as he raced toward them. Lucy was a few steps behind. C.J. opened her mouth to warn him to slow down or he would fall, then pressed her lips together. Every time she made a comment like that both children looked at her as if she were the biggest bitch on the planet. Worse, C.J. was pretty sure they were right.

A small log lay between Tommy and them. The boy jumped over it easily, then came down on both feet. But something happened because, instead of staying solidly planted, his right foot slid out from under him. He threw his arms open wide to try and find his balance. Whatever he'd been holding went flying as he tumbled to his knees and skidded on the dirt.

C.J. winced as he rolled over, and she saw the blood and dirt on his knee. She and Thad started toward him. Thad sprinted ahead and got there first. He sank next to Tommy and pulled him close.

"That had to hurt," he said calmly. "Let's take a look and see what you've done."

Tommy winced as he thrust out his leg. C.J. crouched down and examined the ugly scrape.

"We'll need the first-aid kit," she said. "Cookie said he has one."

Lucy bent over her brother's injury. "You okay?"

He nodded, but didn't speak. C.J. figured he was trying not to cry. She thought about telling him it was okay to cry, that no one would think less of him, but she didn't know how to express herself without coming off as superior. Better to do something practical.

She rose and headed toward the cook fire. She found the old man pouring barbecue sauce over chicken breasts and quickly explained what had happened. Cookie dug out a large first-aid kit and handed it to her.

"Tell the kid it's gonna be okay," the old man said. "We're having strawberry shortcake for dessert."

She wasn't sure that the promise of shortcake was enough to ease Tommy's pain, but it was worth a try. Maybe thinking about it would distract him from the worst of it. They would have to clean the wound. Did the first-aid kit have something that wouldn't sting? She would—

C.J. came to a sudden stop. She and Thad had left their saddlebags in a heap when they'd gone off to take care of their horses. Now Lucy was crouched in front of them. She had the flaps open and was quickly going through the contents.

"I knew it," C.J. breathed. "They stole from us at the party and that girl is doing it again."

She marched toward Lucy. "Just what do you think you're doing?" she demanded as anger surged through her. "Get away from our things."

Lucy spun around, then jumped to her feet and tucked her hands behind her back. "I wasn't doing nothing."

"Sure you weren't."

Lucy's dark eyes flashed with defiance. "I was looking for bandages. For Tommy's knee. It's bleeding real bad."

"Don't lie to me. You heard me say I was getting the first-aid kit from Cookie. There would be bandages inside that."

Her anger grew until she was shaking. Why had she allowed Thad to convince her to come on this trip? So these ingrate children could have a vacation? They were thieves. They'd probably been born that way, and they would no doubt grow up to commit bigger and better crimes.

Lucy's mouth quivered. "You were gone a long time."

"So you decided to take matters into your

own hands and go through our saddle-bags. Is that it? I'm sorry to tell you, Lucy, that we didn't bring any money with us. I had a feeling if we did, you'd just try to steal it."

"I would not. I—" She caught her breath. "You're a mean, old butthead."

With that, Lucy turned and ran away. C.J. swore quietly. She wanted to go home right now. She wanted to have never come on this ridiculous trip. Instead she was stuck with thieving children and rabid vege-tarians. And one of those children was bleeding.

C.J. hurried to the edge of camp. Tommy was still sitting on the ground with Thad's arms around him. She tried not to notice how comfortable her husband looked holding the boy. Chase jogged up and collected the first-aid kit from her.

"Why don't you hold his hand?" he said. "I'll take care of cleaning the wound."

C.J. took a step back. How could she explain that she wasn't the sort of woman who was good at holding children's hands? While she wanted to help, they never seemed comforted. She had hoped that by having her own child, or even adopting a baby, she would be able to figure it all out in time. Once her child loved her, he or she would understand that C.J. cared with all her heart, even if she didn't always know what to say.

"What happened?" Gladys asked as she walked toward them. "Oh, the poor dear. Tommy, did you fall? You're being very brave."

Eddie joined her friend. "What are you going to use on that scrape, Chase? Got any hydrogen peroxide? It won't sting so bad. Plus, Tommy will like the way it bubbles. All that white fizzing and foaming is like a battle going on right there on your knee. The good guys are fighting with the germs. Of course the good guys always win."

"H-how do you know?" Tommy asked.

Eddie crouched next to him. "I've seen plenty of battles on knees in my day. Josh, my boss, takes spills off his bicycle all the time. Never seen one where the good guys didn't kick butt."

C.J. took another step back, then another. No one noticed. She turned and headed for the small stream she'd seen on their way in.

When she got there, she found a flat rock to sit on and folded her arms over her chest. She felt all ragged inside, and her eyes burned as if she wanted to cry.

Stress, she told herself. This wasn't anyone's idea of a relaxing time. Plus she hadn't been sleeping very well. When she got home she would take a couple of days to unwind and get her equilibrium back.

She heard footsteps behind her but didn't turn around. She felt someone sit beside her on the rock. Even without looking, she knew it was Thad.

"Tommy's doing fine," he said. "Chase cleaned out the wound and put on a bandage. The boy's with Gladys and Eddie. They went to see if there were any brownies left from lunch."

He spoke matter-of-factly, as if sharing information. But she wasn't fooled. She heard the criticism hidden in his words. She should have stayed and helped take care of Tommy. She should have been the one to tell him that he would be fine and then get him a snack.

She sighed. That wasn't fair. Thad never judged her. Sometimes she wished that he would.

"I caught Lucy going through our saddlebags," she said. "I told her we hadn't brought any money with us, so there was no point in stealing."

Thad rested his hand on the small of her back. "What did she say?"

"That she wasn't stealing. She claims to have been looking for a bandage for Tommy, but she was right there when I said I was going to get the first-aid kit from Cookie." She squeezed her arms tightly against her chest. "I know you think I was wrong before when I said they stole from us, but I know what I saw."

"You think she was doing it again?"

C.J. shrugged.

"Is it possible she was telling the truth? Looking for a bandage?"

She wanted to say no. She wanted to scream that these were not the children she'd wanted. It wasn't fair. None of it. She and Thad were good people. They were honest and they worked hard. Was it so wrong for them to want a baby?

Pain sliced through her until it was impossible to breathe. Her throat ached. The ever-present anger rose up inside of her until it was all she could think about. There was such coldness in her rage. Such brittleness that sometimes she wondered if she would eventually shatter.

There was a time when she'd been soft and yielding, but not anymore. Not for a long time. Unexpected sadness overwhelmed her. She closed her eyes against it and dropped her chin to her chest.

"I used to laugh," she whispered. "I used to be fun and funny. What happened to me? When did I start changing?"

Thad was silent for a long time. Finally she turned to look at him. His blue eyes never wavered as he studied her.

"Do you really want an answer?"

Did she? Did she want to know what her husband thought of her?

Slowly she nodded.

He shifted so that he was facing her, then cupped her face in his hands. "It wasn't when we found out we couldn't have children. Maybe it started after the cancer. Maybe after what happened in Kazakhstan."

Tears spilled out of her eyes. She couldn't deny his words—he spoke the truth. There had been too many disappointments, too many almosts. Too much pain. Rather than let it overwhelm her, she'd closed her heart.

He pulled her close and wrapped his arms around her. "You'll be fine," he promised.

C.J. wasn't so sure. Something inside of her had died a long time ago. In that space where she'd once held laughter and light, there was only anger. How could a person survive like that?

"I still love you," he said.

She looked at him. She wanted to ask how that was possible. How could he care when she'd become so dark and ugly on the inside?

"I love you, too," she told him, because it was true. He had always been her anchor. Her solid rock. Her life.

But what was she to him? A burden? He was a gentle, kind man burdened with an angry, cold wife. He might love her, but she would bet he didn't like her very much. Not anymore.

Could she blame him? C.J. wasn't sure

she even liked herself these days.

She almost said so to Thad, then stopped. If she confessed her secret, she knew what he would say. He would tell her to change. Easy words, but meaningless. Change? How? Where would she find the key she needed to unlock her heart and let the world back in?

Phoebe stood under a large tree of an undefined nature. She really should have brought a couple of flora and fauna books with her on the trip. She could have used them to identify the plants and trees she saw on the ride. Well, she wasn't completely sure she would be able to read while riding Rocky. Did motion sickness apply to horseback?

She turned around and watched as Zane assembled the tent Lucy and Tommy shared. Zane worked quickly, his muscles bunching and releasing with each movement. There was an air of confidence about him, probably because he knew what he was doing. He was a man comfortable in his world. She, on the other hand, had always felt slightly out of step with her surroundings.

Sunlight filtered through the leaves. They'd stopped a little early today. Her butt appreciated the abbreviated ride nearly as much as it had appreciated the massage the night before. Would Zane be offering again?

Liquid desire trickled through her. As Maya had teased her earlier, she had it bad.

Her gaze drifted over the tents already set out, but not yet put up. Something wasn't right. There was no symmetry to the camp, no sense of flow.

She crossed the grass to stand next to Zane and cleared her throat.

"I've been reading up on feng shui," she said.

Zane straightened, pulled off his hat and slapped it against his thigh. He didn't look wildly excited to see her, but at least he didn't turn his back.

"It's an ancient Chinese way of organizing one's world to make sure the positive energy forces flow correctly." Phoebe hesitated. "I think it's Chinese. For sure it's Asian."

"Good to know."

"Our camp is in the shape of an octagon,

so we just have to find the front door and then we can position the tents so they're in the right area. Tommy and Lucy should sleep in the 'children area' so they stay safe and healthy. I guess I'd want to be in the career area because things aren't exactly great there right now."

Zane's dark gaze never wavered from her face. When she was quiet, he blinked a couple of times. "I thought you said you wanted to stop helping people all the time. You said it got you into trouble."

"I forgot." She sighed. "I just thought..."

"You were trying to help."

She nodded. "It does seem to be a compulsion." She thought about the feng shui and what he must think of it—and her. "I'm not an idiot."

"I never thought you were. Your idea for the campsite is interesting, but it's going to be windy tonight. I'm positioning the tents so that the wind doesn't blow inside or blow them down."

"Oh." She fingered the hem of her T-shirt. "Okay. I guess that works, too."

"Would you hand me that?" he asked, pointing to tent stakes bundled together.

She collected the thin metal hooks and handed them to him. As he secured Lucy and Tommy's tent, she felt the first whisper of breeze drift across her cheek.

"It must be nice to have a place like this for your backyard," she said. "Did you ever go out riding and get lost when you were a kid?"

"Some."

"What happened?"

"Eventually I found my way back."

"I've never had much sense of direction," she said, "which can make showing houses a challenge."

He straightened and stuck the remaining tent stakes into his back pocket, then crossed to stand behind her. When he put his hand on her upper arm, a ribbon of heat wove its way through her body.

"There," he said, turning her and pointing. "See that mountain?"

She raised her gaze to the snow-covered peak. "Uh-huh."

"The ranch is in a valley just at the foot of that mountain. When I was a kid and I'd get turned around, I'd ride for high ground. When I could see the mountain, I knew my way home."

As he spoke she could almost see a younger version of Zane riding a horse through the wilderness, headed for a mountain that would forever mean home.

"I'm not sure that would work with freeway signs," she said.

He squeezed her arm and released her. "Then you'll have to invest in GPS."

"Believe me, I have it. Every real estate agent's best friend." But GPS wasn't nearly as exciting and romantic as a mountain that would always lead one home.

"So one day you'll be telling your children about the mountain," she said. "And they'll want you to tell them about the times you got lost and had to fight off a big black bear with nothing more than a canteen and a broken branch."

"I like to think I'd be smarter than that. A canteen's not much of a weapon."

"What if the bear is thirsty? You could distract it with the promise of water."

Zane turned back to the tents, but not before she saw him smile.

"Good to know," he said. "But I'm not planning on having kids."

"But you have to. If you don't, the family line won't go on. You're the fifth generation. Doesn't there have to be a sixth?"

"Chase can take care of that."

She started to say that his brother didn't seem to be a big fan of ranching, but decided she didn't want to go there with Zane.

"Don't you like kids?" she asked.

"Sure, but liking them isn't the problem."

She eyed his perfectly muscled body and doubted there were any problems there. "So what is? I would think a wife and a few kids would be the next logical step."

He glanced at her. "It's not that easy. Most women find the ranch too isolated."

She wondered if his ex-wife had felt that way. Phoebe thought about the beauty of Zane's place, the history and the feeling of belonging. She thought of family traditions, of never having to fight freeway traffic, of silence and snow and Zane to wake up to each morning. Then she carefully popped her fantasy bubble because she knew better than to dream about things she could never have.

"Where there's love, there's enough of

everything," she said. At least that's what she'd always believed. She'd never actually dared to test the theory for herself.

Zane was looking at her in such a way that her heart suddenly began throwing itself against her ribs. She felt tingly and hot, as if she was getting a fever. Her mouth got dry, but other parts of her did exactly the opposite.

Would Zane mind if she pulled off her shirt?

Before she could ask, Cookie rang the bell for supper. Phoebe turned and ran toward the wagon, leaving temptation and all her impossible fantasies behind.

CHAPTER FOURTEEN

Maya leaned forward and laughed. "He actually accused me of sleeping with the professor to get an A, if you can believe it."

"Was the professor sexy?" Eddie asked.

"What did you do?" Gladys said at the same time.

"I went to my professor and explained what was going on. He was furious. I don't know that he cared about me as much as he resented what the jerk's comments said about him. I'd done all the work, I'd gotten the good grades on the test, and at the end of the term, I'm the one who had the internship."

Gladys patted Maya's arm. "Back in my day a woman had to have real determination to have any kind of professional career. To be honest, I never wanted more than to be Ephraim's wife and stay home to raise our children."

"I've seen mothers with their kids," Maya told her. "I think a career was the easy way out."

All three women laughed. Zane reached for another cup of coffee to hide his smile. He would never in a million years have pictured his high-powered take-no-prisoners ex-stepsister gabbing with two grandmother types—somewhat warped grandmothers, that was—over roasted marshmallows and an open fire. She'd sure mellowed over the past few years, although he knew if he said that to her, she would tell him that he was the one who had changed. Maybe they both had.

He shifted slightly, so that he stretched out on the ground, with his feet pointing toward the fire. Phoebe was across from him and just a little to his right. He could watch her without turning his head.

Firelight brought out hints of red and gold in her dark brown hair. Shadows danced across her cheek. She pulled her long branch from the fire and tested the softness of the marshmallow she'd been roasting. When the hot center gushed out over her fingers, she jerked her hand back and licked the sticky mess from her skin.

The quick movements of her tongue reminded him of kissing her and holding her. The memories had a not-surprising result on his libido and his dick. Half frustrated and half resigned, he shifted so she wasn't in his line of sight. Maybe if he couldn't see what he couldn't have, he wouldn't want her so bad.

Maybe the steers would fly the rest of the way.

He grinned at the thought. Maya glanced at him and raised her eyebrows.

"What's so funny?"

"I'm a man who enjoys life."

She snorted. "Yeah, right. Tell me another one."

"Maybe I'm impressed by all your accomplishments."

Maya made a show of glancing behind her, as if to see who he was talking to. Then she shook her head. "We have children trying to fall asleep in that tent over there, or I would tell you exactly what I thought of that."

"You don't think you impress me?"

"Only with my ignorance."

Gladys handed her another marshmallow. "Of course your brother thinks the world of you, dear. Why wouldn't he?"

"I could list the reasons," Maya muttered.

"You graduated at the top of your class," Zane said. "That's a great accomplishment."

Maya didn't look convinced, but she didn't call him a liar to his face. Chase walked over and sat down between Maya and Zane.

"The cattle are snug in their beds," he said as he grabbed Maya's branch and a handful of marshmallows. "What did I miss?"

Phoebe grinned. "Zane was just telling us that he thinks Maya is brilliant because she graduated at the top of her class in TV school. Maya, of course, doesn't believe the compliment."

"We don't call it TV school, either, but, yeah, that about sums it up," Maya agreed.

"You'd do well to follow Maya's example," Zane said. "She knew what she wanted, and she applied herself."

Chase jabbed his stick toward the fire. "I am applying myself."

"Not in school." Zane sat up straighter. "Chase, you can be anything you want. You have brains and opportunity. But instead of working hard, you take the easy way out and get lousy grades in the subjects you think don't matter. You're going into your senior year of high school. You can't keep screwing around."

Chase pulled back the branch and tugged off the browned marshmallow. "You think I screw around because you don't like the same things I like."

Zane felt the familiar whispers of irritation. He and his brother had gone around and around on this subject. For once, Zane would like Chase to understand what he was saying.

"You've done a great job with your electronics," he said carefully. "You get A's in math and science. But what about English and history? They're important, too."

"Not to me." Chase shoved three marshmallows onto the stick. "I want to go to MIT, and you want me to go to some farm college and study animal breeding. Either way, nobody's gonna care what I got in English."

"Oh, they're **gonna** care," Maya said. "Whether you're working on the ranch or in computers, you need to be a well-rounded person."

Chase snorted.

"Maya's right," Phoebe said quietly. "Better to have too many opportunities than not enough."

Her tone was wistful. Zane wondered what opportunities she'd missed in her life, but before he could ask, Eddie murmured something to Gladys and stood up.

"Today wasn't bad," she said, pointing right at Zane, "but tomorrow, I expect you to show a little skin. We were promised sexy cowboys on this trip. Wouldn't kill you to ride without a shirt for a couple hours."

With a laugh, Phoebe rose, as well. "On that note, I'm turning in, too."

Zane watched her go, then turned his attention back to his brother.

"Maya and Phoebe have a point."

"Figures the only time you'd agree with them is when they're taking your side." He scrambled to his feet and tossed down his stick. "You think I care about any of it? I don't. You know why? Because none of it matters. If you'd just once listen to me instead of always telling me what I'm doing wrong, you might get it. You might see that my robots aren't a hobby. I'm not playing with my computer when I'm up in my room. I'm making something. I'm creating things that didn't exist before. But you don't give a damn about any of it because you're too busy always telling me how I screw up."

Zane took a deep breath and told himself he had to stay calm. Yelling at Chase had never worked.

"I have listened about your robots."

"You've stayed in the room while I was talking, but you don't really care. You think they're a waste of money."

Zane didn't want to get into that now. The costly experiments were the reason Chase had taken money, which had led to the cattle drive. Better not to discuss that in front of everyone.

"Chase, you're not being fair," Maya said quietly. "You shouldn't expect Zane to care about robots the same way you do."

"Why not? He expects me to care about the ranch." He glared at Zane. "I don't. I never will. I hate it. You want me to be like you. I'm not. I'm someone different. You're going to try to force me to do what you want, and that's not going to happen."

Chase turned and stalked off. Maya

scrambled to her feet and hurried after him. Zane didn't know what to do. Stay or go? Finally he sagged back against the log and shook his head. When he and Chase were having it out, the only thing that helped heal things between them was time.

He turned to Gladys, who was the only one left by the fire. C.J. and Thad had turned in after the kids went to bed, and Andrea and Martin had disappeared soon after dinner.

"Sorry about that," Zane said. "Family fights weren't supposed to be part of your vacation package."

Gladys shrugged. "When people live together, they clash from time to time. Chase is still a teenager. That can be a difficult time. Ephraim and I had three daughters, so I'm used to the yelling."

"Three." Zane didn't want to think about that. He had enough trouble with one. Maybe girls were simpler.

"Kids are funny creatures," the older woman said as she pushed a marshmallow onto a stick and held it close to the dying fire. "Or maybe it's just folks in general. Some are easy to love and some are hard."

She glanced at Zane and smiled. "Loving Ephraim was the easiest part of my life. That's why they call it 'falling in love,' 'cause when it's right, it's as effortless as falling..." Her voice trailed off and she sighed.

"We were together since we weren't much older than Chase. We grew up together, really, learning what worked and what made us want to kill each other. He yielded where I wanted to be stubborn, and he stood his ground when I wanted to bend. I trusted that man heart and soul. But kids. That's a whole different kind of love."

Zane shifted uncomfortably, suddenly aware that he was sitting on hard ground. Whatever Gladys had to say, he didn't want to hear it. Not because he was afraid, but because he was uneasy. In his world, no one talked about anything more intimate than problems on the ranch and Chase's latest screwup.

Gladys pulled off the toasted marsh-mallow and took a bite.

"We raised our three exactly the same," she said when she'd chewed and swallowed. "Same house, same parents, same ideas, same schools. Yet they all turned out

different. Two were just fine. But Natalie."
Gladys shook her head. "When she was
little, Ephraim used to say she had a bit of
the devil in her. I suppose that's true. Not a
day went by that Natalie didn't try to raise
some hell."

Zane didn't know what to say. He wished
someone would join them and change
the subject. Barring that, he tried to think
of something relevant to add to the
conversation.

Finally he cleared his throat. "That must
have been hard on you and Ephraim."

Gladys nodded. "She was our middle
child. Folks said they were the easiest, the
peacemakers. But not Natalie. She was
stealing candy before she was eight and
doing drugs by the time she was twelve.
We tried everything. Rehab, tough love,
jail time, threats, bribes. She'd get clean
for a while, and then she'd fall back into it.
We tried not loving her and loving her
too much. She failed at two marriages,
drove while high and killed her only child.
I think that's what pushed her over the
edge. Knowing she'd killed her boy. Two
weeks later, Natalie died of an overdose.

That was in '98."

Zane opened his mouth, then closed it. He'd expected Gladys to give him some tired advice, not share such a personal tragedy.

"I'm sorry," he said, feeling as lame as he sounded.

"It was a time of sorrow," Gladys said. "The pain of it nearly ended things for me and Ephraim. There was so much guilt, so much need. We about sucked the life out of each other."

"Your marriage was in trouble?" Zane said before he could stop himself. "But the way you talk about him..."

"We managed to find our way back to each other. It took time and hard work. I lost him in '04, but I take comfort knowing that when he passed, he knew how much I loved him without a doubt." She threw her stick into the fire. "Just like Natalie needed us to love her, no matter what. And we did. Even when we had to turn our backs on her. Even when she died."

Gladys looked at Zane. "You love Chase. We can all see that. But he tests your patience. I know these seem like dark times, but he's a good kid. He'll get through it. Sometimes they take the easy road and sometimes they take the hard one, but either way, our job is to love them and to keep on trying."

Zane didn't know what he felt about his brother. He knew he wanted to protect Chase as much as he could, keep him from making the same mistakes that had screwed up Zane's life. Was that love? He couldn't relate to what Gladys said about her relationship with her kids.

"My old man wasn't like you and Ephraim," he said at last. "He was hard and distant most of the time. He chewed my ass on a regular basis. The only person who seemed to matter, who touched him, was my mom. He was devoted to her."

Gladys drew her penciled-in eyebrows together. "I know the kind you're talking about. They seem to only have room in their heart for one person. Parents do that some with their kids—love one and ignore the rest. I never could understand it."

Zane swallowed. He didn't talk about personal stuff, not with anyone and certainly not with one of the most notorious gossips in Fool's Gold. Yet now that he'd started speaking, he couldn't make himself stop.

"I could handle most of it," he said. "What really got to me was that he would never let me apologize when I screwed up. That was the worst. The anger, the few times he beat the crap out of me, those didn't matter as much. It was not being able to make it right."

Those times still haunted him.

Gladys nodded slowly. "Forgiveness is a gift given by those with a full heart. To see a mistake and still love the person, I guess that's the best each of us can be. I know I got it right with my other two kids. With Natalie..." She paused and stared into the fire. "I tried. Sometimes I made it work and sometimes I didn't."

The old woman patted Zane's shoulder. "Seems to me you're the kind of man who'll get it right more often than not."

With that she rose and dusted off her fringed leather chaps. "It's late. Sleep well, Zane."

When Gladys was gone, Zane stretched out his legs and stared up at the sky. There were more stars up there than any man could count. More possibilities. On those nights when he'd been a kid and couldn't sleep, he would go outside and study the constellations. Sometimes he would imagine that he could leave earth and go live up there. Things would be different then. Better.

He hadn't thought of his father in years, yet suddenly the old man seemed to be back in his life. He'd never softened, not even at the end when he lay dying.

"I want to go," he'd whispered with his last breath. "I want to be with her."

Not "I'll miss you, son." Not even goodbye. Just a wish to be gone.

Zane told himself it didn't matter. He was grown, and the past couldn't touch him. For the most part he believed that, but what he didn't know for sure was how the past influenced the present. He was so concerned about keeping Chase from making mistakes, yet had he once thought about the fact that he might be treating his brother the same way his father treated him?

Phoebe watched as the sun slowly rose over the trees in the distance. It was cool, clear and intensely quiet. Maybe it was like that in LA before dawn, but as she'd always done her best to never be awake that early, she couldn't be sure. Still there was something to be said for greeting the sun.

"You probably do this all the time," she said aloud. "Wake up before the sun. I'll bet you've seen a bunch of beautiful sunrises."

Manny, intent on his breakfast, didn't give her much more than an ear flicker in response.

Undeterred, Phoebe leaned forward to scratch behind one of those ears. "I didn't think I would like the outdoors at all," she told him. "Too much back to nature. But it's growing on me. I don't think I'll ever prefer a tent and an air mattress to a real house and bed, but I understand the appeal of a couple of nights in the wilderness."

She refused to admit how much of that appeal related to her encounters with Zane. Last night she'd almost been disappointed that she hadn't had to make a midnight potty run. She supposed she could have faked it, in the hopes of seeing him, but somehow that had seemed tacky. Instead she'd lain awake in her tent and listened to the sounds of night, all the while wondering if Zane was thinking about her as much as she was thinking about him.

"It's not just that he's good-looking," she said. "Okay, some of it is that. I mean, have you seen his body?"

Manny raised his head. His big, brown eyes seemed to roll slightly in his head. She grinned.

"I know. He's a guy, you're a guy. You don't have to admit that he's hot, but he is. You're going to have to trust me on that. But it's more than that. He's also really nice. I like how dependable he is and how he's the kind of man who will always be there for his family. He's smart, too. He has a lot of responsibility, but that doesn't seem to bother him."

Thinking about responsibility made her remember hers. All her clients who were having to get by without her. April had promised to handle her houses in escrow. While Phoebe trusted her boss to do the work, she knew April's heart wouldn't be into it. A lot of agents had trouble getting excited about relatively low-priced starter homes when there were multimillion-dollar estates in the neighborhood.

"She doesn't get it," Phoebe told the steer. "April thinks I should concentrate on what will make me the most money. I know that's important, but so is helping people find their first home. They're usually terrified and excited. Then they find out the house is theirs." She sighed. "There's no feeling like that. Not for them or for me. Because I know I was a part of making it happen."

She pulled her legs to her chest and rested her chin on her knees. "I don't know what I'll do if I lose my license. I love what I do. I'm not a great salesperson, but I genuinely care, and I believe that makes a difference. My clients need me."

And being needed was the best part of her day.

"I don't want to think about it," she whispered to the steer. "But I have to. I'll have to find a whole new career."

Doing what? She really didn't have any other training. It wasn't the sales she loved, it was the people. So her experience in real estate wasn't exactly going to translate into selling cars or clothes.

At least her expenses weren't all that

high. She had some savings to tide her over until she found some other line of work. It wasn't as if she had to worry about a house payment.

"Zane was surprised when I told him I didn't own a house," she said. "Being in real estate and all, I guess it makes sense I would have one. I mean, I would be the first to spot a good deal, right? Only I never bothered."

She glanced around to make sure she and Manny were still alone. "Sometimes I don't think I deserve a house. Isn't that crazy? Like I'm not worthy."

She'd sort of hoped saying the words out loud would make her feel foolish, and she would instantly see that she'd been playing a silly game with herself. Instead she was struck by the thought that she'd never felt worthy. That was the reason she was always rescuing the world. She was trying to earn her way into heaven. Barring that, she was trying to earn her way into happiness.

"Not exactly a plan to make me the poster child for mental health," she said.

Manny stopped chewing long enough to

gently butt his head against her arm. She took the action to mean he was offering his own version of cattle comfort.

"I appreciate you listening," she said. "I guess this is hard for you to understand. I've always been looking for a place to belong, and you've always been where you're a part of things." She frowned slightly. "Do you have a family?"

She remembered then that Manny was a steer and, by definition, would not be having children. "I didn't mean kids," she amended quickly. "Just brothers and sisters. Parents. Do you have someone to love?"

There it was. Her big secret. What she wanted more than anything was someone to love who would love her back.

"I want to be first in someone's life," she whispered. "Their most important person. But so far it hasn't happened."

A crashing in the bushes made Phoebe straighten and turn toward the sound. More raccoons looking for accessories? No, it was too big to be a masked bandit. A bear?

Before she could decide if she should panic, or scream, or hide behind Manny, Maya stepped into the clearing. She glanced from Phoebe to the steer and raised her eyebrows.

"Talking to the animals? Is that really how you want to start your day?"

"Manny was helping me get my life back on track. We're discussing life goals and career choices."

Maya held up her hands. "Not before coffee, I beg you."

"But it's an important conversation to have. I'm twenty-seven, and all my life I've wanted a family. So why aren't I married? Am I really that bad at picking guys? Is it something else? Do I feel I don't deserve happiness, so I unconsciously pick the one guy who won't want to commit or will be mean to me? Am I trapped in a female rescue fantasy?" She patted Manny's neck. "I don't think I'm a lesbian."

Maya snorted. "You're not a lesbian. As for picking the wrong guy, you do seem to be gifted in that department. I'm not sure why." She shook her head. "Didn't I say I didn't want to have this conversation until after coffee?"

"But it's important. I want to belong."

"Why? Belonging is highly overrated."

"So it's the rescue fantasy?" Phoebe asked.

"I don't think so. Are you waiting to be rescued? God knows I'm not. I'm plenty able to rescue myself. Besides, you're always rescuing the world. Doesn't that mean you're strong?"

Did it? Or did it mean she wasn't comfortable allowing someone to care about her? Being vulnerable meant opening herself up to hurt. Needing meant risking not getting what she wanted. Far safer to be the giver than the givee.

"You're right," Phoebe said. "We both need coffee."

"And a change in subject. Come on. Zane sent me to find you and bring you back for breakfast." She grinned. "Apparently he's worried about you."

"He worries about everyone," Phoebe said, trying not to be pleased by Maya's words. "It's his nature."

"That's true. Zane would love to be in charge of the world. He gets off on bossing people around."

"It's not that," Phoebe said. "He takes his responsibilities seriously."

"Defending him again?"

Phoebe waved goodbye to Manny and started down the path. "He doesn't need me to defend him. He's strong enough to take care of himself."

"Interesting." Maya walked next to her. "So here's this big, hunky guy who doesn't need you to rescue him. No wonder you're all atwitter around him. You don't know what to do."

Phoebe wanted to kick a rock. It figured Maya would manage to put it all together in about fifteen seconds. It was her own fault for having a smart friend.

Maya was right. If Zane didn't need Phoebe to take care of him, what on earth would he need her for? And if he didn't need her, why would he want her? She understood the theory that some men cared about women just because. That the women didn't have to do anything to earn the affection. It wasn't anything she'd ever experienced in her own life.

"Zane isn't for me," she said firmly.

Maya laughed. "That sounds really good, but I can't help wondering who you're trying to convince."

C.J. knelt in the tent she shared with Thad and finished packing the few items she'd used during the night. Her brain felt foggy, probably from a lack of sleep. She'd lain awake most of the night, staring up at the tent ceiling, examining her life and not liking what she discovered. She'd also thought a lot about how to change. Was there a way to stop her downward spiral into bitterness and anger? Did any of the happy, cheerful, loving person she used to be still exist?

Despite the long hours spent in contemplation, she hadn't come up with an answer to any of those questions, but she knew she had to keep trying to find them. She had to take a first step. Maybe that involved accepting that she and Thad were never going to have a baby. Not theirs, not someone else's.

She knew she hadn't accepted that truth. Not yet. She'd raged, she'd fumed, she'd plotted. She'd folded in on herself. But she'd never actually accepted it and moved on. She'd never tried to heal. She'd convinced herself that without a baby, her life wasn't worth anything, that she wasn't worth anything. And she'd tried to drag Thad into the abyss with her.

If she didn't get a grip on this, she would lose her husband. She might also lose herself.

Finished with the saddlebags, she crawled out of the tent and stood. The morning was crisp and clear. She and Thad didn't get out of the city enough, she thought. They should plan weekends up in the mountains. There were many wonderful places to be found only a few hours outside of San Francisco. They could—

C.J. heard a sound and turned. She saw Lucy backing out of the tent she shared with Tommy. At the sight of the child's slight body and ratty hair, C.J. stiffened. Anger swelled up inside of her. But this time, instead of giving in to the hot emotion, she took a deep breath and tried to figure out why Lucy made her so furious. What about this girl pushed her buttons? Was it the girl's fault that she had no family and no one to take care of her? Was it the girl's fault that Thad liked her?

Had C.J. become so blindly selfish that she resented the child even being alive if she, C.J., couldn't have the baby she wanted?

The possibility shocked her so much, she took an involuntary step back. Lucy glanced in her direction. The child's expression immediately turned wary.

C.J. didn't blame her. She'd been nothing but a nightmare since the second she'd laid eyes on Lucy.

"Good morning," she said, going for a somewhat cheerful voice. She wanted to make amends, not terrify the child.

Lucy blinked at her. She didn't respond, but she also didn't run away.

C.J. tried a slight smile. "Did you sleep well?"

Still looking apprehensive and not the least bit trusting, Lucy nodded slowly. Her matted hair swayed with the movement.

C.J. eyed the dark strands. If combed out, her hair would probably come to the middle of her back. It was a mess and ugly, but with a little care, it could be attractive. Didn't most little girls want to be pretty?

"Lucy, would you like me to braid your hair?" she asked before she could stop herself with second thoughts. "I think that style would look nice on you, and it would keep your hair out of your face while you are riding."

Lucy's mouth twisted as her eyes narrowed. C.J. knew exactly what she was thinking. The kid was trying to figure out how she would use this offer to trip her up.

I am a complete and total bitch, C.J. thought grimly.

"I know how to French braid," she said in a pathetic attempt to make the offer more enticing. Suddenly it was very important to do this for Lucy, although C.J. was not willing to say why.

"I don't have a brush or nothing," the girl said defiantly, as she squared her thin shoulders.

"I have a brush. And a rubber band for the bottom." C.J. bent down and grabbed her saddlebag. "In here. I'd have to get the tangles out of your hair first, but I'd be gentle. I don't want to hurt you."

As she spoke the words, C.J. realized she was telling the truth. She didn't want to hurt Lucy. She didn't want to be a horrible person anymore.

She crossed to a fallen log and sat down.

After patting the space next to herself, she waited.

Lucy sucked in a breath. She glanced around, then looked at the saddlebags. Longing darkened her eyes. Finally she walked forward slowly and perched on the log.

Relief swept over C.J. She fumbled with the buckle, then opened the bag and pulled out a wide-toothed comb.

"I'm going to start at the bottom and work up," she said as she leaned toward the girl. "I'll do my best not to tug too hard, but if it hurts, you tell me and I'll stop."

"Okay." Lucy sounded doubtful.

C.J. began to work. The tangles came out more easily than she'd thought they would. The girl's hair wasn't wiry, only messy. Once combed, it was sleek and shiny.

After a few minutes Lucy reached up and felt the strands that had already been combed. "It feels nice," she said.

"Wait until I put it in a French braid. You're going to look really pretty. I have a mirror with me, so you can see."

Lucy turned slightly to glance at her, then faced front again. "I wasn't stealing yesterday," she blurted out, speaking quickly. "I really was looking for a Band-Aid."

C.J. swallowed. "I know," she whispered, then cleared her throat. "I know. I'm sorry I accused you of stealing. It was very wrong of me, and I hope you'll accept my apology and forgive me."

Lucy sprang to her feet and spun to face her. She looked confused and more than a little stunned. "You're apologizing to me?"

"Yes. I was wrong. I'm sorry."

Lucy opened her mouth, then closed it. C.J. wondered if any adult in the girl's life had ever taken responsibility for making a mistake.

"It's okay," Lucy told her and sat back down.

"Thank you for accepting my apology."

Still sounding startled, Lucy said, "You're welcome."

C.J. continued to work on her hair. Being wrong about yesterday was one thing, she told herself, but what about the picnic? Had she been wrong there, too?

"You must have been very frustrated," C.J. said, hoping she wasn't making a huge mistake in pursuing this line of conversation. "When someone is honest and gets accused of stealing, it's easy for them to get mad."

Lucy stiffened slightly. C.J. kept combing, but then the girl pulled away. She dropped her chin to her chest.

"We steal sometimes," she whispered. "Tommy takes the money while I do something to get everybody's attention. He hates doing it, but I make him." Lucy tilted her head and looked at C.J. "We don't buy candy with the money, or toys. I'm real careful with it."

She made the statement as if wanting to know that made it better.

"So why do you take it?" C.J. asked, not sure why she didn't feel vindicated to have her suspicions confirmed.

"Sometimes we buy food. When Mrs. Fortier gets mad at us, she sends us to bed without supper. That happens a lot and we get real hungry. We try to be quiet, but sometimes we forget, and then she locks us in our room." Lucy sighed. "We're saving the rest for when we're ready to run away and be on our own. Some of it's gonna have to go for a new coat for Tommy. Mrs. Fortier says his old one is just fine, but it's too small. He can barely fit into it, and when it snows and stuff, he needs to be warm."

Anger flooded C.J., but this time it wasn't directed at the child. Instead, she felt a burning need to find the horrible woman who treated these children so badly and lock her in a room without food for a couple of weeks. Then she should spend a good long time in prison.

"I'm glad you and Tommy take care of each other," she said, careful to keep her feelings to herself. If Lucy saw any strong emotion, she would assume C.J. was mad at her. Based on recent events, who could blame the girl?

She slid forward until she could reach the girl's hair and continued combing it. They talked about the horses and how good Cookie's desserts were until C.J. finished with the braid and handed over her mirror.

Lucy stared at herself. Her mouth curved into a delighted smile.

"I have to go show Tommy," she crowed, handed C.J. the mirror, then raced toward the cook wagon. Halfway across the clearing, she turned back.

"Thank you, C.J."

"You're welcome. After dinner, I'll take it out so it's not too lumpy to sleep on, but if you'd like me to put it back in the morning, I will."

Lucy beamed. "I'd like that a lot."

C.J. watched her go, then packed away her mirror and comb. In her world, the act was a small thing, but what was it in Lucy's world?

Thad stepped into the clearing. He carried a mug of coffee in each hand. "I saw your handiwork," he said, handing her the cup. "Lucy's hair looks nice."

C.J. shrugged, not wanting to talk about why she'd done it or what it all meant. If this had been her first baby step back into the world of the humane, she didn't want to look at it too closely for fear of messing up.

"Lucy told me a few things about her foster-care situation," she said and recounted the girl's stories of lack of clothing and being sent to bed without food. "When we get back, I want to report that woman. She shouldn't be allowed to take in children.

Not if she isn't interested in caring for them."

She braced herself for Thad's response. No doubt he would want them to take in the children themselves. While she and her husband had been approved to have foster children, for C.J. it had simply been one more step on the road to getting a baby. She had no intention of taking in older children.

"Good idea," he said instead. "We have our contact in social services. I also know a few lawyers who work in the department. I'll have a word with them, as well. Lucy and Tommy should be with someone who wants them."

C.J. waited, but he only smiled at her and sipped his coffee. That was it? She'd been prepared to fight him on the issue. What had happened? And why did she feel oddly let down?

CHAPTER FIFTEEN

Shortly before lunch Phoebe realized she was missing her pen. She wouldn't have noticed except in an attempt to give herself hope about her employment future, she'd decided to spend some of her riding time brainstorming alternative career options. And as being within sighting distance of Zane caused her brain to shut down in a hormonal rush, she figured she should write those ideas down. Hence the need for a pen. But it was just plain gone.

One advantage of minimal luggage was the ease with which she could sort through her belongings. She had all her clothes, no watch, one silver earring and—

"That is just so annoying," she said aloud, then stomped her foot on the ground. "I mean, how do they know?"

Chase crossed the clearing and headed toward her. "How does who know what?"

"The raccoons," she told him. "My pen is missing."

He grinned. "Let me guess. Shiny?"

"A silver Cross pen. I doubt it's all that expensive, but it was given to me by a client, so it was special." She closed her saddlebag. "What I want to know is how did they get it? Do they paw through my luggage while I'm out eating or something?"

"I'm sure word has gotten around about you," he said and chuckled. "The raccoon grapevine is filled with messages about the dark-haired woman with the endless stash of shiny possessions."

Phoebe didn't doubt that could be very possible. "Think I could get my pen back if I offered them the other earring?"

"We could try to set up a meeting on neutral ground."

Phoebe couldn't help laughing as she pictured herself in a trench coat on a foggy night, crossing a bridge to meet a nervous raccoon.

"Let me know if you make any progress with them," she said.

"Sure thing." Chase settled on the log next to her, straddling it and facing her. "So, tell me about Jonny Blaze. What's he like?"

She wrinkled her nose. "He was fine. I told you, he treated me like his kid sister.

The man actually patted my head. I'm not making that up."

Chase looked disappointed. "So you didn't date?"

"We had a soda once, while we were looking at houses. Does that count?"

"I don't think so. You know any other movie stars?"

"Nope. Just the one. I know that in Beverly Hills I should concentrate on high-end real estate, but I don't. Besides, a lot more of the rich and famous are moving into other areas."

Chase removed his hat and ran his fingers through his hair. "So you have a boyfriend?"

The unexpected question made her laugh. "No. Right now I barely have a houseplant."

"Why not?"

She sighed. "Honestly, I have really bad luck with men. Or maybe I just have lousy taste."

"What goes wrong?"

She wondered if there was enough time left in the universe to discuss that. "Pretty much everything. I tend to pick guys who need to be rescued. You know, there's something wrong in their life. They stay until it's fixed, usually by me, and then they move on."

Often hurting her in the process, she thought sadly. Like Jeff sleeping with the eighteen-year-old intern Phoebe had hired. Okay, the girl had some responsibility in that one. She doubted the discussion of sex had been all one-sided, but the thought that he could have done that with someone who was so young and vulnerable was just plain icky.

"So look for different kinds of guys," Chase told her with the absolute confidence of a young man who had yet to be battered by love. "You're beautiful, smart and funny. Guys like that."

His compliment made her feel good. Not as good as if it had come from Zane, but still, it was nice. "Thanks for the endorsement. Could I get a letter to carry with me and show prospective dates?"

"Sure."

She patted his arm. "You're very sweet, but dating isn't that simple. At least not for me. Maya and I were discussing the fact that I should probably stop finding guys who need rescuing. At least with men who have it all together I would have a whole new set of problems. It might not work any better, but it would be interesting."

Of course she didn't mention the fact that the thought of being with someone who didn't need her practically sent her screaming into the night. If she wasn't fixing some problem, then why would a guy want her around?

"Zane doesn't need rescuing," Chase said. "You could practice on him."

The unexpected statement left Phoebe more than a little flustered. She coughed, cleared her throat and tried to smile. "Yes, well, but I'm not dating Zane, am I?" She didn't think that hot mind-altering kisses counted as actual dates.

"You could." Chase shook his head. "On second thought, that's not such a good idea. The more I think about it, the more I realize Zane is in some need of serious rescuing."

Right, Phoebe thought as she rolled her eyes. Zane needed rescuing, and soon the baby goats would learn to dance like the Rockettes and take the whole family on a road trip.

"Zane is the most together and responsible person I've ever met," she said. "The only thing he needs rescuing from is the rest of us who upset his perfect world."

"You're wrong."

Chase glanced over his shoulder, as if checking to make sure they were alone. Phoebe followed his gaze and saw C.J. and the kids helping Cookie with lunch. The rest of the crew was nowhere to be seen.

"Zane's not very good with women," Chase said, his voice low.

Phoebe, having been in Zane's presence while his mouth was on hers and his hand was between her legs, snorted in disbelief. "That is so not true."

Chase raised his eyebrows.

Nanoseconds later, she realized that maybe she shouldn't have sounded so adamant about her statement. She slid back on the log.

"Okay, well, not that I would know or anything. But he's just so in charge and women really like that. Plus, he's good-looking. There's the whole cowboy thing." She let her voice trail off and hoped she didn't sound as lame as she felt.

Chase continued to stare at her. She'd never been very good with the whole "silence as power" concept. As always, she found herself stumbling over her words in an effort to fill the empty space.

"Your brother is great with women. Maya told me he was voted the guy all the girls in high school most wanted to—er—be with."

Chase actually chuckled at that one. "Not women who know him. Maya knows Zane needs help as much as I do. It's like when he got married. Could Zane have screwed up more?"

Phoebe felt as neatly divided as a classic schizophrenic. On the one hand, she knew it was wrong to gossip about Zane's personal life. On the other hand, she desperately wanted to know more about Zane. Besides, Maya had already told a few things, so this wasn't really gossiping, was it?

Need beat out the moral high road by a three to one margin. She sighed in defeat.

"I know he was married, and it didn't go well," she said.

"There's an understatement," Chase told her. "Sally was pretty and really nice. She was obviously crazy about Zane, which is why she accepted his marriage proposal."

Phoebe pressed a hand to her stomach, as if the movement could still the jealousy churning there. Well, she'd been the one who had wanted details.

"I'm glad his marriage started on a high note," she said, almost speaking the truth. "It's sad that it had to end."

Chase snorted. "You're missing my point. Here's Zane with this perfect setup. A beautiful woman who was more than willing to keep his bed warm at night. She cooked, she cleaned, she baked cookies."

Phoebe winced. She wasn't sure she could stand to hear anymore. Not that she was interested, but if she was, there was no way she could compete with this paragon of virtue.

"Then Zane completely blew it," Chase said. "Sally wanted to have kids, and when she kept pressing him, he told her the truth."

Phoebe's breath caught. "That he didn't love her."

"Exactly. He flat-out told her he didn't want to have children with her because he'd only married her to have a woman around to act like a mother to me. Is that dumb or what? All he had to do was have a kid or two with Sally, and he would have been set for the rest of his life."

"But if he didn't love her..."

"Zane doesn't know what love is. He could have learned to love her. Or lied. What did it matter? Sally wasn't asking for much."

"He was honest. I respect that."

"You would," Chase told her. "But it was stupid. Sally was hurt and mad. Who can blame her? She'd been used. Like I said, my brother's pretty backward when it comes to women."

Phoebe felt sorry for both Zane and Sally, although she had to admit she didn't mind that the other woman was out of the picture. If she'd still been around, there wouldn't have been any soul-stirring kisses, or that whole hand-down-the-pants thing that still made her tingle.

Chase's gaze turned speculative. "Now Zane is even more cautious when it comes to the ladies. Which is why he hasn't told you he likes you."

Phoebe's mouth dropped open. She made a sincere effort to close it, but as she couldn't actually feel her lips, she wasn't sure if she succeeded.

Zane liked her? She wanted it to be true so much, her teeth hurt. But did he? Really?

She shook her head. "Zane's being very nice to me because he's an excellent host. There's nothing between us." She was sort of telling the truth and sort of hoping Chase would prove her wrong. Which made her feel about as sophisticated as a thirteen-year-old at her first boy-girl party.

Chase grinned. "Want to bet? He's always looking at you. I've seen him. Plus he kissed you."

Stunned, Phoebe scooted back on the log. Unfortunately there wasn't all that much log left, and she landed right on her fanny in the dirt. From her undignified position, she stared at Chase.

"How do you know that?"

He shrugged. "I saw you walking back to your tent a couple of nights ago. You had the look of a woman who'd been well kissed. A couple of minutes later, my brother appeared. Let's just say he was distracted."

She was thrilled, embarrassed and terrified. Thrilled that Chase thought Zane liked her, embarrassed about his knowledge of the kisses and terrified by the thought that Zane might actually be attracted to her.

Sure he was everything she wanted, but she doubted she came close to fulfilling his wish list. He was capable, strong, determined. His ideal partner would be someone completely together and unflappable. Someone who didn't talk to animals and lose her possessions to marauding raccoon gangs.

Chase sighed. "I get it. You're not interested. I feel kind of bad for Zane, but I get where you're coming from. He doesn't talk, and when he does, he's critical. He has no sense of humor. As for being romantic, you'd find more passion in a rock."

Phoebe scrambled to her feet. "That's not fair. You're judging Zane as your older brother. You don't know what he's like with women, and you don't see him the way I do. He's not any of those things. He's very handsome and strong and sexy, and we've had a lot of personal conversations and he was never critical. As for him being romantic or passionate—"

She had the sudden thought that she

might have taken her defensive position just a little too far. Clearing her throat, she brushed off her backside.

"Let's just say the old saying about still waters is true," she finished primly.

"Cool." Chase stood. "I thought you liked him."

Phoebe felt the trap neatly close. "I... he..." She stomped her foot. "Dammit, Chase, that's not fair."

He patted her shoulder. "Don't worry, kid, I won't say anything."

"Good. Not that there's anything to say."

"Of course not."

"Zane and I are friends."

"Right."

"Good friends."

"Of course." Chase winked. "But if things get hot and heavy, remind him I've got condoms in my saddlebags."

Phoebe shrieked and covered her cheeks with her hands. "I can't believe you said that."

"Hey, I like to be prepared. We could have run into a group of college girls out camping or something."

"That's not what I meant," she mumbled

and was more than a little grateful when Cookie rang the bell for lunch.

Zane spent the first part of the after-noon trying to forget what he'd seen before lunch and the second part telling himself he didn't give a damn. He wasn't success-ful either time. There was no way to block out the vision of Phoebe and Chase sitting together, heads bent close as they had a very private conversation. He'd been too far away to hear what they were saying, but he'd heard the laughter.

There was still a tightness in his gut that he refused to acknowledge. No way was he going to be jealous of his own brother. Besides, Phoebe wasn't the type of woman to go after a kid. So they'd been talking. Nothing more.

But it had been an easy conversation. Chase was good at that. Half the time, Zane stood next to Phoebe as silent and stupid as a tree, because he couldn't think of anything to say. Or if she started talking, it was about feng shui or making friends with stumps or something that surprised him into silence. It delighted him, too, but he'd never told her that. He didn't know how.

He swore under his breath, going through multiple combinations of words until he'd run out of all that he knew. Feeling marginally better, he pushed Phoebe from his mind and concentrated on reaching the campsite by four.

Fifteen minutes later, Maya rode up next to him. She gave him one of her sassy smiles.

"So, big guy, how's it hanging?"

He didn't even look at her.

"Not feeling chatty, huh?" She sighed. "That's hardly noteworthy. I know you probably think I'm here to bug you, but if that happens during this conversation, it's only a side benefit. My actual point is to say that everything seems to be going well. You must be pleased."

He eyed her warily. "I'm hopeful we'll make it through without a disaster. We've been lucky, so far. Frank said there's a big storm due in, but I'm hoping it will stay away until Saturday."

"I'm betting our luck will hold. You'll get the greenhorns back to the ranch without them being the wiser as to their purpose. Best of all, I think Chase has learned his lesson."

Zane wasn't so sure.

Maya sighed. "Come on, Zane. Give the kid a break. You've busted his ass and he's come through. He earned all the punishment you gave him, but you have to admit he's done well. Every now and then there's stark panic in his eyes. That has to make you feel good."

Zane allowed himself a slight smile. "Panic's good."

"So you'll give Chase credit?"

The smile faded. "He's taking his punishment like a man. I wouldn't expect any less of him, but if he hadn't screwed up in the first place, we wouldn't be having this conversation."

She took off her hat and slapped him on the arm with it. "You're so stubborn. If I thought I could take you, I'd pull you off your horse right now and beat the crap out of you."

Zane looked at her.

She shook her head. "I said 'if.' I just wish you could see things differently. You complain that I only look for the best things in Chase, but I swear you're always looking for the bad."

"That's not true. I see both sides." He hesitated, remembering his conversation with Gladys. "I care about him."

Care. It was as much as he could say. Love would be better, but that word had never passed Zane's lips. He'd only heard it once in his life—from Sally. She'd screamed it at him the day she'd found out why he'd really married her.

You sonofabitch, I loved you. Doesn't that matter?

He'd been so shocked, he hadn't known what to say. By the time he'd realized it had mattered a little, she'd been long gone. Then winter had set in, and if he'd had any thoughts of going after her, they faded with time, telling him they hadn't been that strong in the first place.

"I don't want Chase to have regrets," he said.

"What are your regrets?" Maya asked.

He didn't answer.

"Zane? Tell me."

"No."

She made a strangled sound low in her throat. "You are the most stubborn man. It's that great mystery I've heard whispers about, isn't it? That's what you regret?"

He didn't speak. No way he was going to talk about that with her.

"Did you kill a man?" she asked.

"No. I didn't kill a man."

"Then what?"

After a couple of minutes, she gave up waiting and returned to the subject at hand. "You need to give Chase room to succeed as well as screw up."

"I'm happy to do both, but so far he's only doing the screwing up. You're pretty quick to pass judgments, considering you're here for all of a weekend a couple times a year, then you take off."

"That should make you happy," she said curtly. "You never wanted me around."

He considered her statement. "That's not true. I liked having you around, and I missed you when you were gone."

"Yeah. Like a rash."

He slowed his horse and turned to her. "No, Maya. Not like a rash. I missed you. This was your home, and I always wanted you to feel welcome here."

Her green eyes widened. "For real?"

He nodded.

She swore. "Don't you dare get all mushy on me, Zane. It would completely creep me out." She rubbed her nose. "Okay. Maybe I knew this was my home. I liked being here. Not just with Chase, but with you, too. I always admired you, and if you tell anyone I said that, I swear I'll castrate your prize steer."

He grinned. "Castrating a steer would be tough, but I won't repeat it. Besides, who would believe me?"

"Good point." She pressed her lips together. "You've done good with Chase. I wish you could let yourself see it."

"That's not part of the job."

"Then it should be."

He hadn't thought of it that way. "Maybe you're right."

She touched her chest. "Be still, my heart."

Phoebe felt like a character in a musical. Everything in her day made her want to break into song. Zane liked her. At least Chase thought he did, and she was gone enough on the man to be willing to accept the gospel truth from a seventeen-year-old.

That being the case, when she walked into the clearing before dinner and saw Zane sitting in a camp chair with an empty seat so conveniently next to him, she gathered her courage and walked straight toward it.

"Hi," she said as she sat next to him.

Zane nodded.

Trying not to be discouraged—just because she knew he liked her didn't mean that he knew she knew—she offered a bright smile.

"Things went well today."

"Uh-huh."

Okay, so maybe Chase was right. Maybe Zane wasn't that great around women. Maybe he was shy.

She squirmed slightly, not sure she could reconcile "shy" with the intense passion she'd felt during their kisses. But if not shy, then what?

Uninterested in her was the most logical explanation, but she didn't want to go there.

She nodded toward the small group by

the campfire. "I've noticed C.J. spending more time with Lucy and Tommy. At first I thought she didn't really like kids, which is weird for someone who's a foster parent. But I guess strange things like that happen. Anyway, it's better now, don't you think?"

Zane pulled off his hat and ran his fingers through his thick, dark hair. Then he stared at her.

"C.J. braided Lucy's hair this morning."

Phoebe beamed. "I noticed that, too. Didn't it just give you a lump in your throat?" She fingered her own hair. "When I was little, I would have loved a braid like that. With a ribbon on the end." She stared at the fire. "A green ribbon."

But ribbons and braids hadn't been a part of her life, and now that she could do that sort of thing herself, it wasn't that important. But the memory would have been nice.

She leaned close to Zane. "Martin ate chicken at lunch. When Andrea went off to chant to the trees or something, he took a piece of fried chicken. I was so proud."

"Andrea can't be an easy woman to live with."

Phoebe glanced at the woman in question. She was hovering by Cookie, no doubt asking questions about the meal.

Zane followed her gaze and sighed. "I'd best take care of that before the old man gets violent."

With that he rose and crossed to the cook fire.

Phoebe watched him go. Once she was able to pull her attention away from the fine shape of his butt and his long-legged walk, she sagged back in her chair.

They'd been talking. Sort of. Zane had actually been chatty, in his taciturn, cowboy kind of way. But she hadn't been able to figure out what he was thinking. Did he really like her, or was Chase just saying what she wanted to hear? If only she could get someone else's opinion on that.

She thought of Maya, but dismissed the idea immediately. Her friend was already suspicious, and confirming her affection for Zane would mean opening herself up to friendly teasing for the rest of the trip. She loved Maya and normally wouldn't have minded, but her feelings for him were too tender to appreciate mocking, however gently meant. She only knew one other source of information.

The cattle had stopped in an open field for the night. Phoebe found Manny right away and crossed to stand next to him.

He acknowledged her with a soft head bump, followed by a brush with his shoulder. Unfortunately the latter sent her staggering back a couple of feet, but she knew he meant well. She scratched his ears.

"It's Zane," she said softly, knowing her voice could carry in the early evening. "Chase said he likes me, but I'm not sure. What do you think?"

Manny raised his head and gazed at her soulfully.

Phoebe bit her lower lip. "Okay. Was that a yes or a no?" She sighed. "Wait. Don't tell me. I don't want to get my hopes up. It's just..." She paused, not sure how to explain her feelings to herself, let alone a steer.

"Something happens when we're together. I like how I feel when I'm around him. He's so tough and strong and together, and yet I feel there's something underneath all that I connect with. Is that too crazy?"

She smiled, knowing Maya would point

out it wasn't much stranger than talking to a steer in the first place.

"The thing is, everyone else belongs. Martin and Andrea, C.J. and Thad. The kids have each other, Maya has Chase. Eddie and Gladys are almost like family to each other." She glanced around at the herd. "You have your friends here. Sometimes I don't feel like I have anyone. And I know this is really weird, but I sense the same thing about Zane. Sure, he's got the ranch and everything, but that's not always enough. It's like there's this empty place inside, and when I'm with him, it gets filled up."

She leaned against Manny and rested her head on his back. He was warm, if a little dusty, and she could hear the faint beating of his heart.

"You're a great listener," she murmured.

Manny munched on grass while she contemplated her next move.

"So what are the odds of you letting me ride you?" she asked.

"I wouldn't try it," Zane said.

She jumped and screamed, then turned and saw him standing right behind her.

"I didn't hear you," she said, wondering how foolish she'd looked draped across the steer.

"I didn't want to interrupt your bonding."

She squinted, trying to tell if he was teasing or making fun of her.

"Manny and I like hanging out," she said, tucking her hands into her back pockets. "So I was wondering. You said that each of the members of the herd has his own place and that if they get sick and fall back, they'll return to it when they're better."

Zane looked more than a little cautious. "Right."

"What happens if Manny gets sick? Who takes his place? Do you have a leader in training?"

"We make do until Manny's better. If he weren't a part of the herd, another steer would take his place."

She considered that and had a bad feeling that "not part of the herd" meant something really permanent, like death. Better to not go there.

"Cookie's about ready with dinner," he said.

"That's subtle," she told him and gave

Manny a last pat before heading for the campsite. "See you in the morning," she told the steer.

Zane fell into step beside her. After a couple of seconds he said, "You know Manny can't actually understand what you're saying, don't you?"

She grinned. "I have an active imagination, but I'm not an idiot. Yes, I know that."

Zane looked relieved. "I'm sure he likes you and all…" His voice trailed off as if he'd just realized what he'd admitted.

"I like him, too," she said, keeping her expression serious. "We're friends."

Zane muttered something under his breath, then turned to her. "I can't figure you out. You're not crazy, but sometimes you're strange." He shrugged. "I don't get it. Or you."

"I like to connect with people or animals. So I talk to them. Sometimes they talk back."

"The people, right?"

"Sometimes the animals whisper me a secret or two."

One corner of his mouth curved up, then the other. When Zane smiled, her entire body felt lighter. Almost as if she was filled with helium and could float.

"I've never met anyone like you," he admitted.

"Is that good or bad?"

His dark gaze zeroed in on her mouth. "Good. Definitely good."

Her throat twisted up tight, and her skin tingled all over. "Even though you think I could bond with a rock?"

"Rocks need friends, too. You have the biggest heart of anyone I know."

She figured that had to be a compliment. After all, being told she had a big heart was nothing like hearing she had a big butt.

She thought of Chase's words, that Zane liked her. Maybe, just maybe, it was true. Wouldn't that be the coolest thing ever? Because she sure liked him. More than a little. And she wasn't just talking about the tingles, either.

Phoebe took a step toward him. At that same second, there was a noise in the bushes next to them. Off balance, she started to turn and found herself falling over a partially covered log. She fell at an awkward angle and landed directly on her back. All the air rushed out of her. She couldn't speak, couldn't breathe, couldn't do anything but lie there gasping.

Zane bent toward her just as Chase burst through the bushes. He took in the scene and lunged for his brother.

"What did you do to her?" he demanded, grabbing Zane by his shirtfront. "What is wrong with you?"

CHAPTER SIXTEEN

Phoebe felt as if Manny had plopped down on her chest. After a couple of seconds of ineffectual gasping, she managed to draw air into her lungs. When she was breathing regularly, she realized that Zane and Chase were scrambling around together. On the ground!

Maya rushed over with Thad right behind her. Cookie followed. Seconds later, Zane had Chase pinned. Both brothers were breathing hard, glaring at each other.

"What the hell?" Maya demanded.

Cookie threatened both of them with a frying pan to the head if they didn't stop. Phoebe still couldn't believe what she was seeing. Nor did she understand what was happening or why.

"Do it," Chase taunted from his place flat on the ground. "Hit me. You know you want to."

Zane's tight expression was unreadable. Tension crackled in the air.

"Dammit all to hell, hit me!"

Zane released his brother and stood up. Then without saying anything, he stalked away. Maya dropped to her knees next to her stepbrother.

"What's going on? Why are you two fighting?"

Chase pointed at Phoebe. "Ask her."

Everyone turned to stare. Phoebe scrambled to her feet and brushed off her fanny. "Me? I didn't do anything." She pointed at the log. "Okay, I tripped and fell and got the wind knocked out of me. What does that have to do with anything?"

Chase's mouth dropped open. "You tripped?"

Phoebe sighed. "So I'm not the most graceful person here. Why is that such a big deal?"

Maya stood and put her hands on her hips. "Kid, you just screwed up big-time."

Chase groaned and flopped back on the ground. "No. I thought... She was on her back and upset and he was bending over her."

Thad and Cookie backed away from the scene. Phoebe looked from them to Chase as all the pieces fell into place.

"You thought he'd hurt me? Zane? Your brother? Has he ever once in his entire life touched a woman?"

Maya shook her head. "Not in a bad way. According to Sally, he was pretty decent in—"

Phoebe held up her hand. She did not want to hear about Zane's lovemaking skills through the grapevine.

She turned back to Chase. "You're always complaining that Zane doesn't see the good in you, but you're just as guilty. Why would you assume something like that about him? He's your brother. You should know he'd never hurt a woman."

Chase sat up and dropped his head to his chest. "I do. It's just—I can't explain it. You were on the ground, and Zane looked, I don't know. Different. Furious."

"He's not the only one," Phoebe told him, before heading off. "You owe your brother an apology."

She crashed through the bushes, hoping Zane hadn't suddenly changed direction. If he had, she would get lost before finding him. On the bright side, maybe she would stumble upon the raccoon thieves and be able to bargain for the release of her pen.

Zane heard the thrashing long before anyone appeared in the clearing. After a couple of minutes he figured out who it was by the soft bits of conversation during which Phoebe apologized to the trees and bushes she trampled.

"Over here," he called, taking pity on her. And maybe himself. For once he didn't want to be alone.

He still couldn't believe Chase had come after him like that. He'd known what his brother was thinking the second he saw his face. That shocked him. Did Chase really think he was such a monster?

Phoebe broke through the underbrush and stepped into the clearing. Twigs and leaves stuck in her hair and on her shirt. She came to a stop when she saw him and began brushing off her clothes.

"I wanted to make sure you were okay," she said.

Zane offered a humorous smile. "He didn't get a shot."

Phoebe crossed to the log and sat next to him. "I'm more concerned about your emotional spirit than whether you were hit."

He looked at her face—at the big eyes and full lips, at the concern. In his world of ranching and outdoor life, Phoebe was useless if decorative. From what he could tell, she hadn't been very monetarily successful in her career, and according to Maya, she was a disaster at relationships.

But to him, she was probably the strongest person he'd ever known. She led with her heart, coming back again and again, regardless of how the organ got bruised. She had a well of courage that left him in awe.

"Nobody worries about me," he told her.

"I do." She took one of his hands in hers. "You'd never hurt me, or any woman. I don't know why Chase jumped to that conclusion."

Zane did his best to ignore the heat pouring into him. Just the light touch of her small fingers was enough to get him hard. He had to get this under control.

"You were on the ground and hurt. I was just standing there. It looked bad."

She dismissed his statement. "I don't care how it looked. I care about how it was."

"Thanks." He squeezed her fingers, then pulled free before he did something stupid like ripping off her jeans and making love to her right there on the ground.

"Oh, Zane."

Phoebe sighed his name in a way that made him want to spill all the dark secrets of his soul. While he couldn't risk that, he was willing to bring one to the light of day.

"If he'd been anyone else, I would have taken him on."

She looked at him. "You would have fought him?"

He nodded. "Right now I could use a good fight."

He expected her to bolt for safety or at least disapprove. Instead she leaned against him, resting her head on his upper arm.

"It's the stress, isn't it?" she asked softly. "You have all of us to worry about. I know why you wanted to teach Chase a lesson, but once you saw everyone and realized all the stuff that could go wrong, I'm sure you figured grounding him for ten years would have been a better option."

He nodded slowly. "Yeah. I don't want anyone to get hurt."

She raised her head and smiled at him. "We're doing okay, and for what it's worth, I think everyone is having a really good time."

"I worry about Chase, too."

He couldn't believe he'd said that. What was wrong with him? But there was something about being around Phoebe. Something that made him relax inside.

"I know he makes mistakes, but basically he's a good kid," she told him. "Trust him, and trust yourself."

She looked so earnest, he thought, as aroused as he was amused.

"You're the one who shouldn't be trusting me," he told her, right before he kissed her.

As he lowered his mouth to hers, he wrapped his arms around her and drew her close. She leaned into him, her slender body warm and supple in his embrace. Her lips clung, then parted. When he swept inside, she was hot, sweet and more than willing to take him on.

The second his tongue touched hers, she moaned. Her fingers dug into his shoulders, and he felt a shudder ripple through her body. He went from hard to ready to explode in two seconds.

The way they were next to each other on a log didn't allow him to explore her the way he wanted, so he broke the kiss and pulled her to her feet.

Phoebe went willingly, if a little unsteadily. When they were both standing, he pressed his mouth to her jaw before sliding to her neck.

She moaned and leaned back her head. Their lower bodies brushed against each other. When her belly came in contact with his erection, it was his turn to groan.

He slid one hand from her waist up to her breast and cupped the feminine curve. Even through the layers of her shirt and bra, he could feel her tight nipple. One sweep of his thumb against it had her gasping.

She touched his head and guided his mouth back to hers. This time when he entered her, she closed her lips around his tongue and sucked. He dropped his free hand to the small of her back, holding her in place so he could rub against her.

The thick ropes of his control began to unravel. When she curled both arms around his neck, it seemed natural to place his around her waist and pick her up. She wrapped her legs around his hips, bringing herself in direct contact with his hard-on.

It was paradise. It was pure torture.

He swore. She broke the kiss and smiled at him.

"So you find me annoying, but you still want me," she whispered.

"I don't find you annoying." He pushed against her crotch.

"I don't find you annoying, either."

He read the passion in her eyes and knew she was more than willing to take things to the next level.

He glanced around, searching for a soft, private spot, only to realize they were out in the open and likely to be discovered any second. It wasn't romantic, it wasn't smart, and he didn't have a condom with him. Phoebe deserved a whole lot better.

"I want you," he told her.

She tightened her legs around him. "Me, too." Color stained her cheeks. "I've never said that to a man before."

Zane realized he hadn't told a woman, either. He'd shown her, but he'd never actually spoken the words. Phoebe was changing him in all kinds of ways.

He wanted her with a desperation he'd never felt before. And yet...

"We can't," he said gently, ignoring the hardness and the pain in his groin. "You deserve better than something hot and fast up against a tree."

She swallowed. "I'm not so sure about that."

"I am."

"Oh."

She sounded disappointed. Had she been anyone else, he would have said the hell with it and taken what she offered. But she was Phoebe.

From behind them came the sound of a car horn honking, and then another. They couldn't see anything through the trees, but they heard laughter drifting toward them as at least a couple of off-road vehicles drove slowly past.

"Sounds like we have company," he said. "We're close to Stryker land. Guess they decided to say hi. You go on ahead. I need a few minutes."

When he pointed at the front of his jeans, she blushed. "Oh. I see your problem. Well, you could walk right behind me and no one would notice."

He chuckled. "I'll wait it out. Go on."

"Okay."

She headed toward camp. Zane watched her go, taking in the sway of her hips and the wave she gave him right before she disappeared.

Getting involved with her would be stupid. He doubted Phoebe understood about easy, short-term affairs. But how was he supposed to resist those big eyes and that mouth of hers? Just touching her made him want her more than he'd ever wanted in his life. He'd walked away from so many things in the name of getting it right, but he wasn't sure he could walk away from her.

Phoebe emerged from the trees to find people pouring out of four rugged-looking vehicles. She stopped counting when she got to twenty, then stepped toward the laughing guests.

After a couple of days on the range with their small group, the noise level was a little shocking. It seemed like organized chaos as the people called out to each other, setting up two portable picnic tables and loading them with food.

The sun was still visible low on the horizon, painting the Western sky in warm purples and reds. The soft light on a summer night in the mountains filled Phoebe with a feeling of contentment.

"Reese!" Chase called out in a voice about an octave lower than normal. He and a gangly teen did a complicated hand-shake that devolved into fake punches.

"Phoebe, over here!" Maya said. "I want to introduce you to my bestie from tenth grade. This is Dellina Hopkins."

She had her arm around the shoulders of a pretty woman with long, brown hair.

"Dellina Ridge now," her friend said.

Maya grabbed Dellina's left hand and whistled at the beautiful ring set flashing on her fourth finger.

"My husband's over there," Dellina said, pointing toward a black Jeep with flames on the side, where two men were lifting out a heavy cooler from the back.

Eddie and Gladys were behind the men. Gladys was holding up a lantern while Eddie was getting close-up video of their butts.

"That's Ford Hendrix," Maya said. "So you must be married to the other guy— Wait a minute! Is that—? You're married to Sam Ridge? The football player? I've done a couple of stories about him and that tell-all his ex-wife wrote."

Dellina laughed. "We don't talk about that."

"Ohmigosh," Maya said breathlessly. "Is that Mayor Marsha?"

She grabbed Phoebe's hand and pulled her toward a lovely silver-haired woman who was standing with Andrea near one of the tables. The woman was dressed with casual elegance in lightweight gray slacks and a teal-colored sweater set. Around her neck, she wore pearls, and Phoebe wondered whether she should warn her about the raccoons.

"I brought Baked Ziti with Butternut Squash and Risotto," Mayor Marsha told Andrea. "The recipe is from the **Fool's Gold Cookbook**. I hoped you might like it because there's no meat."

Andrea looked nonplussed. "How did you know?"

"Maya," Mayor Marsha said as she pulled

her into a warm embrace. "What a pleasure. And you must be Phoebe. Welcome to Fool's Gold."

"Mayor Marsha is the longest-serving mayor in California," Maya said.

Phoebe enjoyed her friend's enthusiasm. She'd never lived in a small town before, but she thought she might like it. In LA, she rarely bumped into friends. The city was so large and spread out, they had to make appointments to see each other, and the appointments had to be scheduled around the flow of traffic. Life seemed simpler here.

"I have something I'd like to talk to you about," the mayor said to Maya. "Come to my office when you're done with the cattle drive."

"Will do." Maya turned to Phoebe. "You doing okay?"

"Sure. This is fun. A little strange to have all these people show up in the middle of our cattle drive."

"It's Fool's Gold. You gotta go with it."

"What most people don't know is that Cinderella had a brother," Thad said.

Tommy looked surprised by the news, but Lucy simply snorted.

"She did not," the little girl told him. "She had wicked stepsisters. There weren't any boys."

Thad smiled. "Her brother had been sent away by the wicked stepmother. He was working in the castle as a groom for the horses, when he heard about a tournament. It was being held the day of the ball."

C.J. continued to stroke the brush through Lucy's hair. After playing all evening with a few of the children from Fool's Gold, Lucy and Tommy seemed quite content to sit near the dying fire with her and Thad. The party had broken up about fifteen minutes ago, and Thad wanted to tell the children a story before bed.

"It's true," she said. "He wanted to win for the glory, but also because the prize money would mean he could finally rescue his sister."

Tommy nodded, as if that made perfect sense, but Lucy looked skeptical.

"That's not the real story," she complained. "You're supposed to talk about the fairy godmother and the glass slipper and stuff."

"I'll get to that," he promised.

C.J. glanced at her husband. He sat on a blanket in front of the fire. Tommy leaned against him. C.J. and Lucy were next to them. She'd already unfastened the girl's braid. As she continued to brush her long hair, she admired the glow of the fire in the dark strands.

"I'll bet her hair wasn't nearly as pretty as yours," C.J. told the girl.

Lucy turned around and stared at her in surprise. Her mouth parted slightly, but she didn't speak.

C.J. felt badly that a simple compliment would be so unexpected. For the first time she wondered where Lucy and Tommy had come from. Where were their biological parents? Had Lucy and Tommy been abandoned? Had their parents died? What circumstances had forced them into foster care?

She looked at both kids, noticing how small they seemed in the vast darkness of the night. They were enthralled by Thad's twisted version of Cinderella.

Watching them set up a familiar longing deep inside. A need for a baby of her own to hold and love and see grow. She wanted to hold the sweet-smelling infant and listen to the steady breathing. She wanted to be there for the first smile, first word, first step.

She put down her brush and stared at the fire. Pain swept through her as she acknowledged it was never going to happen. For reasons she couldn't control, through circumstances that were no one's fault, there would never be a baby in her arms.

Emptiness surrounded her until it was big enough to crush her into dust. No child, no family. No memories, no hopes, no dreams.

She and Thad were good people. They didn't deserve what had happened.

A soft sound caught her attention. She turned and saw Lucy laughing at something Thad had said. C.J. studied the girl's profile, her pretty face and the hunger that never faded from her eyes.

What did Lucy want? When she was alone at night, what dreams did she have?

A family, C.J. decided. The girl would want a family and to feel safe. Would that ever happen? She sighed. Given the children's mixed heritage and their age, it was unlikely. So she and Lucy had at least one thing in common—they were both caught up in wishing for what they would never have.

While C.J. didn't enjoy her own fate, she knew she could survive it. But what about Lucy and Tommy? How would they make it to adulthood only dependent on each other? Alone and unloved in a world that preyed on the lonely.

The solution to all their problems was right in front of her. She acknowledged it even as she rejected it. She might have to give up her dream, but she wasn't ready to accept something else instead. Not yet. Maybe not ever.

Chase waited until Thad and C.J. got the kids settled for the night, and Eddie and Gladys made one last trip into the bushes, chattering all the way there and all the way back. Then he walked toward the fire. Zane was there, as he was every night. He was always the last one to go to bed and the first one up in the morning. Chase had the sudden thought that his brother must spend a lot of his life tired of being the responsible one.

He crossed the bare dirt until he reached the fire. His brother didn't look up as he approached, but he didn't walk away, either. Chase figured that was about as good as it was going to get.

He stood there, shifting his weight, then finally cleared his throat.

"I'm sorry about before," he said gruffly. "I misread the situation. I can't figure out why I did. I know you wouldn't hurt Phoebe. It's just...I saw her laying there and I reacted." He shrugged. "I'm sorry," he repeated.

He knew Zane wasn't going to say anything. Apologizing for screwing up never made it better.

His brother looked at him for a long time. Finally Zane tossed the last of his coffee into the fire and rose.

"I know I can be a real bastard," Zane said. "And I know why you thought something had happened with Phoebe. It's okay."

Chase blinked. He couldn't believe it. "You mean you're not mad?"

"It was an honest mistake. One that could have cost you your pretty face, but that's another story."

Chase grinned. "You saying you could take me, old man?"

"In a heartbeat."

Chase knew he was tall, but he hadn't filled out yet. Zane had a couple of inches and about forty pounds of muscle on him. Still, he couldn't help taking a boxer's stance and raising his fists.

"When and where," he joked.

Zane chuckled. "Get some sleep."

Chase nodded. "'Night."

He headed to his tent, feeling better than he had in a long time.

The following morning, Phoebe shared her dilemma with Rocky.

"I'm not sure how much Zane likes me," she told the gelding, "but he wants me, which is a good thing, right? I mean sexual attraction is exciting."

She thought of the horse's limitation in that department. "Am I making you feel bad by discussing this?"

Rocky stomped one of his hooves, which she took to mean it was fine.

"So I was wondering if I should, you know, ride close to Zane this morning." She buckled the saddle into place and checked the stirrups. "Is that too forward? I don't want him to think I'm easy."

She thought about what had happened the previous day. How she'd practically rubbed herself against him like a cat in heat.

"It might be too late for that."

Rocky shook his head, which she took to be an equine version of "go for it."

"Okay. If you say so."

She led Rocky to a stump. She climbed up on it and managed a semi-graceful mount. Once she was settled in her saddle, she urged him forward and joined up with the milling cattle. Zane's call of "move 'em out" sent a thrill through her, as always.

Manny started out at a slow walk. The other steers fell into place. Phoebe took up her spot, then glanced around casually to see if anyone was paying attention to her. When she was sure she was unobserved, she gave Rocky a very light tap with her heels. He picked up the pace.

After three minutes of bone-jarring trot, she was even with Zane and able to slow to a more manageable walk. Of course now that she was here, she didn't know what to say.

She settled on a simple, "'Morning."

He responded with one of his familiar grunts.

Phoebe reminded herself of his claim to want her and how hard he'd gotten while they'd been kissing and how he'd touched her breast. Courage in place, she sucked in a breath.

"Do you mind if I ride up with you for a while?" she asked.

"I'd like that."

Pleasure made her beam. "How'd you sleep?"

He chuckled. "Like hell. You?"

She thought of her erotic dreams. "I might have tossed and turned a little."

"Good."

She glanced at him and saw him flash a smile. She grinned back. Contentment made her relax.

"So what was it like growing up around here?" she asked. "The ranch is pretty far from town. Did you have a long trip to school?"

"I took the bus. It was about forty-five minutes each way because of all the stops, unless the weather was bad. After some storms I couldn't get to classes, or if it got bad during the day, I spent the night at a friend's house."

"Wow. Really?" The worst she'd ever faced was a twenty-minute walk or a canceled day because of an earthquake. "Did you have a lot of friends on the bus?"

"Sure. We'd tease the girls, or the littler kids."

"You mean torture."

His smile returned. "That, too."

"I know Chase is your half brother. Why didn't your parents have more children together?" She bit her lower lip. "Is that too personal? I mean, did your mom die when you were really young?"

"I was twelve," he said. "The town got me through. All the women brought us food. My friends' families had me over so I could get away from the sadness."

"I'm sorry you had to go through that, but I'm glad you had support."

"Me, too." He glanced at her, then away. "As to why my parents didn't have other kids before Mom died, I guess it was because they would be in the way."

"Of what? It's a ranch. Isn't there plenty of room?"

Zane stared straight ahead. "My parents loved each other more than they loved anything else. Or anyone. Having other people around was a distraction they didn't want."

Phoebe couldn't imagine such a thing. "But you were their child."

"I know. My mom was better than my dad. She took care of me and we were close. But when she was dying, my dad couldn't handle it. He was desperate without her. After she was gone, he didn't know how to survive."

Phoebe could see how the ranch could get lonely for a man on his own. "But he had you."

"You'd think."

She didn't know what to make of that. "Then he met and married Chase's mother, right?"

Zane nodded. "She stuck around for a few years before she took off. Maya's mother was next. There were a couple more after that. Eventually my old man stopped trying to replace my mom. He simply waited to die, so he could be with her again."

"I guess he loved her a lot," Phoebe said, then shuddered. "But it sounds like a scary kind of love. I like what Thad and C.J. have. They obviously adore each other, but there's plenty of room for other people."

"I agree with you. What my parents had was…I don't know." He shook his head. "I wouldn't want that."

"What would you want?" she asked before she could stop herself. "How would you like to love a woman?"

"I haven't thought about it."

She swallowed her fear and plunged ahead. "Have you been in love before?"

He glanced at her. "No. You?"

She sighed. "No. There were a couple of times I came close, but it didn't work out. Sometimes I want it more than anything, and sometimes I find the concept terrifying. I don't want to be that vulnerable."

She braced herself for him to be critical, but all he said was, "Makes sense."

They rode in silence for a while. Finally Zane spoke.

"What will you do if you lose your real estate license?"

"I've been trying to figure that out. I need to have a plan. So far, nothing's been coming to me. I was talking to Manny about it and—" She broke off. "Just so you know, Manny doesn't answer."

"Good thing. If he did, I'd worry about you both."

"I would hope so. Anyway, I don't have a plan yet. I always thought I'd stay in LA, but having been out here has shown me that maybe I'd like something different. Fool's Gold seems like a special place." She smiled. "Think I could get a job rustling cattle?"

"Rustling? That's stealing."

"Oh. I mean taking care of them."

"You'd better learn your terms before you apply."

"I guess." She tugged at her hat. "Chase will be going off to college next year, right? What will you do?"

"What I've always done."

She knew what that meant. Work the land, breed cattle, raise the goats. By himself.

"Won't you be lonely?"

He glanced at her. "Probably."

The single word tugged at her heart more than any declaration of affection ever had. She wanted to crawl up on his horse and hold him close. She wanted to promise that she would be there for him, if he was interested. She wanted a lot of things.

"This is all I know," he said.

"Plus, it's what you love. It's not as if you feel trapped by your destiny or anything."

Zane didn't answer. She looked at him.

"Do you feel trapped?"

"Not in the way you mean. But there are times..." His mouth twisted at the corners, but he didn't smile. "When I was about Chase's age, my father decided to improve the bloodline in our horses, so he went out and bought an expensive stallion. The ranch was in trouble—he couldn't afford the horse, but he was determined."

Phoebe frowned slightly. The ranch looked plenty prosperous to her. Was that a recent development?

"That stallion was a real beauty," Zane continued. "Spirited, strong and stubborn. He wasn't to be ridden. My dad laid down the law on that one right away."

She got a bad feeling in her belly. "You

rode him, didn't you?"

Zane shrugged. "Sure. I was a kid. Impulsive, plus I hated that my old man didn't trust me. I took him out that first afternoon. He moved like the wind. He took fences and gullies. I'd never felt such speed or drive in a horse before. But we'd been having some heavy rains, and the horse slipped in the mud. I went flying and he fell. I broke an arm, and he broke two legs."

She winced. "That must have hurt."

"I got over my break easily enough, but the stallion had to be put down. My dad was furious. He hadn't called the insurance company yet, so we weren't covered. He still owed more money than we had, and without stud fees, there was no way to make the payments. He ended up selling some land to cover the costs."

Phoebe shivered slightly. She didn't have to ask about the rest of it—she'd already figured out that Zane's father was a hard man who didn't excuse mistakes or those who made them.

"He never said a word," Zane said quietly. "That was the worst of it. He never let me say I was sorry, or make up for it. For him, I didn't exist anymore."

"But you were his son."

He glanced at her. "That didn't matter. I did my best to never screw up again, but it was too late. Every day I walked to the fence line and stared at the land we'd lost. I was determined to get it back."

She had a thousand questions. "The ranch is okay now, right?"

"Yeah. It took me a few years, but we're profitable."

"And this is why you're so hard on Chase. You don't want him to go through what you went through."

"Right. I tried talking to my dad before he died, but he wouldn't listen. He said it didn't matter, but I knew it did."

She felt his pain and wanted to make it better. She wanted to go back in time and hold the young man he'd been, telling him that he'd made a mistake—nothing more. The punishment he'd endured didn't fit the crime.

"Your father was wrong," she told him. "You're worth more than any horse or any piece of land."

"I appreciate the vote of confidence, but

I don't know if it's true. Maybe if I'd been able to get the land back."

"Why can't you?"

"The man who bought it—Reilly Konopka —won't sell it to me." He sounded grim. "I saved until I had enough, but when I approached him, he wouldn't sell. He wanted to give it to me."

Phoebe blinked. "As a gift?"

"I couldn't take it that way. But he wouldn't let me, the old bastard. So he still owns the land, and I still fight the ghosts."

She didn't know what to say. Knowing Zane as she did, she understood the problem—Zane couldn't accept the land without earning it. In his mind, he had to make peace with the past, and that was his only way.

She ached for him. Why couldn't he see that he would never be able to make things right with his father—he could only make them right with himself? That this wasn't about land, but about forgiveness and love.

"I go see Reilly every couple of years, and he pisses me off by refusing my money."

Phoebe wondered how much of the

problem was Zane's neighbor acting more like a father than Zane's own flesh and blood.

"Eventually I'll wear him down," he said. "I'll beat this."

Phoebe wasn't so sure. Winning a battle was more difficult when the opponent refused to participate in the fight.

CHAPTER SEVENTEEN

The fire snapped and danced, creating shadows on the ground. Zane leaned back against a log and sipped his coffee. The night was still and cool, with no hint of stars above the cloud cover. The forecasted rain had yet to fall, and he was beginning to believe that they were going to get through the cattle drive without some kind of disaster.

Even as the thought formed, he made a fist and knocked on the log. No point in tempting fate. Not when there were still two days and plenty of miles between his greenhorns and the safety of the house.

He glanced around at the people sitting by the fire. They were all there. Even Cookie had pulled up an old stump and taken a seat.

Maya sat with Phoebe and Chase. He didn't linger on that group, because he knew what would happen. His gaze would settle on Phoebe, and he wouldn't want to look away. Not with the firelight making her eyes shine and her skin glow. Not with the sound of her voice easing inside of him and tying him up in knots. She was five kinds of temptation with just enough hell thrown in to make things interesting.

Funny—he would have thought telling her the truth about his past would have changed things. That he would feel distant or angry. Instead he found he didn't mind her knowing. Phoebe had reacted true to form—with acceptance and a full heart.

Where did she get the courage to be so open?

Maya glanced up and saw him watching. She nudged Phoebe. "Zane has all the cattle bloodlines on the computer."

"Isn't that complicated? How would the program work?"

"I have no idea," he told her, trying not to get lost in her pretty eyes. "Chase designed it."

She turned to his brother. "Is that true? You designed the program?"

"Sure. It was no big deal."

"I think it's amazing."

Chase lifted a shoulder, as if it didn't matter, but Zane saw the pleasure he took in the compliment.

"Zane's not much into computers, so I made it extra user-friendly," Chase continued. "He just inputs the number of the animal in question, and the program leads him through a series of prompts."

"Sounds great," Phoebe said. "Can I see it in action when we get back to the house?"

Chase looked at Zane, who nodded. "Sure."

"In some ways technology is making life easier," Maya said, stretching her long legs out in front of her. "But it can also create trouble. This guy I work with accidentally left his phone at his girlfriend's house. She went through the calendar and found out about all the other women he was dating."

Phoebe winced. "I'm not sure that can be blamed on the phone. Maybe he should have been more honest." She hesitated. "Of course his girlfriend shouldn't have gone through his things."

"If he hadn't forgotten it in the first place," Maya pointed out. "Nothing would have happened."

Phoebe looked shocked. "You think it's

all right for a man to date more than one woman at a time?"

"If they're not exclusive, what does it matter? She can do the same thing."

Phoebe swallowed. "That's just so…"

"Sophisticated?" Maya asked with a grin.

"Icky," Phoebe told her.

Zane smiled. For all her years in the city, Phoebe was a simple girl at heart. She believed in honesty, one man and one woman and talking to anything that moved. Her heart was so big, it was no wonder she was always finding it bruised. Life didn't offer many rewards for those who led with their emotions.

She couldn't be more different, he thought. He lived in a world where emotions were irrelevant.

Tommy slid closer to Chase. "Do you write other kinds of programs?"

"Sure." Chase ruffled the boy's hair. "But programs are easy. Right now a buddy and me are working on a robotic cat."

Tommy's eyes widened. "Whatta ya mean?"

"You know those robot dogs you can buy? You teach 'em tricks and stuff?"

Tommy nodded.

"We're building a cat, only way more sophisticated than that." Chase's face lit with excitement. "We've got some software bugs. I want the cat to chase mice."

"Real ones?" the kid asked

"Yeah. We've started with little stuffed mice we've rigged up to move, but so far the cat's not interested."

Lucy moved next to her brother. "It won't hurt the mice, will it?"

He shook his head. "Nah. We just want the cat to be able to catch them."

He continued talking, explaining about the various programs, the problem of building custom parts. The adults didn't pay attention, but Tommy and Lucy were riveted.

Zane had heard it all before. How many times had his brother talked through dinner, gesturing, making sketches on napkins and explaining technical details until his meal got cold? Zane had listened, but he'd never understood what Chase saw in it all. To him it was just mechanical parts— only interesting because of what they could do. He didn't get the fun in putting them all together.

But he wasn't Chase, and Chase wasn't him.

"When do you think you're gonna get it working?" Tommy asked.

Chase's animated expression went flat. "I don't know. We had a pretty serious crash and burn last week. I'd wanted to get it fixed this summer but..." He poked at the ground. "I have a lot of chores."

"Too bad," Tommy said.

Zane watched his brother. The chores in question were ranch work—both to pull his weight and to pay off the extra cost for the saddles and tents needed for the cattle drive.

While he knew it was important that Chase learn about responsibility and consequences, for the first time he realized that Chase's interest in computers wasn't a passing phase. It was what he wanted to do with his life.

Maybe he'd always known the truth, but he hadn't wanted to see it. Maybe he'd hoped his brother would stick around for a while. But that wasn't going to happen. Chase would never be happy at a small agriculture college. Instead he wanted to head east to attend MIT. Given his skills with and love of computers, Zane couldn't blame him.

Thad checked his watch and rose. "Okay, kids. Time for bed."

Tommy scrambled to his feet. "Thad, no. Give us a few more minutes. I want to hear more about Chase's robot cat."

"You can hear about it in the morning."

"He's right," C.J. said.

Tommy looked at her, then smiled. "Okay."

Lucy hugged C.J. before standing and following her brother toward the tents.

Zane had seen the evolution of C.J. and Thad's relationship with the kids but hadn't realized they'd gotten so close. He wasn't sure how it had happened but figured it beat the palpable hostility he'd felt between them earlier in the week.

Everyone else followed the kids' example. Andrea and Martin excused themselves, followed by Eddie and Gladys. Maya paused to have a word with Cookie while Phoebe stood and wiped off her rear.

"'Night," she said to no one in particular.

As Zane watched, she took a step, then

turned and glanced at him. Her mouth curved into a full smile that made his gut ache.

"'Night, Zane," she murmured.

He winked.

The gesture surprised them both, but he wasn't the one who stumbled slightly, caught her breath, then waved before disappearing into the darkness. He had a moment's regret that he hadn't given in to instinct and simply started undressing her when he'd had the chance. He didn't doubt she'd been as ready and willing as he had been.

"Stupid principles," he muttered under his breath.

He finished his coffee and rose. As Chase walked by, Zane grabbed his brother's arm.

"Got a second?" he asked, dropping his hand to his side.

Chase looked wary, but nodded. "Sure."

"I've been thinking. We're probably going to break even on the cattle drive. So there's no reason for you to work extra hours to pay off the saddles and the tents. When we get back, you still need to do your regular chores, but that's all. You can spend the rest of your time with your computers and your robotic cat."

Chase stared at him. "I don't get it."

Zane grinned. "I figured you for the smart one in the family. Guess I was wrong."

Chase blinked a couple of times as understanding dawned. "You mean it, Zane? You're not gonna make me work a sixty-hour week in the barns?"

Zane set his mug on the table by Cookie's wagon. "When have I ever done that?"

Chase smiled. "You know what I mean."

"Yeah, I do. Like I said, just do your regular chores. I'll handle the rest. And when we get back, give me a list of everything you're going to need to make the cat work and what it's all going to cost. Paying for it myself is a whole lot cheaper than any scheme you'll come up with."

Chase whooped with delight. "You mean it? That's so great. You're the best." He slapped his brother's back. "I can't wait to get home and get to work on the cat. Thanks, Zane."

He yelled again, then ran toward his tent. At the entrance, he paused and gave Zane a thumbs-up before ducking inside.

Zane watched him go. Chase was still a kid, but like Maya had been telling him for years, he was a good one. Funny how he hadn't seen that before. He'd been so caught up in keeping Chase from having regrets that he'd forgotten to let him have a life. Until Phoebe had reminded him what was really important.

Phoebe found it difficult to fall asleep, but that was pretty much her life lately. There was something about being around Zane that set her body to humming. And once that humming started, there was no way to block out the sound or vibration.

Torn between sexual longing and emotional connection, she took the route most likely to lead to sleep and thought about what he'd told her of his past. No wonder he wanted to keep Chase on the straight and narrow. Zane had been forced to live with a single mistake for years.

His father had been wrong not to forgive him. Phoebe wanted to face the man and give him a piece of her mind—a desire complicated by death and distance. She wanted Zane to understand he didn't have to prove anything anymore. That he could let the past go. She wanted a lot of things where he was concerned.

Foolish wants and desires, she reminded herself. Although when he'd been kissing her, the passion had felt so right. And while she'd appreciated his concerns about making love out there in the open, she wasn't completely sure she would have minded.

She needed him. Embarrassing but true. She couldn't remember ever needing a man before. And she wasn't just talking about clever conversation or a warm, fuzzy hug. Nope, she actually meant she needed "it."

There wasn't a part of her body that didn't long to be caressed. At this point in time, she wouldn't be picky. Even a foot rub would be too erotic for words. Unfortunately Zane wasn't likely to come calling, and there was no way she could simply walk up to his tent and announce herself. Not only was it not within the working parameters of her personality, but the night was so quiet out here. Everyone in a three mile radius would know what was going on.

Phoebe turned restlessly in her sleeping bag. At least there weren't any rocks under her tonight. She'd picked a section of soft mossy ground when they'd pitched the tents. Zane had tried to talk her out of it, but she'd insisted. She was tired of something sharp jabbing her in her hip or her shoulder, every time she tried to doze off to sleep. She also liked being a little ways away from the rest of the camp. It felt more private.

Unfortunately, private didn't equate to sleepy. She turned again, then sighed heavily. She needed a man...bad. But not just any man. Zane. Only Zane.

After several more minutes of tossing and turning, Phoebe tried to meditate her way to sleep. She pictured herself in a beautiful mountain meadow. She could hear the sound of birds and feel the sun's warmth on her arms. The scent of the flowers surrounded her. Everything was perfect... right up until a woodpecker took up residence.

A woodpecker?

Phoebe opened her eyes and realized it

had started to rain. The noise she'd heard was rain gently pattering against her tent. She felt along the seams and was grateful when they turned out to be watertight. At least she wasn't going to get soaked.

She closed her eyes again and relaxed. The rain was kind of nice. Soothing. It was just the right rhythm to lull her off to sleep.

Until the rushing river of water that coursed through her tent about forty minutes later woke her right up.

Phoebe sat up with a muffled shriek. She was drowning and intensely cold. Something damp brushed against her face. She couldn't see, couldn't figure out where she was and—

Memory returned and with it the realization that there was freezing water racing into her tent. She was immersed in it and soaked.

Several things occurred to her at once. First, Zane had warned her about the mossy ground being a seasonal stream, or river in this case. Second, that she was never, ever going to be warm again. Third, and perhaps most important, she had to get out of here.

If getting into her snug sleeping bag was difficult, getting out of it while both of them were drenched was nearly impossible. She shimmied and shoved and squirmed and swore. Finally, she freed herself. Dressed only in a shirt, panties and socks, she stepped out into the rain and found herself more than ankle deep in water.

She could feel her hair plastering to her head and the shivers rippling through her body. Grabbing the tent with both hands, she tugged and pulled, but it wouldn't budge. Giving up on it, she ducked back inside and dragged out her saddlebags and duffel, her jeans and boots. Then she slogged through the rain and muddy ground to the closest tent.

"Z-Zane," she said, her teeth chattering as she stood there in the darkness. "M-my t-tent is f-flooded."

She heard a heavy sigh, then his voice. "You're just standing out there getting wet, aren't you?"

She nodded before she realized he couldn't see her. "I was wet b-before. There's a river in my tent."

A flashlight clicked on, then the tent flap opened. "Leave your gear and get in here."

Phoebe hesitated, not wanting to abandon her belongings, but the sight of Zane holding a large, dry towel was too much for her to resist. She dropped everything and ducked inside.

The tent was slightly larger than her own, but still a pinch for two, especially when she was soaking wet, on her knees and trying not to drip on everything. Zane wrapped the towel around her and grabbed his boots.

"Is your tent still standing?" he asked.

She nodded because her teeth were chattering too much for her to speak. Though the sight of him with his shirt unbuttoned was doing a lot to warm her up. His chest had just a smattering of hair at the top that veed over his flat stomach toward his jeans.

He gave her a quick glance. "You're soaked to the bone, aren't you?"

She nodded again.

He muttered something that sounded like "Figures" or maybe it was "damn fool woman"—she wasn't sure. He fingered her dripping shirt, then shook his head.

"Take off your clothes, get dry, then crawl into my sleeping bag. It'll warm you up. I'm going to put your gear into Cookie's wagon where it'll have a chance to dry off by morning. After I take down your tent, I'll be back."

He closed his shirt and put on his cowboy hat. As he started to crawl outside, he paused and looked back at her. "I'd appreciate it if you'd stay out of trouble between now and then."

"O-okay," she managed between lips numb with cold.

When Zane was gone, Phoebe did as he'd told her. She peeled off her wet socks and stretched them out by the flap. She hesitated over her shirt, but the dripping cold material sucked the heat from her already chilled body. Abandoning modesty, she wrestled the buttons open and pushed off the garment.

As her panties were only slightly damp and she couldn't imagine actually getting completely naked under circumstances like these, she left them in place. She wrapped the towel around her wet hair and slid into Zane's sleeping bag.

Instantly warmth enveloped her. The soft material was toasty and smelled of Zane's body. It was like being in his arms... sort of. She imagined nestling her cheek against his muscled chest.

She curled up into a ball and willed herself to stop shaking. The towel fell off, but she couldn't unfold her arms long enough to put it back in place. Then she decided to just leave it because it would protect his pillow from her damp hair.

There were noises from outside. The faint sounds told her Zane was dragging her tent to safety. She felt really bad for getting him up in the middle of a stormy night, and more than a little stupid for not listening when he'd told her not to put her tent on a dry streambed.

She was well into her course of self-recrimination when he returned. The flap parted, and a very wet Zane crawled in beside her.

"You okay?" he asked, as he set down the flashlight and touched her cheek. "Getting warm?"

She nodded, then sniffed. "I'm sorry."

His dark eyes crinkled slightly as he smiled. "It was worth it."

"What?"

"I get to say I told you so."

She sniffed again. "You're not mad?"

"Because I had to go out in the rain, in the middle of the night, pull up the stakes on your tent, resecure it somewhere else so it would dry out, then cart your saddle-bags over to Cookie's wagon, wake him up and then listen to him complain?"

She winced. "Those would be the reasons."

"I'm not mad."

She couldn't believe it. "But I was stupid."

"You're a greenhorn. You didn't know any better."

"You tried to tell me. I should have listened."

He smiled. "That'll teach you. The man always knows best."

"That's so not true."

"It is in this case. So are you naked?"

The switch in topic caught her unaware. She shimmied a little deeper into the sleeping bag. "I, ah, left on my panties."

Zane swore softly. "I guess I deserved

that for asking."

"Deserved what?"

"You don't want to know."

Suddenly she did. Very much. But she didn't know how to ask. So she tried a different subject.

"Are we going to share the sleeping bag?"

"I thought I'd go stay with Cookie."

"Oh." Disappointment flooded her way more than the river had. It was just as cold, but not as wet.

"Phoebe, we talked about this," he reminded her. "You deserve better than a quickie out in the open."

"We're in a tent," she said before she could stop herself. "And it doesn't have to be quick."

As soon as the words were out, she wanted to pull the sleeping bag over her head and disappear. Instead, she closed her eyes and waited for Zane to stalk off in disgust. When he didn't move, she opened first one eye, then the other.

He was staring at her with the hungry expression of a man who has been starving all his life. The need burning in his dark irises warmed her way more than the sleeping bag.

He wanted her. She could feel his desire all the way to her toes. She wasn't sure why he wanted her or for how long, but she couldn't worry about any of that now.

She watched the battle rage inside of him. Base need fought his desire to be a gentleman. She wasn't exactly sure how to influence the outcome, but she was determined to get her way in this. After considering several options, she settled on a simple, yet direct approach. She unzipped the sleeping bag and sat up.

While she was sure her hair was wet and spiky and that the flashlight didn't exactly flatter her skin tone, Zane didn't seem to notice any of that. His gaze dropped to her bare breasts and didn't budge. There was an audible exhalation of air, a swear-word, then a low groan that sounded very much like surrender.

A heartbeat later, the flashlight clicked off.

Phoebe blinked in the darkness. "Zane?"

"We're gonna have to do this by feel. Otherwise we'll be putting on a show."

She thought about how flashlights in

the tents created detailed shadows and blushed at the thought of entertaining the others.

Before she could figure out some kind of response, she both felt and heard movement. Instinctively, she pulled the sleeping bag up over her chest.

"What are you doing?" she asked.

"Taking off my jacket. It's soaked."

"Oh."

There was a bit more rustling, then a warm hand settled on her shoulder.

"You okay with this?" he asked.

"Yes," she whispered, nearly meaning it. Sure, she wanted to be with him in the most intimate way possible, but wanting it and talking about it were two different things.

He chuckled. "Second thoughts?"

"Not exactly."

"Then what, exactly?"

But she never got to say. Apparently he'd been moving closer as they spoke, and before she could form a word, his mouth settled on hers.

The man had great aim, she thought as firm, tender lips claimed her own. Her body melted in anticipation, which made it difficult to stay upright. Rather than puddle into the sleeping bag, she simply leaned against him.

Even as he moved back and forth on her mouth, he brought his strong arms around her. She felt the soft, well-washed cotton of his shirt and the strength of his muscles. She always felt at home in his arms, so it was only natural to release her death grip on the sleeping bag and wrap her arms around his neck. Which meant her bare chest was pressed against his material-covered one, but once he stroked her lower lip with his tongue, none of that seemed to matter.

She'd always had the best time in Zane's arms, she thought hazily as she parted her mouth and waited for him to sweep inside. He kissed like someone who had invented the activity. If kissing was a sport, then Zane was an Olympic-class athlete.

He teased her by nipping on her lower lip before he brushed his tongue against hers. She sighed in a delicious combination of passion and anticipation.

Heat flared, chasing away the last of the

chill. His hands rubbed against her bare back, one going lower, one going higher. She ran her fingers through his hair, then squeezed the muscles in his shoulders. Wanting grew until it was uncontrollable. Fortunately he read her mind.

He broke the kiss. He was still close enough that she could feel his warm breath on her neck, which was all the warning she had before he pressed his mouth against the underside of her jaw. Shivers rippled through her. She arched back her head, even as she wanted to get closer.

As he kissed and nibbled his way to her ear, he lowered her onto the sleeping bag. There was more movement. She wasn't sure what he was doing because he never stopped kissing her.

When he took her earlobe into his mouth and sucked, she had to bite her lower lip to keep from crying out. When she felt the weight of him as he stretched out next to her, it was all she could do to stop her legs from falling open in a shameless invitation. It didn't matter that she was still wearing panties, or that he was fully dressed. She wanted him...all of him...on top, inside, pleasuring them both into madness.

Thoughts of what they would do later faded when his kisses moved lower and lower. Her breath caught as he neared her breasts, then came out in a hiss as his lips closed over her tight, sensitive nipple.

She was drowning in pleasure, she thought, clutching his head and holding him in place. It was good—too good.

"More," she breathed.

He sucked and licked and teased her nipple with his mouth and tongue, then shifted to her other breast and repeated the erotic torture.

She could feel herself swelling for him. Between her legs there was heat and dampness. Her panties were too much of a barrier, and the sleeping bag was a straitjacket. She fought to find the zipper, then tugged it lower.

When she was able to kick free of the covering, she reached for his shirt. He continued to pleasure her breasts, which meant after a couple of halfhearted attempts with his buttons, she had to let her hands fall back to her sides while she reveled in what he could do to her.

"This can't be legal," she whispered.

He raised his head. "Why not?"

"It feels too good."

He chuckled. She heard the sound, felt the soft exhalation of cool air on her bare, damp breasts, but she couldn't see anything. Not him, not herself. It was strange, but in a good way. The darkness gave her courage.

"Take your clothes off," she said, knowing that she would never have managed the words in the light.

"Yes, ma'am."

There was rustling, then nothing, then the distinctive sound of a zipper being pulled down.

Her heart thundered in her chest. She tried to imagine him naked. What would he look like? Thinking about him naked made her imagine him standing in front of her—erect. And thinking about that made her think about him pushing inside of her. Filling her. Making her—

"Condom," she gasped.

A movement stopped.

"What?"

Phoebe felt the earth open up in preparation of swallowing her. How could she have not mentioned this before?

"I'm not on anything right now," she whispered. "Birth control. I'm not on the Pill." She gestured helplessly.

"Shit, fuck, damn."

Disappointment tied her in knots. "I was really only interested in that middle part," she joked.

There was a second of silence, followed by a low chuckle. "You're never predictable, Phoebe. I'll give you that. Cross your fingers."

"What?"

"Cross your fingers. I might have a condom in my shaving kit."

There was movement and rustling, then the sound of a zipper being opened.

"I'm going to have to put on the light."

She briefly debated being polite and closing her eyes, but who was she kidding? She wanted to see Zane naked. In preparation, she raised up on one elbow and stared in his general direction. When the light came on, she saw all she wanted and more.

He was kneeling at the end of the sleeping bag. Naked, aroused and more physically perfect than any man had a right to be. She saw the definition in his arms, the broad strength of his chest and his flat stomach before lowering her attention to his large, hard penis.

The physical proof of his desire for her made her so happy, she nearly cried. Her other instinct was to part her legs, tell him never mind with birth control and protection and demand he take her right there.

As that last bit was only ever going to happen in her fantasies, she contented herself with stretching out her arm and lightly grazing the tip of him with her fingers.

He stiffened instantly, then turned to look at her.

If she'd had any doubts about his willingness to participate, they were put to rest by the fire in his eyes and the tightness of his expression. He was a man on the sexual edge, and she couldn't wait to push him over.

He shook his head and forced his attention back to the shaving kit. At first he set the various items on the foot of the sleeping bag, but after a couple of seconds, he simply turned the container over and dumped out the contents.

"Be here, be here, be here," he muttered as he pawed through everything. Then he grabbed a square packet in triumph. "Got one."

She couldn't help smiling. "Only one?"

He grinned. "We'll have to be creative after that."

He handed her the condom, then clicked off the light. "Where was I?" he asked.

"You can pretty much be anywhere you want to be," she told him.

"Good. Then I want to be here."

He pulled off her panties in one smooth move. Then there was nothing. She tensed in anticipation. A whisper of breath was her only warning. One second he was beside her, the next, he kissed the inside of her ankle. She jumped in surprise.

"What are you doing?" she asked, even as she parted her thighs.

"You're a smart woman. You figure it out."

He kissed his way up to her knee, then moved between her legs and nibbled higher. Up and up and up until he pressed an openmouthed kiss just at that hollow by her hip.

"That's not right," he teased, even as he licked her tummy. "I was looking for something else."

Anticipation had reached such a fevered pitch that Phoebe wasn't sure she could talk—even to give directions. She could only send loud telepathic messages instructing Zane on the right place to press that tongue of his. Fortunately, the man was pretty darned good at mind reading.

He slipped from her tummy to the promised land in three seconds flat. This time, she didn't have warning, but that was okay. She didn't mind the surprise of his gentle caress pleasuring the most intimate parts of her.

She parted her legs even more and raised her hips in a silent invitation. He moved slowly, discovering, tasting, whispering how good this all was for him.

She wanted to tell him he should try it from her perspective, but she couldn't form words. She couldn't even think. All she could do was feel the liquid heat spiraling through her. Feel the tensing of her muscles as he explored all of her before settling on that one spot designed to send her into paradise. Feel the heavenly pressure of the finger he slipped inside her.

He moved in tandem, slow, then a little faster. She rocked her head back and forth, her breathing increasing. Her eyes opened, but in the darkness there was nothing to see.

Her climax approached with a speed that left her breathless. She couldn't be ready so soon, but she couldn't—didn't want—to make him stop.

"Zane," she whispered. "I can't—"

He didn't respond. Probably a good thing, she thought with her last bit of conscious-ness, right before she lost control and gave herself over to her release.

Every cell in her body became caught up in the abandon that was her orgasm. Pleasure encompassed her. There was so much inside her, it went on and on, Zane drawing it out, moving slower, more gently, silently urging her to surrender all she had to him.

At last, when she could breathe and think and move, she sighed.

"That was amazing," she told him.

He kissed the top of her thigh. "For me,

too."

She heard him sit up and prepared to pass over the condom. But before she could, she felt his finger enter her again. Just the finger.

It shouldn't have been that exciting, but there was something about the way he touched her. She'd just had more than her fill of orgasms, but she couldn't help clamping around him, drawing him in deeper.

"Good?" he asked.

"Oh, yeah. Don't stop."

Without thinking, she reached down and grabbed his wrist. Holding his hand still, she thrust her hips forward and back, finding the right pace until the heavy tension returned, and she felt the telltale contractions begin again.

He swore softly. "Can you do that while I'm inside of you?"

"Absolutely."

She pulled his hand free and pressed the condom into his palm. "Can you put this on in the dark?"

He chuckled. "With you as motivation, I could probably put it on after I was dead."

Then he was pressing against her.

She reached between them and guided him inside of her. As he entered her, she contracted around him. He filled her slowly, stretching her, delighting her. Each thrust was enough to send her flying.

Zane shifted so he could hold on to her hips. "I can feel you coming," he murmured. "You're killing me. I can't hold on much longer."

"Go for it," she told him.

He took her at her word. Moving faster and faster, he pulled out of her, then slipped back inside. She lost herself in the movement, in what she was feeling. The pleasure was greater than any she'd ever experienced. Maybe it was a fluke. Maybe it was something about being outdoors or the placement of the moon. Whatever. At this point, she didn't much care.

Instead, as she felt Zane tensing for his own release, she wrapped her legs around him and pulled him close. One last shudder rippled through her. She gave herself up to the feel of him, to the sudden weight as he wrapped his arms around her and groaned his surrender.

CHAPTER EIGHTEEN

Phoebe had always dreaded the awkward moments of "after." After making love. Not that she had a lot of experience with that sort of thing. She'd had lovers before, just not tons. And in her world, the after part was fraught with peril.

Usually there was the whole cuddle versus not cuddle. Plus the conversation. Often the conversation went along the lines of "was it good for you?" Because it wasn't always. Sometimes it wasn't at all. Generally she walked around the truth, not wanting to hurt anyone's feelings.

For an assortment of reasons, she often wished to avoid the whole postcoital chit-chat. So she'd never once in her entire life had to lie there, flushed with an incredibly relaxed feeling while fighting growing humiliation over her body's inability to stop having orgasms.

"I'm sorry," she whispered.

Zane shifted off of her. "What?"

"I shouldn't have done that."

"Done what?"

She heard the caution in his voice.

"I was too...you know."

"I don't know," he said. "Too, what?"

"Wanton."

There wasn't any sound. Not even a hint of sound. Then he laughed. It wasn't a chuckle. It was a huge, from-the-belly laugh. The kind that made it impossible for the person laughing to move or breathe or even stop.

"Zane?" She shook his arm.

He continued to laugh. The sound seemed to echo all around them.

"Zane, stop. You'll wake up everyone."

That seemed to get his attention. She sensed his attempt to control himself, although a few guffaws escaped.

"This isn't funny," she told him in a heated whisper.

He leaned close. She couldn't see him, but she could feel him.

"Phoebe, you're the most amazing lover I've ever had. You're sexy, responsive to the point of being a lethal weapon, sweet, funny, caring and if I had a box of condoms, I'd use every single one before sunup. But you're not wanton."

His words made her feel a little better, but only a little. "I don't usually, you know, climax that much. Or at all."

"You did with me."

"I know."

"I wanted to please you."

She smiled. "I could tell."

"So what's the problem?"

"I don't want you to think less of me."

He touched her cheek, then outlined her mouth. "I think the world of you."

Her concern faded like mist in sunlight. "Really?"

He kissed her. "Absolutely."

Zane should have known Phoebe wouldn't be like other women, he thought as he settled next to her and pulled her against him. Not out of bed and certainly not in it.

"Anything else you want to worry about?" he asked, sure there was.

"Well…" She sighed. "I know guys aren't into the whole all-night thing. I should probably go stay with Maya until morning."

They were lying naked on his sleeping bag, their legs tangled, his fingers in her hair. He could smell her and their recent lovemaking. After sex most women wanted to talk, and he didn't doubt that Phoebe was in the mood for a lengthy discussion on emotions—particularly his.

Normally that would send him running for the hills. He liked his relationships easy, with well-defined rules. No caring, no commitments and definitely no spending the night.

Which meant it was crazy for him to say, "You can stay here if you don't mind the cramped quarters."

She shifted in his arms. He guessed she was peering at him in the darkness. "Really?"

"Sure."

"Okay. I'd like that. But we have to get up early so no one knows I spent the night here."

"Cookie's going to figure it out when I don't show up to share the wagon with him in this rain, but don't worry. He won't say anything."

"Good."

They made their way into the sleeping bag. It was crowded, and she was still naked, so it only took about three seconds for him to get hard again.

She reached between them. "Are you sure there aren't any more condoms?"

He flexed at her words, then groaned softly. It was going to be a long night. "Positive."

He was torn between asking her to stop tormenting him and begging her to keep on doing it. The outcome of the latter was inevitable, and in a sleeping bag, more than a little messy.

Just a few seconds more, he told himself as he closed his eyes and gave himself up to the steady stroking of her hand. He would stop her before things got out of control.

But Phoebe being Phoebe and his attraction to her being what it was, that point of "out of control" arrived a lot faster than he would have realized. Painfully aroused and right on the edge, he grabbed her wrist.

"You're killing me."

"So not my purpose."

Then she stunned him by opening the sleeping bag, pushing it away and sliding down between his legs. As her fingers toyed with his testicles, her mouth settled on his erection. From there it was a thirty-seven-second journey to heaven.

Later, when he'd returned the favor and they were back in the sleeping bag and tangled together, Zane allowed himself to wonder what life would be like with Phoebe. Would she enjoy his world or would the wide-open spaces wear on her? He had a feeling she would hold genealogy classes for the goats and self-actualization classes for the steers. She would make him crazy, and she would make him laugh.

She would love him.

Phoebe was the kind of woman who, once she committed to a man, would give her heart completely. She would love with her whole being, and forever, unless the guy was a complete jerk and broke her heart. Phoebe was made to love and be loved.

She could never be for him. He didn't want to love anyone—ever. Love was isolation and danger and pain. Which meant he should have told her to head over to Maya's tent. Safer for him and for her.

Instead he pulled her sleeping body close to his and lightly kissed her hair.

Tomorrow, he promised himself. He would end this tomorrow. Was it so wrong to want to have this one night to remember?

Zane awakened them both early. By the time Chase stirred, he had both their tents down and was on his third cup of coffee. Phoebe had promised she could act completely normal, but looking at her from across the fire, he wasn't so sure. There was no way anyone could see her dreamy expression and not know something was different.

She tucked a strand of hair behind her ear. "What? You keep looking at me. I know my makeup can't be smudged. I'm not wearing any."

It didn't matter; she was still beautiful.

"You look different," he told her. "Satisfied."

Color flared on her cheeks. "You're only saying that because you know the truth."

"Uh-huh."

He doubted that, but maybe she was right. Or maybe the weather would be enough of a distraction to keep everyone from figuring out the truth.

"How long is it going to rain?" she asked

as she fingered a pole holding up the canvas sheet they put up to protect the fire and the seating area around it. "It sure got cold and damp in a hurry."

Zane shrugged. "No way to tell. The storm is supposed to hang around for a few days, but maybe it will blow over."

He hoped it would. Traveling in the rain wouldn't be fun for anyone. And he couldn't simply turn them around, head to the ranch and be there in time for lunch. They were at the farthest point from his house. It was a full two-day ride back.

Phoebe finished her coffee. "I'm going to check and see if my things are dry," she said as she stood.

He nodded, then watched her go.

Cookie had started a second campfire on the far side of camp. Phoebe's clothes and sleeping bag were getting a dose of smoky warm air in an attempt to get them dry before they headed out. Zane knew the old man wouldn't tease Phoebe. Instead he would save his comments for Zane.

"Hey," Chase said as he approached. "The rain sucks."

"Agreed."

His younger brother settled on a log. "I checked on the cattle. They're fine. The clouds don't look like there's going to be any lightning or thunder, but they look plenty wet."

Zane nodded. "Storm's supposed to last two days. I was hoping it would hold off until Saturday."

Chase sipped his coffee. "Everybody okay?"

There was something about the question. Zane stared at him. "What do you mean?"

"Nothing. Just checking."

Had Chase heard something in the night? Zane shook his head. Not possible. His tent had been some distance from the others, and the rain had blocked out a lot of noise. Nothing about his brother's expression told what he was thinking.

"We're heading back today, right?" Chase said.

"That's the plan. I wish it wasn't a two-day ride."

"There's—"

Chase stopped speaking and stared at his coffee. Zane knew what he'd been about to say. Reilly's place. It was only about an hour's ride. The old man would give them shelter until the worst of the storm passed, and even send out a few of his men to watch over the cattle until then.

But Zane wasn't about to impose on his neighbor. Not now and not ever.

He glanced at the sky and wondered how long he could take a stand in weather like this. Whatever his issues with Reilly, his guests' safety came first.

"I better see how everyone's doing," he said as he tossed the rest of his coffee into the fire.

"Before you go," Chase said and held out something in his hand. "I wasn't sure if you had enough with you."

Zane stared at the three condoms resting on his brother's palm. Then he glanced at Chase, who was grinning.

"Way to go, big brother."

Not knowing what to say, Zane rose and stalked off. But not before he took the condoms. He might be stubborn, but he wasn't a fool.

For the first time since starting on the cattle drive, Phoebe wasn't having fun. It was wet and cold, and the bad weather showed no signs of letting up.

Lucy rode next to her. The girl was soaked to the skin, and Phoebe was afraid she'd started to shiver.

"Are you all right?" she asked.

Lucy nodded, but when she tried to speak, her teeth chattered.

This couldn't be good. Right now Phoebe was so darned happy that she could have survived a seven-day blizzard, keeping warm on the glow left over from her night with Zane, but there were more people on this cattle drive than just herself.

C.J. rode up. Her face tightened with obvious concern. "Lucy, honey, don't you have a raincoat? Your jacket is dripping."

"I'm ok-kay," the girl muttered. "I'm having fun."

C.J. glanced at Phoebe. "We can't go on like this," she said. "The kids will get sick."

Phoebe nodded, but before she could decide what to do, Rocky slipped in the thick mud on the trail.

The large horse sidestepped quickly and nearly went down. Phoebe shrieked as she clung to the saddle. After a couple of steps the long-legged horse managed to catch his balance. When she was able to breathe and relax her death grip, she looked up and saw Zane riding up.

"Everyone gather round," he yelled. "Chase, bring Martin and Thad over."

He wore a thick coat that looked as if it could repel any liquid known to man. His cowboy hat protected his face and neck and his leather gloves probably kept his hands warm.

So there was more to this Western wear than just fashion, Phoebe thought humorously. After last night, she could even understand the appeal of shirts with snaps. The easier to get undressed quickly.

Maya rode up and stopped next to her.

"This sucks," she said sourly. "I hate being wet."

Phoebe nodded. "It's no fun."

"I doubt it's going to get any better. I have no idea where we are, which probably means we're not that close to the ranch."

When all the folks had moved close to Zane, he spoke.

"We've hit a patch of bad weather, and I doubt it's going to let up anytime soon. We need to get to cover. The ranch is a good two-day ride from here."

Maya didn't look surprised at the news, but several people groaned.

Eddie shook her head. "Gladys and I are up for it, people. So you have to be, too."

Zane held up a gloved hand. "Don't worry. I'm not going to make you stay out in the rain that long. There's another ranch about an hour from here. We'll leave Chase and Cookie with the cattle and ride directly there. We should arrive before lunch."

Phoebe was stunned. "Reilly's place?"

Maya stared at her. "How do you know about Reilly?"

"He told me—about what happened before and why they don't get along."

Maya's eyes widened. "Wait a minute. He **told** you? Chase doesn't even know what happened. Tell me."

Phoebe wasn't about to betray Zane's confidence, but before she could say that, he spoke again.

"Thad will take one of the kids, and I'll take the other. We'll tie their horses to the back of Cookie's wagon."

"Why?" C.J. asked.

"Hypothermia. They're too small to survive in the rain and cold on their own."

C.J.'s face paled as she stared at Lucy
and Tommy. "I had no idea. Are they going
to be all right? I don't want anything to
happen to them."

Phoebe was warmed by her concern.
She'd come a long way in a short time.

"They'll be fine," Zane promised.

Thad slid off his horse and walked toward
Tommy. "Hey, big guy. You and me are
going to have some fun."

The boy was shivering too hard to do
much more than nod as Thad plucked him
off his mount. Zane moved his horse
next to Lucy's and simply grabbed the girl
around the waist. When she settled on the
saddle in front of him, he unbuttoned his
coat, tucked it around her, then fastened
the bottom three buttons.

"I wish he could do that with me," Maya
said with a shiver. She narrowed her gaze.
"But don't for a minute think all this means
I've forgotten. I want to know the secret."

"Later," Phoebe said, knowing she was
putting off the inevitable confrontation with
her friend.

But she didn't want to get into it now and have an audience while she explained that while she hadn't actually promised to keep Zane's secret, she felt obligated to protect him and his past. Her heart ached when she thought about all that had happened to him when he'd been Chase's age.

Thad wrapped Tommy in his coat and put a protective arm around the boy. C.J. leaned close and smoothed his hair off his face.

"You'll be warm soon," she promised.

Phoebe moved next to Zane. She smiled reassuringly at Lucy, then lowered her voice. "Reilly won't have a problem taking us in?" she asked.

He shook his head. "This is Fool's Gold. We look out for each other." His mouth curved in a smile. "I may be forced to bunk down in the barn, but you'll all be treated like honored guests."

Chase rode up. "All ready?"

"Just about. Grab the kids' horses. I'll be back in the morning. Stay sharp."

Chase grinned. "Cookie and I will hunker down in his wagon. Don't sweat it. We'll play cards."

"Not for money," Zane told him.

"Are you kidding? I don't want to get more in debt."

Cookie poked his head out from the wagon cover. "He'll be fine. I'll take good care of the boy. There's plenty of grazing for the steers, and God knows, they don't seem to notice the rain. Just get on back here tomorrow so we can head home."

"Will do," Zane promised and turned back to the group. "Let's go."

Phoebe waved goodbye to Manny, then urged Rocky forward.

Zane kept them at a walk until they'd left the herd behind, then he kicked his mount into a trot. Phoebe winced as her backside slapped against the hard saddle.

"S-sorry, buddy," she told Rocky. "I know this can't be pleasant for you."

She clung on as best she could while her insides were being pummeled into the consistency of a smoothie. When they'd cleared the trees, Zane urged his horse faster still.

She felt Rocky speed up, and suddenly his gait smoothed out. There was a back and forth rocking, but it was easy to stay in place. Plus, it felt like they were going really fast.

"Are we galloping?" she yelled to Maya.

Her friend grinned. "Not even close. This is a nice slow canter."

"I like this."

"Yeah. It cuts down on bruising."

They rode on through the rain, but knowing they were going to be out of it soon made Phoebe not mind about the damp cold. Whenever she started to shiver, she thought about the previous night, when she'd lost herself in Zane's arms. It wasn't just that he'd made her feel so good, it was that she'd felt so safe with him. Like she could say or be anything.

When the sensual memories got to be too much, she wondered if he was worried about facing Reilly again after all these years. Would the old man welcome him with open arms or torment him about the past? Phoebe found herself hoping Reilly would be kind.

At last they crested a rise, and she saw a well-tended ranch stretching out before them. She took in the tidy pastures, the secure fencing and the charm of the sprawling ranch house. A few minutes later they were sliding off their horses while Zane walked to the freshly painted red front door. It opened before he got there, and an old man stepped out.

He was thin and bent, with thick gray hair and dark eyes that seemed able to see through solid objects. He and Zane stared at each other for a long time before the old man spoke.

"Well, lookee here. Didn't expect to see you dripping on my front porch, Zane. What can I do you for?"

The words were pleasant, as was the man's smile. Phoebe relaxed a little even as she saw the tension in Zane's shoulders and heard the stiffness in his voice as he spoke.

"I need your help," he said, then explained what had gone wrong.

"Greenhorns on a cattle drive," Reilly said with a shake of his head. "I never thought I'd live to see the day." He looked past Zane and gestured everyone inside. "No sense in freezing off your privates. Get in here. I'll tell Matilda we've got company.

She'll be pleased. She gets tired of cooking for an old man with not much appetite."

They all trooped inside, introducing themselves as they passed their host. When it was Phoebe's turn, Reilly gave her a warm smile.

"Welcome to my home," he said.

"Thank you. You're very kind to offer us shelter."

He shrugged off her words. "Don't worry about that, little girl. I appreciate the company."

When Maya shook his hand, he frowned. "I've seen you before."

"I used to be Zane's stepsister."

Reilly grinned. "And your mama was that showgirl, right? Whoee, did she have some legs on her."

"Yeah, they were terrific," Maya muttered.

"Haven't seen you in town in a while," Eddie said to Reilly.

"Got no use for them festivals," he said. "Tourists make too much traffic."

Phoebe suppressed a smile. If he thought Fool's Gold traffic was bad, what would he think of LA rush hour?

When they'd all been introduced, Reilly

let them into a massive great room. There was a big fireplace at one end, with several large crackling logs. Phoebe joined the group as they headed directly for the smoky warmth. C.J. crouched down with Lucy and Tommy, rubbing their backs and hands to chase away the chill.

Reilly counted heads. "Hmm, a few of you are going to have to double up. I have a big place, but not that many bedrooms."

"We appreciate any hospitality you can offer us," Zane said stiffly.

Instinctively, Phoebe moved next to him. She wanted to take his hand, but wasn't sure if he would appreciate that. Instead she settled on standing close and offering silent moral support.

"I'm glad for the company, son. Now, who is married to whom? I want to get the bedroom situation right."

As Reilly figured out the sleeping arrangements, Phoebe gazed at the soaring ceilings and large windows. Even on such a gray and stormy day, light filtered into the house. There were exposed beams, old hardwood floors that were beautiful enough to belong in a museum and dozens of stunning antiques. From the center of the great room, she could see into a dining room and a library that were just as impressive. A place like this would be at least fifteen million in Beverly Hills. She figured it would have to be well into seven figures even outside a small town in the mountains of Northern California.

"Isn't it gorgeous?" Maya said as she moved nearer to Phoebe. "I always heard old man Reilly was loaded. Apparently his grandfather hit it rich in a gold rush or two. He's only spent his life herding cattle because he likes it. Oh, we're sharing a room. We'll each have a real bed. Doesn't that sound like heaven?"

Phoebe nodded, but what she was thinking was that however much she liked her friend, she would rather share a room with Zane. Speaking of which...

"Are you okay?" she asked him, her voice low.

"Fine."

She couldn't tell from looking at him, nor did she know what he was thinking. Still, this wasn't exactly the time or place to discuss something so personal and she couldn't figure out a way to point out that Reilly was being great about the unexpected invasion.

"Now, you folks probably want to get to your rooms and dry off," Reilly said. "Let me show you where those are. Danny will bring in your things when he puts up the horses."

"I can do that," Zane said.

Reilly slapped him on the back. "You're a guest, son. I'll take care it."

Zane offered a gruff, "Thank you."

Reilly led the way upstairs. The kids' room was first, with C.J. and Thad across the hall. Next up were Eddie and Gladys, then Phoebe and Maya.

"This is my grandson's old room," Reilly told them. "Ryder's in Kenya now, taking pictures for **National Geographic**. He's single, you know. I keep tellin' him he needs to find a woman and settle down." He winked as he spoke. "Now, you let me know if you need anything."

"He's charming," Maya said when they were alone. "I can't believe he and Zane are fighting." She plopped down on one of the beds and stared meaningfully at

Phoebe. "So? Start talking."

Phoebe felt her stomach clench. "I can't. Zane told me in confidence."

Maya raised her eyebrows. "Am I or am I not your best friend?"

She winced. "We both know you can probably guilt it out of me, but I wish you wouldn't. I don't want to betray Zane."

Maya studied her. "So things have progressed even further than I thought."

"I... We..." Phoebe sank onto the other bed and covered her face with her hands. "Help."

Maya surprised her by laughing. "Okay, kid. I'm giving you a break because we are best friends, and I don't want to snap your moral backbone. But you owe me."

"Forever," Phoebe promised, grateful to be off the hook.

While Maya dried her hair, Phoebe took a couple of minutes to explore the room. Framed nature photographs covered almost every inch of wall space. The frames looked homemade, and she could imagine Reilly building one every time his grandson sent a new picture.

There was a close-up of a polar bear,

every ice-white hair on its massive body in sharp focus. Next to it, a baby monkey clung to its mother as she leaped between trees. Over the dresser was an oversize print of a daredevil in a skintight platinum-colored bodysuit, riding a surfboard in the sky. The color and the daring combined to make Phoebe catch her breath. And on the nightstand, there was a portrait of Reilly with the man she assumed was his grand-son, Ryder. He looked to be about twenty in the picture, though she assumed with all of his world traveling that he was older now.

A bathroom was attached to the bed-room. After sighing over the thrill of indoor plumbing and coming up with a schedule for the shower and Jacuzzi tub, they headed down to lunch.

Matilda might have only had forty-five minutes' notice, but she'd still managed to put together a lunch that rivaled Cookie's best meal.

There was stew, and spaghetti and garlic bread, a salad, cut-up fruit and chocolate cake for dessert. Phoebe slid into a high wood chair across from Zane and offered him a smile.

"This is really nice," she said.

He grunted.

She studied his tight expression and the wariness in his eyes. Obviously his claim to be "fine" was overstated.

But before she could say anything, the rest of their group entered the room and took seats. Then Reilly joined them.

There was plenty of food to go around, and lots of conversation. Reilly entertained them with stories about Ryder's photo adventures around the world. He found out a little about each guest, then turned his attention to Zane.

"I didn't know you'd started offering cattle drives," he said.

Zane grunted. Phoebe wasn't surprised he didn't respond any other way. He didn't want everyone to know why they were on the cattle drive.

Reilly looked as if he might probe a little, so Phoebe tried to change the topic.

"Your house is beautiful," she said. "The craftsmanship is amazing, and there are so many unique architectural elements."

"Well, thank you, Phoebe. A lot of that is

my mother's doing. She had big plans and a real eye for detail. To me this was always the place where I grew up. Now, with my kids and grandson gone, it's a big, empty house. Ryder insists he's never going to want to settle down. That boy was born with itchy feet. I'm thinking about selling." He shrugged. "If the right offer came along, I'd take it."

Across from her, Zane stiffened, but Phoebe barely noticed. A picture had flashed in her brain. A picture of a man describing his dream house, including the isolated location, with plenty of land. But something unique.

She looked around at the carved molding in the dining room and the inlaid flooring. Was this the place Jonny Blaze had been talking about?

Zane wandered restlessly through the house. He hated being here nearly as much as he hated being indebted to Reilly. No doubt the old bastard was gloating. Once again he'd gotten the better of him.

He crossed to a window and stared out at the storm. The afternoon was gray and cold. He knew he didn't have to worry about Chase. The kid would be fine. Cookie's wagon was more than enough protection for the two of them. And in this kind of rain, the cattle weren't likely to do much more than hunker down and endure. But he couldn't help worrying. And thinking. The past was always close, and in this house, it threatened to overwhelm him.

Determined not to give in, he went searching for Phoebe. He found her in a back office by the kitchen. She was working on a computer.

"Hey," he said as he entered.

She glanced up and practically beamed. "Oh, Zane, isn't this place amazing? And you know what? Reilly has Wi-Fi. I've already sent off pictures of the inside. I didn't want to get any of the exterior, what with it raining and all, but Reilly had some and I scanned those in. I even caught Jonny Blaze at home. He's thrilled by what he's seen so far. In fact he's talking about making an offer, sight unseen. Is that just the best? Of course I'd have to get the deal through before I get my license revoked, but still. Reilly will get what he wants, Jonny

Blaze will have his private retreat and I'll get a commission that is..."

She sucked in a breath. "Well, I can't do the math in my head, but it's going to be a lot, which is so cool."

He stared at her, unable to believe what she was saying. "Jonny Blaze?"

"You remember."

"I sure as hell do. You can't sell this place to some movie star."

The words came out as a roar. Phoebe's eyes darkened with confusion, and she slowly rose.

"What's wrong? Zane? Are you worried he's going to throw parties and put up a theme park or something? It won't be like that. Jonny really respects the environment. He wants the acreage for privacy. In fact he'd probably be delighted to sell you his cattle and let them run on this land. Do cattle run? Is **graze** a better word?" Her expression softened. "Don't worry, Zane. I've already told Jonny that there's a strip of land he can't have. If this deal goes through, you'll get it back."

"Like charity?"

"No. Of course not. It's yours. It's always

been yours. I thought…"

"The hell you did." He glared at her. "You can't do this."

"Why not?"

A voice came from behind them. "You gonna tell her, boy? Or am I?"

CHAPTER NINETEEN

Zane spun around and saw Reilly standing in the doorway. Figured the old man would show up now.

"She already knows."

Reilly shrugged. "So what's the big deal? We all get what we want."

Zane couldn't explain. What words would tell either of them that he had to earn back the land? That only through pain and suffering could he make it right. Even then —who knew if the ghosts would be happy at last?

He tried to tell himself that it didn't matter. Not after all this time. The thing was, he couldn't make himself believe it.

Reilly was going to sell the land to some movie star, and Zane would never get the chance to make things right. Sure, Phoebe would make sure he got his acreage back, but that wasn't enough. He wouldn't have proved anything.

"Crazy," he muttered to himself as he stared out the window at the rain. "You're more than crazy."

Zane knew it to be true. His father had been dead for years. What was there to prove and make right? Were there any ghosts outside of those he'd created himself? So what did the land really mean after all this time? He'd done fine without it. Better than fine. He'd done the one thing his father had never been able to do—run the ranch at a profit.

Zane had inherited acres of land and enough debt to sink it, but he'd managed to pull off the impossible. He'd paid off every penny and now had enough in the bank to secure the future of several generations. So why wasn't that enough? Why did he feel the coldness of his father's disappointment breathing down his neck?

Phoebe moved close and wrapped her arms around him. He accepted the embrace for a second, then stepped back. Her dark eyes widened.

"I need to think this through," he said. "Alone."

He saw the pain in her expression and wished he could make it better. But how? He'd learned over and over that there was no way to fix what had been done and that forgiveness was a gift always withheld.

She swallowed. "If you change your mind, if you want to talk, you know how to find me."

Her acceptance both awed and annoyed him. "Don't you ever stop giving?"

She considered the question. "I don't think I can. It's a part of who I am."

Of course, he thought, seeing the truth for the first time. Phoebe was light. She was bright and good and loving. Whatever the circumstances of her life, she could be proud of who she was and what she brought to this world.

And what was he? What kind of man had he become?

Phoebe thought she would sleep, what with having been awake most of the previous night. But instead of drifting off like Maya had done within fifteen seconds of them turning out the lights, she'd lain on her back and stared up at the dark ceiling.

She couldn't stop thinking about Zane. Nothing new, she told herself. The man had become an important part of her world. For a while she'd had a simple crush on him. Then she'd started to think the attraction was mutual. Then they'd made love, and she hadn't needed to think aside from the fact that she was blissfully happy, and now she was confused. Again.

She knew he was in pain—both about the land and what had happened with his father. She'd recognized the pain in his eyes. She'd wanted to comfort him, but he wasn't the kind of man who welcomed that sort of intimacy. If only he was.

With a sigh she rose and pulled on jeans, then replaced her sleep shirt with a long-sleeved T-shirt. Barefoot, she walked to the door and let herself out into the hall-way, one of the books she'd purchased in Fool's Gold tucked under her elbow. If she couldn't think herself to sleep, maybe she could find a quiet place to read.

She made it to the top of the stairs before she heard something. A slight creaking made her turn around while a dark shadow loomed in the darkness.

"Phoebe?"

Her breath caught as she recognized the voice. "Zane? What are you doing up?"

"I can't sleep. I was lurking outside of your room, trying to figure out how to talk to you without waking Maya."

He wanted to talk to her? Really?

She moved toward him. "Here I am."

Instead of saying anything, he took her hand and led her down the hall. They entered the bedroom he'd been given, and when he'd closed the door behind them, he hit the light switch.

One of the bedside lamps came on, illuminating the small room. There was a double bed, a dresser and a door to a bathroom.

She turned to ask him what he wanted, but before she could speak, he took the book from her and set it aside, wrapped his arms around her and pulled her close.

"I'm sorry," he whispered, pressing his cheek against her hair. "I'm such a jackass."

She rubbed her hands up and down his back. He was warm and alive and next to her. Nothing else really mattered.

"Jackass seems strong," she murmured.

"How about a first-class screwup?"

"If you're going to do a job, then do it the best you can."

He chuckled low in his throat. "Gee, thanks."

"You're welcome."

He drew back and took her hand. Tugging her along, he walked to the bed, then pulled her down next to him.

"You're a hell of a woman," he said as he brushed the hair from her face.

Her? "I'm not all that special."

"Sure you are. You're fearless."

"So are you."

He shook his head. "Not even close. I'm sorry I pushed you away before. I'm not used to sharing my troubles. When I was a kid—" He shrugged. "I was a complete screwup. Just like Chase. My old man never understood. Whenever things went bad, he'd give me this look. I think I have it, too. Chase calls it the 'death-ray look.'"

Phoebe angled toward him, shifted so she tucked one foot under her. "It's tough when we disappoint a parent."

"Worse than tough," he said, staring past her.

Her heart ached for him. Phoebe took his hand and squeezed. "Your father was wrong. He sounds like a difficult, mean man who couldn't see how he was destroying his son."

"This isn't about me."

"Of course it is. There's a part of you deep inside that still hurts." She released his hand and cupped his face. "I would do anything to go back in time and hold that little boy and tell him it's okay."

Zane started to pull back. She didn't want to let him go. Not just yet. Not while he was hurting so much she could feel the pain surrounding him. His wound ate away at him, making him hollow. She wanted to crawl inside and fill that space.

"Don't you ever give up?" he asked hoarsely.

"Not really. It's a flaw."

"No, it's not."

He reached for her and pulled her close. Then they were stretched out on the bed, their arms around each other and nothing in the world mattered but being together.

She surged forward as he dropped his head, and they met in a kiss that quickly consumed them. Heat, need and desire exploded into an out-of-control fire.

He touched her everywhere, and she

touched him back. Breasts, chest, back, hips, legs. She felt the length of his muscles, the power of his shoulders. Her mouth parted as he plunged inside of her. Tongues met, stroked, danced, as her blood pounded and flowed in a hot, passionate river of wanting.

His long fingers found her breasts and squeezed them. Her nipples were already hard, and the brush of his thumbs against the tight tips made her whimper. She hadn't pulled on a bra, and she was desperate to feel his hands on her bare skin.

"Naked," she whispered against his mouth.

She wasn't sure if she meant him or herself. Nor did it matter. He pulled back enough to allow her to drag off her T-shirt.

While his gaze devoured her bare chest, he worked the buttons of his shirt, then jerked off the garment. She had already unfastened her jeans and quickly pushed them and her panties off. Even as he reached for his belt, he scrambled off the bed and headed for the bathroom. Seconds later he was back, naked and clutching a handful of condoms.

"Don't ask," he said when she glanced at them and raised her eyebrows.

She decided it didn't matter how or where he'd gotten them. All that was important was that he put one on and get inside of her right now!

She moved to the center of the bed as he flung himself beside her. The square packets of protection went flying. One landed on her belly, and she grabbed for it.

Zane raised himself on an elbow and bent over her. His mouth brushed against hers before moving lower to her neck. He licked and kissed and nibbled his way to the sensitive skin below her ear, then lower still to her chest. At the same time, he ran his hand down her belly.

She parted her legs long before he arrived. His fingers found her center at the exact moment his mouth closed over her left nipple. Breath escaped as she moaned her pleasure.

Tongue and fingers moved in tandem, circling, rubbing, teasing, pleasuring. She reached between them and took his erection in her hand. He was already rock hard. As she closed around him, he shuddered.

His touch between her legs slowed slightly, then the pace resumed.

He shifted so he could rub her with his thumb while pushing two fingers inside her. At the same time he kissed his way up her chest and neck until he reached her ear.

"I want you to come for me," he whispered. "Now. I want to feel your muscles contract around my fingers. I want to hear your breathing catch, and I want you to scream."

The erotic image of his words made her shiver, then tense. She opened her eyes and realized that, unlike the previous night in the tent, this time she could see him. All of him. And that he could see her. And that he was looking.

Their gazes locked as he continued to touch her. He moved a little faster, pushed a little harder until she felt herself losing control. Then he kissed her, dipping into her mouth, mimicking the actions between her legs.

It was just enough to send her over the edge. She felt her eyes flutter closed as her release claimed her.

Pleasure rushed through her in waves of contractions. She arched her body toward him, sucked in her breath and maybe even screamed. Fortunately the sound was muffled by Zane's kiss.

He continued to touch her, gentling the contact, slowing, until every last shudder had stilled, and she could think again.

"You're so beautiful," he told her when she looked at him. "All of you."

She made a leisurely, visual exploration of his muscled chest, his flat belly, his jutting erection. He was a man who worked hard, and it showed.

"So are you." She touched a scar on his thigh. "Want to tell me how you got that?"

"Not right now."

He knelt between her legs, and she handed him the condom. As he ripped open the package, she brushed her fingers against the tip of his arousal. He flexed in response.

Anticipation filled her. She wanted him inside her. She wanted to feel him getting closer, even as she lost herself in what they were doing. She wanted to touch him everywhere, to be held by him. She wanted to love him.

Words clogged her throat, and then he

was pushing inside her and speaking didn't matter anymore.

Her body stretched to accommodate him. She drew her legs back to bring him in deeper. More. She wanted more.

When his arms came around her, she clutched his hips. They kissed. The rhythm of his body filling her made her pulse her hips. Anticipation spiraled to tension. He moved harder and faster, making her suck on his tongue. She dug her fingers into him.

The bed creaked, and outside thunder shattered the silence of the night. Phoebe didn't care. There was only the moment, the man and what they were doing together. Then she lost control. Her orgasm claimed her, shattering her. She could only cling to him as he called out her name and sank into his own release.

Later, when they'd turned out the lights and found their way under the covers, she snuggled close to him. The sound of his heartbeat filled her with contentment.

He was asleep. She could tell by his steady breathing. By the way he stirred in his dreams. While he slept, she laced their fingers together and spoke the words she hadn't found the courage to say any other time.

"I love you."

The arm around her tightened. His leg moved against hers, and he sighed.

"Love you, too, Phoebe."

His voice, thick and barely audible, made her heart stop. Her eyes popped open, and she couldn't seem to catch her breath.

Had he really said the words or had she imagined them? If he had said them, was it something he'd mumbled in his sleep? An almost automatic response? Or had he meant them?

The questions haunted her for hours, until sometime before dawn when exhaustion gave way to slumber, and she finally relaxed against him.

A loud pounding pushed Zane into consciousness. In less than two seconds he was aware of a very naked Phoebe curled up against him and the sound of his brother's voice calling his name.

"Hold on," he yelled back and reached

for his jeans.

As he stumbled from the bed, Phoebe stirred. "What is it?"

"Trouble."

Zane knew Chase would never leave the cattle if something wasn't wrong.

He collected his jeans and pulled them on, then walked to the door.

"What?" he asked as he opened the door and slipped into the hallway. He was careful to make sure Chase couldn't see Phoebe in his bed.

His brother looked wet and miserable. "The water's rising," he said quickly. "Fast. Cookie's moving the wagon. We need to get some men out there right now, Zane. We've got an hour at most."

Zane swore. He'd been aware of the steady rain, but he hadn't thought the rivers would swell up so fast. **Must still be some runoff pouring in**, he thought.

Up and down the hallway, doors opened. Martin stepped out of his room, as did Thad. Maya stumbled out, as well.

"What's going on?" Thad asked.

"Water's rising," Chase said. "We have to move the cattle."

"I'll talk to Reilly," Zane said. "Get some of his men to help."

The old man appeared. He'd pulled a bathrobe over pajamas. "I heard," he said when Chase started to explain. He shook his head. "Zane, I'm sorry, but I sent two crews out to repair fences and gave everyone else a long weekend. There's no one here but me and old Danny who looks after the horses. He's so bent with arthritis, he can't ride anymore. But I'll come help."

Zane groaned. The three of them weren't enough to get fifty head of wet cattle moving. Not when they had to cross a river to get to safety.

He looked at Chase and saw panic in his brother's eyes. "That's not enough," Chase said.

"Should I call the Strykers?" Eddie asked, her phone at the ready.

"Yeah, call them, thanks. But we don't have time to wait, and I don't know if they're going to be able to find us in time. They can't come in Jeeps this time. They're going to have to ride, and we're clear on the other side of the spread."

"I'll go," Thad said.

Zane looked at him in surprise. "I appreciate the offer, but this isn't part of your vacation. This is hard, dangerous work. Cold and wet, too."

Thad shrugged. "I want to help. I can ride and point the steers in the right direction. Will that be enough?"

"I'll go, too," Martin said.

"Me, too."

The last voice came from behind him. Zane turned to see Phoebe leaning against the wall.

Maya groaned. "Dammit, Phoebe, if you go, I'll have to, as well. Do you know what this weather is going to do to my hair?"

Phoebe smiled. "Wear a hat."

"Oh, yeah, that'll help in this rain."

"You don't have to do this," Zane said. "Not any of you."

"We know that," Thad said. "We're all in this together. Now I say we head out and save us some cattle."

Chase nodded. "They're greenhorns, Zane, but there's plenty of them. Without them, we can't get the herd to safety."

Zane knew his brother was right. He didn't have a choice. Not if he wanted to save the steers.

"Get the horses saddled up," he told Chase. "We'll be out in five minutes." He turned back to everyone else. "Dress warmly. Make the top layer as waterproof as you can." He nodded at Eddie and Gladys. "We'll need some food."

Eddie nodded, then grabbed Andrea and C.J. and pulled them toward the stairs.

Zane turned to Phoebe, who smiled at him. "They're going to help," she said.

He frowned. "I know."

"They like you. We all like you."

"Oh. My. God."

He turned and saw Maya staring at him.

"I just got it," she said. "You had sex with Phoebe." She looked at Phoebe. "You had sex with Zane. I can't decide if this is great or too gross for words."

Phoebe laughed.

Zane walked toward his room. "Just get dressed."

CHAPTER TWENTY

Phoebe knew that it had to be after dawn. There was a milky quality to the horizon that hinted at light somewhere above the thick, gray clouds, but she was beginning to feel she would never see the sun again. She was also wetter and colder than she'd believed possible. Her clothes were soaked, and her body temperature had dropped from freezing to pain. She found it difficult to hold on to her reins, even with the gloves Reilly had given her to wear.

Water dripped off her hat and splashed onto Rocky. She'd given up apologizing to the horse. She knew he was as miserable as she was, and there weren't any words to make up for that.

But still she followed Martin, who followed Zane. She forced herself to stay positive, to think about last night rather than the moment. To remember the passion she and Zane had shared. To recall him saying he loved her. Even if he hadn't meant it, those were words she would treasure forever.

Finally, after what felt like hours, they reached the cattle. Phoebe was stunned to find the animals standing in knee-deep water. She could see the rushing current as the area flooded, and for the first time, she was afraid.

"Gather round," Zane yelled, motioning for them to get closer.

When everyone had huddled together, he called out their instructions over the drumming of the rain.

"The cattle are restless from the water," he told them. "Stay alert. Given the choice between losing one of them and losing one of you, I want you to save yourself."

"Good to know," Maya muttered from Phoebe's left. "What if it's the choice between me and two steers?"

Zane either didn't hear her or ignored her.

"We're going to head for higher ground. We have to cross a stream and then head through an open pasture. The pasture slopes up, and we'll be safe once we're there. But to get there, we're heading downhill."

Phoebe glanced at the swirling water all

around them and swallowed hard. Downhill would not have been her first choice.

"We're going to work in groups," Zane said loudly. "Reilly will take Martin and Maya. I'll take Thad. Chase—" he looked at his brother "—you've got Phoebe."

Phoebe was about to ask why she needed her own personal escort when Zane swung around to face her. "I want you up front with Manny. You and Chase are going to lead the herd. Manny knows you and Rocky, and he'll follow you. It's dangerous, Phoebe. You're going to have to be careful. No stopping to talk to trees. I mean it."

She nodded.

Zane turned to his brother. "Chase, you know what you're up against."

"Yeah."

He jerked his head in her direction. "I'm counting on you to keep her safe."

Phoebe felt her heart stumble over a beat. A thousand thoughts flashed through her mind—all thrilling, all wonderful. Zane wanted her kept safe? He was trusting his brother with her? Feelings of love and happiness rose faster than the water, but before she could dwell on any one, Zane yelled for them to move on out. Suddenly Chase was at her side and pointing in the direction they were to go.

As she turned her horse, she realized they were going to ride into the rain. The driving cold water found her nose and eyes, no matter how low she pulled her hat. Her feet were painful blocks of ice, her thighs ached.

They circled the herd until they were in front, then Chase cut in and found Manny. He gave the steer a push with his foot. Manny didn't budge.

Chase swore loud enough for Phoebe to hear, but Manny wasn't impressed. The steer just settled his shoulders into what looked like a very stubborn stance and mooed pathetically.

Without thinking, Phoebe swung down from Rocky. The water came past the top of her boots and poured inside. It was colder than she would have believed possible—so cold that she couldn't breathe. But she forced herself to wade through it toward Manny, dragging her horse with her.

She could feel a current sucking at her

with each step. Once she nearly went down, and she had to grab on to Rocky to stay standing. Finally she reached Manny and got right in his face.

When he saw her, he reared back and got a really mean look on his face. Phoebe panicked for a second, then remembered she was wearing a hat. Quickly, she tore it off and tossed it away, letting the rain pour directly on her head.

But Manny recognized her, which was all that mattered. He sniffed at her wet coat, then lowered his head and bumped against her. She nearly fell on her butt.

"We have to get out of here," she told him, yelling directly into his ear. "I'm not kidding. If you stay here, you're going to drown."

Moisture dripped down her cheeks, and she realized she'd started crying.

"I don't want you to die. You hear me, Manny? So we're leaving. Right now. Come on."

She grabbed the collar around his n eck and pulled. Without his cooperation, she knew it was an impossible task, but surprisingly he took a step, then another.

Soon he was walking next to her, and the whole herd fell into place behind him.

After a couple of minutes, Chase moved in and dismounted. He swore as he sank into the water.

"Goddamn weather," he muttered. "Get on your horse, Phoebe."

"What if Manny won't follow Rocky?"

"You can't stay in the water. You'll die."

She tried to answer, but her teeth were chattering too hard. So when Chase laced his fingers together to give her a leg up, she stepped into his hands. Water splashed in an arc out of her boot as she swung her leg over the saddle.

Rocky didn't need much urging to head through the water. She watched over her shoulder and sighed in gratitude when she saw Manny following her. They were moving again. They were going to save the cattle.

It was only then that she realized how much she was shaking. There were no words to describe the level of cold she felt. Each breath was painful.

Chase pointed toward a grove of trees. "Go that way," he yelled. "To the left of them."

She nodded because she couldn't speak.

And so they rode for what felt like days. The rain lessened, then stopped altogether, but the water kept rising. In a way, that was more terrifying, because she had no idea where it was coming from or how much more was coming.

On and on, with Zane coming up to check on them every fifteen minutes or so. Hours passed. As he paused by her, she did her best to smile and say she was fine, even though she knew she was never going to be warm again. All that mattered right now was getting the cattle to safety. So, as often as Chase glanced toward her to make sure she was still there, she looked over her shoulder to see Manny walking behind Rocky.

Finally the sun broke through the clouds. Phoebe sighed in relief as the bright light heated her, although she was surprised by the position of the sun. It was later than she thought. Still, her spirits lifted as she realized they were climbing, and the water was quickly falling off.

"Are we there?" she asked Chase. "Have we done it?"

He shook his head. "We're nearly at the creek. Once we're on the other side, it's a straight climb up to safety. But we have to cross while we still have light. We don't have a choice. All this will be underwater by morning."

Underwater? She didn't like the sound of that. She was about to tell him when she realized she could hear something. Rushing water. And it sure didn't sound like a creek to her.

Phoebe nearly fainted when she crested the rise and saw the raging river in front of them. Water raced south, ripping at branches, pulling small trees into the bubbling, muddy flow.

"We can't cross that," she said.

"Sure we can. No problem."

Chase said the right words, but his voice told her he was more than worried. He was afraid.

Zane rode up. "How does it look?"

"There's no way," Phoebe said, pointing to the wide, angry river.

Zane looked from her to Chase. "I'll see if we can cross it. You stay here. If something happens..." He stared at his brother.

"Leave the cattle. They'll have to swim for it as the water rises. Ride south as fast as you can. You'll be able to find a place to cross farther downstream."

Phoebe stared at him. "Zane, no! Don't do this. We'll all go downstream. Together."

"We don't have much time. We have to try to save the cattle."

She didn't like this. Not any of it. But as she turned, she saw Manny and knew she couldn't abandon him. Not without trying to save him and his friends.

Then Zane was gone, heading toward the water. Phoebe held her breath as he entered the swirling, muddy current.

She wanted to yell out for him to be safe. She wanted to tell him that she loved him. But she didn't want to distract him, and she was busy praying for his safety.

She promised God just about anything He could possibly want if only He would keep Zane safe. She twisted the reins and willed her strength into Zane. Then she stopped breathing.

Zane's horse walked into the river and immediately stumbled. The animal righted itself, but not before Phoebe died at least twice. Zane guided the animal through the swirling water. When the horse began to swim, she thought she was going to faint.

"What's going— Holy shit," Maya breathed as she rode up next to Phoebe. "No way we're crossing that."

Phoebe didn't speak. She was too busy watching Zane. His horse went sideways two feet for every foot it moved forward, but finally it could reach ground, and it surged out the other side.

He took off his hat and waved it. "Piece of cake," he yelled.

"Talk about a liar," Maya muttered.

Twenty minutes later, Zane had ridden across the river to their side and rejoined them. A quick search of the banks found a nice low place to head into the water with a gradual bank on the other side.

"Here's how we're going to do it," Zane said as he rode up next to Phoebe. "Chase will go in first, then you. Manny will follow. I want the steer on your left, so he's downstream. If he loses his footing, I don't want him falling into you. Understand?"

She nodded because she was too scared to speak.

"Chase will be downstream of you both, so if something happens, relax. He'll catch you. Trust Rocky. He has long legs, and he'll only have to swim for a few feet." Zane hesitated. "You probably won't like what it feels like when he's swimming, but don't panic. Hold on to the saddle and go with it. He's strong, and he wants to get to the other side as much as you do."

Zane's fierce expression softened a little. "You can do this, Phoebe."

She looked at Manny and the other steers milling behind him. They were all counting on her, and she wasn't going to let them down.

"I'll be fine," she lied.

"Good. Now let me go tell everyone else what we're doing."

Phoebe only half listened while Zane explained the plan. He, Chase and Reilly would be downstream, while Martin, Thad and Maya would ride upstream of the herd. He warned them that the water was cold, to trust their horses and head for the bank. Then it was time to head out.

Phoebe waited for Chase to lead the way. When he hit the water, he started swearing.

His combinations were so colorful that she started to laugh...right up until the icy river reached her feet and instantly soaked her boots. It was even colder than the last time.

The water sucked the breath right out of her. She wanted to turn back and say she couldn't do this, but she didn't. Instead she thought of Zane, of Manny and all the steers. She had to be brave. This mattered.

As Rocky moved forward, she turned to see Manny entering the water. The steer stopped. Phoebe reined in Rocky.

"Come on, Manny," she called. "You can do it."

The steer shuddered, then slowly moved toward her.

"That's it," she yelled. "Manny. Come on, big guy. Race you to the other side."

The next few steers entered the water.

Phoebe was so intent on urging Manny forward that she forgot to watch where they were going. Suddenly Rocky stumbled, then lurched. She was nearly thrown.

"Phoebe!"

She heard Zane cry out, but she couldn't answer. She reached for the saddle, the reins, anything. But her cold fingers wouldn't cooperate. She felt herself falling into the icy, rushing water.

"Chase!" Zane yelled.

"I see her. Phoebe, grab on."

She was trying. Desperately. She scrambled to stay in the saddle. She could almost reach the edge of the leather, but just then Rocky began to swim. The change in movement made her slip more.

Something large hit her in the back of the thigh, and she was thrust forward and up. Her fingers grabbed for the saddle, and this time she connected with the wet, slippery leather. She regained her balance. It was only when she was hanging on that she was able to glance down and see Manny right next to her horse. The old steer looked up, and in that second, Phoebe would swear that he was smiling.

Just as Rocky and Manny dragged themselves out of the water on the far bank, a group of riders appeared at the top of the hill. The Strykers had arrived. There was little for them to do, other than wait while the bedraggled riders made their way across the creek, one by one.

The oldest brother—Rafe, she thought—

handed her a heavy blanket to drape over her shoulders. When that was in place, he passed over a thermos of coffee.

"Th-thank you," she said.

"Looked like we might have to call search and rescue there for a minute," he said.

"You saw that?"

"First time I ever saw a steer save somebody." He patted her back and left her so he could bring coffee to the others.

The hot liquid warmed her hands and stomach and eased some of her shaking. The blanket was old and musty, but at this point she wouldn't care if she had to share it with an entire mouse family.

How nice to live in a town where you could count on people to help when help was needed, she thought. Fool's Gold was that kind of place. Back at Reilly's house, there'd been no question about whether the Strykers would jump in, only about whether they would get there in time.

Phoebe watched the last of the cattle reach the safe side of the river. No matter how cold she was, she knew she would never forget this day or the knowledge that she'd made a difference. They all had.

• • •

"It stopped raining," Lucy said from her seat by the window. "Maybe they'll be back soon."

C.J. patted the sofa cushion next to her. "Thad said they'd call when they were heading back."

Lucy sighed, then walked toward her. "Are they okay?"

C.J. ignored the fear inside of her and nodded. "Sure. They're fine. Zane's been a cowboy all his life. He's not going to let anything happen to anyone."

Lucy's light brown eyes filled with tears. "Promise?"

Without thinking, C.J. held open her arms. Lucy rushed into her embrace. Tommy, sitting next to her, snuggled close.

"I don't want Thad to drown," the boy whispered.

"It's just a little rain," C.J. told him, trying not to think about flooding streams or snow runoff. "I'm sure they'll be wet and cold, but they'll survive. You'll see. And when they all get back here, we'll listen while they tell us everything."

Both children stared at her. C.J. willed them to believe her or at least to pretend to. Keeping up her spirits and acting calm when all she wanted to do was pace sucked up a lot of energy.

Lucy burrowed into her side. "Okay," the girl whispered. "Want to read us a story?"

"Sure."

Tommy stood and raced off to get a book from the library. They'd found a stash of them there earlier that morning. Probably leftovers from when the old man's grandson had been little.

While the boy was gone, C.J. smoothed Lucy's hair off her face.

"You need to think good thoughts," she said. "Sometimes that helps."

"Not always," the child told her.

C.J. stared into Lucy's face and knew the girl had seen things she, C.J., could never imagine. She and her brother had faced horrors no child should have to deal with. And if she and Thad didn't do something, they would return to a life in hell.

Her throat tightened, and her voice got thick.

"I always wanted a little baby of my own,"

she said softly. "Not because babies are that special, but because I never thought I was very good with children. You know? I don't ever know what to say or how to act. I thought if I had a baby, I would raise it so that it knew I loved it, even when I made a mistake."

Lucy looked away. "Yeah. A lot of people want babies."

"Sometimes what we want isn't the right thing for us to have," C.J. continued. "There was this boy I really liked in high school. I desperately wanted him to ask me out, and when he didn't, I thought I would die. I was so heartbroken. Then I met Thad, and I loved him so much more than that other boy. It turned out he loved me, too, and he wanted to marry me. If I'd gone out with the first boy, I would have gone to a different college, and I never would have met Thad. So not getting what I thought I wanted was a good thing. Does that make sense?"

Lucy stared at her. "I guess. Maybe."

C.J. stroked her cheek. "I thought I wanted a baby. If I'd had one, or if Thad and I had adopted one, we never would have come on this cattle drive. We never would have met you and Tommy."

The hope in Lucy's eyes was so bright, it was painful to see.

"You mean not getting what you wanted was a good thing?" she asked quietly, almost fearfully.

"Absolutely," C.J. told her, then hugged her close. "I want you and Tommy to come live with us. I may not always do the right thing or say the right thing, but that's because I've never been a mom before. It's not because I don't care. Can you remember that?"

Lucy nodded, then caught her breath on a sob.

Tommy walked back in the living room. "What?" he asked as he set down his book. "What happened?"

"I told Lucy that I'd like you two to come live with me and Thad."

Tommy's smile was pure joy. He whooped loudly and flung himself at C.J. She felt herself being crushed and strangled by skinny little kid arms. Their warm bodies pressed close. Life had never been so good.

The cattle made it to higher ground by sunset. Wet, tired and shivering with cold, the riders rode through the growing darkness, back to Reilly's house.

The Strykers had volunteered to stay with the herd, and Zane had gladly accepted. He considered getting everyone warm and fed his priority.

Three hours after Phoebe had nearly fallen in the river, he still couldn't draw in a full breath. When she'd slipped, he'd known he could never survive losing her. If she'd been hurt, or worse, it would have been his fault. All of it. Because he'd been so determined to teach Chase a lesson. The irony was Zane had been the one to learn a thing or two in the past week.

He checked his cell phone, and when they were within range of a tower, he handed it over to Reilly who called to let the folks at the house know they were on their way back.

The moon rose in a clear sky, allowing them to see the trail back. The horses sensed their destination and cantered the last five miles.

Zane and his crew arrived wet, tired,

hungry and proud. C.J., the kids, Andrea, Matilda, Eddie and Gladys greeted them. Danny and Chase took the horses. Zane helped Maya down from her horse, then reached for Phoebe. He was stunned when he felt her cold, soaked clothes.

"Run a bath," he yelled to the housekeeper. He turned back to Phoebe. "Can you feel your toes?"

"No, and I don't want to. They're going to hurt."

Maya came over and wrapped an arm around her. "Don't sweat it, Zane. I'll make sure she gets warmed up. See what happens when you cross a river. When I get back to the city, I'm not leaving my house for at least six weeks. And I'm going to spend all my time ordering things delivered. There will be no roughing it for me."

Phoebe shivered as she walked toward the house. "I liked it. It was all very exciting. Well, not the river, but the rest of it. Wasn't Manny brave? And he saved my life. I need to get him a gift. What do you think he'd like?"

"His balls back."

Zane followed them into the house. He found Martin, Reilly and Thad telling the women what had happened. They stopped talking when he entered and surrounded him.

"That was great, Zane," Martin said. "Talk about an adventure."

"I've never experienced anything like this," Thad said, as he wiped mud from his face. He turned to his wife. "Honey, you should have been there. The water was rising, the cattle were restless. I wasn't sure we were going to make it."

"You could try to sound a little less excited about dying," C.J. told him.

Thad grinned and caught her up in his arms. "I missed you and the kids."

"We missed you, too."

"You did good, Zane," Gladys said, drawing his attention away from Thad and C.J.

Zane shook his head. "I messed up big-time. I'm sorry."

Gladys brushed off the apology. "You might think you're perfect, son, but that's not the case. You're just as flawed as the rest of us. And you know how to show folks a good time. Eddie and I will never forget this vacation. In fact, if you want to do it again next year, count us in."

"That's right," Martin said. "Only no rain."

Zane held up his hands. "I'll see what I can do."

Everyone laughed and talked. Zane backed out of the room and turned to go help in the barn. As he reached for the front door, it opened and Chase stepped inside.

"The horses are all in stalls," he said. "Danny's going to rub them down and feed them. I'm going to change my clothes, then I'll head back out to help him."

"I'll go with you."

They walked toward the stairs. At the foot, Zane paused and touched his brother's arm. "You did good today."

Chase shook his head. "No, Zane. I made a big mistake. Phoebe could have died out there. We could have lost the steers. All because I pulled some stupid stunt. I'm sorry."

Zane's throat tightened. He tried to speak but couldn't. So he wrapped his arms around Chase and pulled him close.

"It's okay," he managed at last, his voice hoarse. "I screw up all the time, too. The thing is, I never let you see that."

Chase hugged him back. "For real?"

They straightened and stared at each other. He quickly told Chase the story of the stallion and how their father had reacted.

"I didn't want you to have regrets," Zane said. "Not like I did. But I've been so busy trying to save you, I've made your life hell."

His brother's eyes filled with tears. "Thanks."

"You're a good kid." He shook his head. "Sorry. A good man. I'm proud you're my brother and..." He hesitated for a second. "I love you, Chase."

His brother sucked in a breath, then hugged him tight. "I love you, too, Zane."

CHAPTER TWENTY-ONE

Phoebe sank onto the top stair and stared down to the great room below. When Zane and Chase hugged, she felt as if her heart was going to overflow with emotion. Or maybe she would just burst into tears.

"Are you coming or what?" Maya asked from the doorway to their bedroom. "There's a bath waiting for you. I think you have hypothermia, Phoebe. You've got to get warmed up."

It was true that every part of her body shivered and ached and that she couldn't much feel her feet or hands, but none of that mattered.

"They're going to be okay," she whispered happily. Knowing the man she loved was happy made her want to glow.

"Of course they're okay. Now come on!"

Phoebe glanced back at Maya. "They love each other. Zane and Chase. They're hugging."

Maya moved over to the railing and glanced down. "That's not something you see every day. I wonder what happened."

"Zane forgave Chase. That's all they each needed. To forgive and be forgiven. Of course Zane still needs to be forgiven from before, but I don't know how to make that happen. His father is dead."

Maya frowned at her. "You're not making much sense."

Phoebe rested her head against the railing. "I wonder if he'll miss me."

"Are you going somewhere?"

"Sure. Back to my regular life."

She tried to stand and couldn't seem to manage it. Maya stepped behind her and helped her to her feet, then escorted her into the bathroom.

The tub was nearly full, and steam fogged the mirror.

"Take your clothes off," Maya said, "and get in the water. It's probably going to hurt at first, but it will warm you up. Do you mind if I borrow your laptop to check in with work?"

"Go for it."

Maya left her alone in the bathroom.

Phoebe fumbled with her layers of damp clothing. As the steam heated her a little, she started to shake. Feeling came back into her hands and feet, and she wished it hadn't. The first sensations were a tingling, but that quickly changed to a needlelike burning.

When she was naked, she stared at the water and sucked in a breath, then stepped into the tub.

The instant pain nearly made her cry out. She settled for a few whimpers and tried to regulate her breathing.

"It will get better," she told herself.

After about five minutes, she found she could stand to keep her hands and feet in the tub. Ten minutes after that, she felt pleasantly toasty all over, and her brain had cleared. Unfortunately clarity brought with it hard, difficult truths.

She loved Zane. She'd probably loved him from the first time she'd met him. He was an irresistible combination of loner and lonely. She didn't just want to take care of him, she wanted to crawl inside and heal him.

She liked how he was capable and strong, smart and at times even funny. He was quietly nurturing, taking care of others without them even realizing what he was doing. She wanted desperately to be the woman who took care of him. He was an honorable man, and how many of those had she met in her life?

But was there a future for her here? Oh, sure, she loved the outdoors and the cattle. She was pretty sure she could even bond with the goats. The thought of long winter nights spent with Zane thrilled her. But she doubted he would see the potential. Instead he would remember that she was the one who lost her belongings to raccoons and pitched her tent in a river. He would see her as frivolous and incompetent. He might enjoy her in his bed, but she doubted he wanted her in his life. He might say he loved her while he slept, but what about while he was awake?

She was going to find out, she told herelf. She was going to talk to Zane and tell him how she felt and then hear what he had to say. He was too important for her to simply accept whatever might happen.

"Phoebe, are you about done in there?" Maya called through the door. "You need to come out right now. But put some clothes on first. Reilly's here, and I don't want you to give him a heart attack."

"I think I could stand the shock," the old man said with a chuckle.

"What's wrong?" Phoebe asked, her mind instantly going to Zane.

"When I logged on to your computer, you got a couple of emails. You need to read them."

Phoebe wrapped herself in a fluffy towel, then tugged on a thick, terry-cloth robe that had been hanging on the back of the door. She stepped into the bedroom.

"Who's sending me emails?" she asked.

Maya sat on one of the beds with the laptop beside her, while Reilly leaned against the door frame.

"Read this one first," her friend said as she turned the laptop to face Phoebe.

Phoebe scanned the contents. Jonny Blaze had sent a signed offer for the property. The dollar amount nearly made her eyes bug out. After she saw that he had cc'd Reilly, she glanced at the old man.

"Are you going to accept?"

"I was thinking I might. I see you held out a certain piece of land. I'm guessing it's for that young man of yours."

She sighed. "Zane isn't my young man, but, yes, I want him to have it. Are you going to fuss with me about that?"

Reilly smiled. "I never fuss."

"Good."

While she couldn't make up for Zane's past, she could do a little something to ease the hurt. At least he would have closure. After all he'd been through he deserved that.

She read the rest of the email. "Jonny's giving you forty-eight hours to consider his offer. You don't have to respond right away." She wrinkled her nose. "I'm really his agent on this property. You'll want to talk to someone else. Maybe a real estate lawyer."

"I trust you, Phoebe."

His words made her feel good. "Thanks."

Maya groaned. "I really hate to spoil the feel-good moment, but you need to read the next one, too."

"What?"

Phoebe clicked the next button. The first sentence made her heart stop. The second had her collapsing on the bed.

The hearing to revoke her license had been moved up to tomorrow at noon.

Tears filled her eyes. "I'll never make it." And if she wasn't there, the board would rule against her in absentia.

"Sure you will," Reilly said briskly. "I'll call Finn Andersson. He runs a charter company. Pack your things. I'll drive you to the airport, and you'll be in Los Angeles by midnight."

"You can grab a couple of hours of sleep, then be at the meeting in plenty of time," Maya told her. "You'll be fine."

Phoebe didn't feel fine. She didn't feel anything but empty.

She didn't want to have to fight for her license, not when she hadn't done anything wrong. Not when fighting meant leaving.

"We have to get going," Reilly told her. "There's another storm coming through. You'll need to be wheels up in less than an hour, and it's a half an hour's drive to the airport."

Phoebe stared at him. "But I have to say goodbye to everyone."

"You don't have time," Maya said. "I'll give them all hugs and kisses. Come on, Phoebe.

This is your real life calling. Now get dressed."

The next fourteen hours passed in a blur. Phoebe managed to scramble into clothes and jump into the car with Reilly. She hadn't had any time to find Zane and talk to him, not that she was sure what she was going to say. Would he consider her affections important or just an inconvenience? Had she managed to touch him in any way, or would he simply be grateful to have her gone?

A problem she would deal with after she saved her career, she told herself. She'd managed a few hours of sleep, then got up, showered and dressed in her best suit. There was still time before she had to leave for the meeting, so she began to make phone calls.

When this had all started, she'd accepted her fate without a whimper. But not anymore. She wasn't the same passive, accepting person she'd been in court. Somehow she'd learned she was strong, and that she mattered. Jeff might try to take her down, and he might succeed, but not without a fight. This time there wasn't a warmhearted steer to save her butt, so she was going to have to do it herself.

She finished her last call at eleven, which didn't give her much time to get to the noon hearing. She made it to the licensing offices quickly and waited in the foyer. So far no one had shown up, but she told herself they would. They'd always believed in her—now she just had to believe in herself.

When she walked into the conference room, Jeff was already there. One look at his face told her that there was nothing she could say or do to convince him to change his mind. For reasons she didn't understand, he wanted to destroy her.

He'd been the one to lie and cheat in their relationship. So why was he punishing her? Why—

Who cared why, she told herself. She'd just spent a week on a cattle drive. She'd saved fifty steers from drowning. She'd crossed a raging river and had lived to tell the tale. Jeff was beneath her notice.

If she lost her license, she would find something better to do with her life.

Something that made her just as happy. Because she'd learned that she could do anything.

The board entered the room and called the meeting to order. Phoebe was asked to stand and state her name. She rose to her feet, but before she could speak, the rear doors flew open and several dozen people entered.

Phoebe smiled as her former clients began to fill the room. Everyone she'd phoned had been more than willing to speak on her behalf. The Majoys who had three kids and barely got by. Betty Whiles, a single mother and diabetic. The Abbotts, the Tennants. Even Jonny Blaze had come. He gave her a big smile and two thumbs-up. She heard a couple of board members catch their breath when they recognized the movie star. Los Angelenos were not impressed by minor celebrity, but someone of Jonny Blaze's stature still managed to get them excited.

A clerk entered the room and handed Phoebe a thick sheaf of papers. The emails she'd asked for from the people who couldn't make the meeting. There were over a dozen glowing testimonials. The last person to enter the room was April, her boss.

Phoebe squared her shoulders and faced the board. There were seven of them, all well dressed and official-looking. She stated her name and gave them a copy of her license.

Jeff waited until she'd finished before standing. "Ms. Kitzke isn't allowed to bring witnesses to her hearing."

Phoebe ignored him. "I understand the rules of the hearing. However, as my competency is being questioned, there was no other way to prove myself. These former clients wish to speak on my behalf. I also have letters. They're not only from clients, but also from financial officers explaining how I always went the extra mile to find the right loan at the best price."

Jeff glared at her. "It's all bullshit."

"No, it's the truth."

April cleared her throat. "I brought my signed affidavit, Phoebe. Just like you asked." She turned to the board. "The mistake with the paperwork was mine. Phoebe caught it and wanted to correct it, but I didn't listen. I was scared I'd lose my job, so I lied."

The head of the board, a stern-looking woman in her midfifties, dropped her half-glasses on the desk in front of her and stared at Jeff.

"I've investigated Phoebe Kitzke myself. She seems to be a credit to the industry. Why exactly have you brought charges against her to revoke her license?"

Just then the rear doors of the conference room opened. Everyone turned. Phoebe was stunned to see Maya walk in, wearing the elegant designer suit she'd bought for her interview with the network. She was trailed by about a dozen people. C.J. and Thad were there with the kids, along with Eddie and Gladys and Andrea and Martin. And...Mayor Marsha?

"How?" she mouthed to Maya. How had she convinced these people to come to LA on her behalf? How had they made it here so soon? Maya shrugged and smiled.

Phoebe returned her attention to the board. "I don't know why Jeff's doing this. We had a relationship and it ended badly. So maybe this is personal." She shook her head. "That doesn't matter. What you need to know about me is that I love my job. I've always given a hundred and ten percent because that's who I am. My clients mattered more than anything. Even more than myself."

She glanced at the people behind her, at her friends…in a way, her family. "Not that I didn't love every minute."

She turned back to the board. "I'm here because I'm not going down without a fight. I do good work. I make a difference. I care and I'm honest. I matter."

There was more to say, but suddenly it wasn't important. She crossed to stand next to Maya.

"That really is a great suit," she murmured.

Her friend stared at her. "Great speech. You're a new and improved version."

"A cattle drive can work miracles."

"So I've heard."

Phoebe waited while the board deliberated. A calm had settled over her, and she felt that there wasn't one thing they could say that would upset her. If they allowed her to keep her license, she would transfer it to the Fool's Gold area. If not, she would move there and find another way to earn a living. She had no doubt that the small community would help her get on her feet. Maybe this was why she had never purchased a home for herself, because in her heart, she had always sensed that Los Angeles wasn't her home. The home she'd been looking for was a small town with a heart big enough to welcome any wounded soul in need.

It took less than five minutes for them to dismiss all charges. She was relieved but not particularly excited, even when the woman in charge called Jeff into her office for an explanation. Phoebe greeted her friends, thanked everyone for coming and promised to join them for a late lunch to celebrate.

When her clients had gone, Eddie and Gladys rushed forward to congratulate her. C.J. and Thad followed.

"I'm so happy for you," C.J. said. "You're an amazing person. I wanted to thank you for what you said to me at the beginning of the cattle drive. About Lucy and Tommy needing a home." Her smile broadened. "Thad and I are going to adopt them. Isn't that wonderful?"

Phoebe clutched her hand. "You're going to be a terrific mother."

C.J. shook her head. "I'm sure I'll make a lot of mistakes, but the kids have promised to be patient with me. We're going to take them as foster children while we work on all the forms and everything."

Thad winked. "I know a few people in high places. We'll pull some strings."

"Good for you."

Phoebe walked with the group to the underground parking garage.

"Aren't you going to ask about him?" Maya paused by her car and grinned. "You know you're dying to."

Phoebe shook her head. If she talked about Zane, she would start to miss him. And if she missed him too much, she wasn't sure she could go on.

"Not yet," she whispered. "This is a happy time, and I don't want to cry."

Maya's smile faded. "Oh, Phoebe, I knew you had it, but I didn't know it was bad."

Phoebe swallowed. "I love him and I don't know if he loves me back."

"You need a drink. Follow me to the

restaurant. After we have lunch and celebrate, you and I will hang out and get drunk."

The last thing she wanted to do was
celebrate, but Phoebe knew she should
be very grateful for all that had happened
to her today. Not only had she retained
her license, but she'd found out that
people cared about what she'd done. Her
helping had really mattered. It should be
more than enough.

And it would be, she told herself. In
time. It was just that right now she wanted
to be with Zane more than she wanted
anything else.

Would he call, she wondered as she
drove the two blocks to the restaurant.
Would they stay in touch? Would they date
when she moved to Fool's Gold? Had their
time together meant anything to him? Was
she wishing for the moon?

She pulled her car behind Maya's and
waited for the valet to hand her a ticket. But
instead of a young man in a red jacket
stepping up to open her door, a tall, handsome cowboy reached for the door handle.

Phoebe didn't know what to think. She
couldn't think. She couldn't breathe. She

could only stare unbelievingly.

The door opened, and Zane held out his hand.

She took it and stood.

"What are you doing here? You hate LA."

"I'm here because you're here."

God, he looked great. She wanted to stare at him for hours. She wanted to run her hands up and down his powerful arms. She wanted to laugh, to cry, to beg, to plead.

"I heard what you did," he said. "How those folks came through for you. I'm not surprised."

She smiled. "I was a little scared when I made the first call," she admitted, "but then it was okay."

"You always lead with your heart."

"I don't know any other way."

He smiled. "Not a surprise." The smile faded. "I love you, Phoebe. You're crazy and beautiful and you make me feel things I didn't know existed. You've shown me possibilities. For the first time in my life I want to do more than just get by."

His words made her want to float or even fly.

"Me, too," she whispered as she stared into his blue eyes. "About all of it. I love you, too."

He cupped her face. "You're the best person I've ever known." He swallowed. "I want to marry you, Phoebe, and I'd love for you to come live on the ranch with me. But if you need the big city, we can settle in LA and I'll put Frank in charge of the ranch."

She flung herself at him. He caught her in his arms and pulled her close.

"I don't want to live in a city," she whispered in his ear. "I want to live on the ranch and learn about breeding horses and cashmere goats and have babies, and when we want some excitement, we can go to Fool's Gold to have dinner. Or invite some friends over for a sing-along around the campfire. Oh, and I want to learn to bake bread. And maybe redo the dining room. But that's all. No other changes. I swear."

She was lying, Zane thought happily as he lowered his head and kissed her. She would turn his world upside down, and he couldn't wait.

He drew back. "This isn't about the land. You know that, right?" He kissed her again. "Although I'm grateful for what you did." He grinned sheepishly. "Reilly showed me the contract with Jonny Blaze and said I'd be a fool not to take the land and just say thank you. I'm guessing he was right."

She stared into his eyes. "Can you do that? Make peace with the past?"

He nodded. "I want to let it go, Phoebe. You've shown me what real love is. I can't change what my father was, but I can stop being angry and start feeling sorry for the old man. He's the one who missed out."

"Oh, Zane!"

He kissed her again, pulling her up against him and running his hands up and down her back. As he deepened the kiss, he became aware of clapping, cheers and catcalls. No doubt Chase had gone into the restaurant and rounded up the whole Fool's Gold crowd to come watch the show. Zane figured they might as well get their money's worth.

He pulled back slightly and took her hand in his as he lowered himself to one knee. He took off his hat and said, "Phoebe, will you marry me?"

Her eyes widened, then filled with tears. "Yes, I will."

Contentment filled him, blending with the love already in his heart.

He pulled the small box from his jacket pocket. While Maya had been busy running to the meeting, Zane had spent some time on Rodeo Drive. The Tiffany's store had a nice collection of engagement rings. He'd chosen a perfect round diamond set on a platinum band that looked like braided rope.

He slipped the ring on her finger, and she gasped.

"It's so beautiful."

"I'm glad you like it. Now keep it away from the raccoons."

"I'll never take it off. Ever." She stared at him. "I really love you, Zane."

He didn't doubt her for a second and knew that he never would. He and Phoebe would be together for the rest of their lives. It was going to be a hell of a ride, and he couldn't wait to see what happened next.